wonderdog

"*Wonderdog* reads as if narrated by the ne'er-do-well, incorrigible, and brilliant wastrel cousin of W. Percy's Binx Bolling. But Inman Majors has a brilliant voice all his own—cockeyed, very funny, and deeply cognizant of the tender mercies. This book's a hell of a read. I loved it."　　—Brad Watson, author of *The Heaven of Mercury*

"*Wonderdog* reads like Charles Portis cross-pollinated with full-tilt Barry Hannah, but Major's voice is his own, and his picaresque tale of Dev Degraw and his adventures among the various high-lifes and lowlifes of Tuscaloosa, Alabama, linger in the mind long after the last page is turned."
—William Gay, author of *The Long Home* and *Provinces of Night*

"High marks for humor and originality."　　　—*Inside Bay Area*

"A Southern comedy for sure."　　　　—*Cincinnati CityBeat*

"If [Barry] Hannah is Southern fiction's Howlin' Wolf, then Majors may well prove to be its B. B. King...Quick-witted, irreverent."　　　　　—*Planet Weekly* (Jackson, MS)

"Majors' wild riffing style runs breathless from drunk good ol' boys to Abercrombie toys to an overeducated doctoral candidate's pretentious ploys. All of it leads, rather remarkably, to a modestly noble vision, in the midst of scandal and sarcasm, of what the best public servants can be."　　　—*Creative Loafing* (Atlanta)

"Expect the unexpected: unstoppered sarcasm laced with real feeling from the mind and mouth of Devaney Degraw, a wise guy whose catalog of complaints runs just this side of stream-of-consciousness (punctuation optional) in a funny, full-tilt second novel from the author of the underrecognized *Swimming in Sky*."

—*The Memphis Flyer*

"*Wonderdog* is a hilariously unruly novel in the fine tradition of Padgett Powell—smart, Southern, inventive, and mean. Majors has written a seriously funny book."

—James Whorton, Jr., author of *Approximately Heaven*

"I ventured a cautious nose between the covers of *Wonderdog,* and immediately this voice, this outrageous voice, reminded me, for some reason, of Old Jones in *A Confederacy of Dunces*. Maybe I shot a look over my shoulder a time or two—okay, maybe I gawked—at the characters parading by, but I wasn't about to get up until the crazy tale was told."

—Sonny Brewer, author of *The Poet of Tolstoy Park* and editor of *Stories from the Blue Moon Café*

"Inman Majors shows how politics will drive a governor's ex-spouse into hiding in a house trailer and [drive] their wiseacre son crazy. A knowing and funny book."

—Ann Richards, former governor of Texas

wonderdog

wonderdog

wonderdog

inman majors

A HARVEST BOOK • HARCOURT, INC.

Orlando Austin New York San Diego Toronto London

www.HarcourtBooks.com

First published by St. Martin's Press in 2004

Library of Congress Cataloging-in-Publication Data
Majors, Inman.
Wonderdog/Inman Majors.—1st Harvest ed.
p.   cm.
"A Harvest Book."
1. Divorced fathers—Fiction.   2. Children of governors—Fiction.
3. Governors—Election—Fiction.   4. Political campaigns—Fiction.
5. Tuscaloosa (Ala.)—Fiction.   6. Fathers and sons—Fiction.   7. Child
actors—Fiction.   I. Title.
PS3563.A3927W66   2005
813'.6—dc22   2005017539
ISBN-13: 978-0156-03090-8   ISBN-10: 0-15-603090-X

Text set in Adobe Caslon

Printed in the United States of America

First Harvest edition 2005
K J I H G F E D C B A

For Christy,

THE ORIGINAL M.D.

acknowledgments

A huge thank you to David McCormick and Pete Wolverton for their support, enthusiasm, and expert advice. Thanks, especially, for taking a chance on my book in the first place and for all you've done to bring it to fruition.

I also need to thank the following for reading early, very rough drafts and for offering such excellent editorial advice: Christy Majors, Frank Majors, Chris Vescovo, Ray Murray, Barry Paige, and Jon Rovner.

Thanks, as always, to Nina, Dad, Mom and Stan, Kent and Brenda, Allen Wier, Kathie Lang, and all my other relatives and friends who have kept the faith.

Finally, I'd like to send out a special Roll Tide to John Barret, Tony Brusate, Alan May, Ray Murray, Ted Sabarese, John Sisson, and Rob Trucks—Tuscaloosa aberrants all—and to thank you for your assistance with the fundamental research that this project required.

And thanks, of course, to Tessa Rane and Max, who always keep things lively.

wonderdog

The
Queen
Bee

Like everyone else in the world I am a lawyer.

And like everyone else in the world, I'd rather do just about anything else than practice law. Be that as it may, a client, or rather a potential client, has managed to slip past my normally reliable secretary and now waits, litigation etched across his yeoman face, for perhaps the worst legal advice the state of Alabama has to offer. Seriously, I'm not good.

Could you repeat that Mr. Wilson, I ask.

I said I want to sue the son of a bitch.

Yes, I say, I heard that. What for is what I'd like you to repeat.

For parking on my lawn.

He's parking his truck on your lawn?

That's right.

In the middle of your lawn?

Naw, says Mr. Wilson. Over on the edge.

But his whole truck is in your yard?

Just two wheels. The rest is in his driveway.

I nod in a fair impersonation of considered silence. What I'm considering is why Mr. Wilson has nothing better to do than to sue his next-door neighbor. That and why he'd want me as his legal counsel, walking in as he did to my gently napping form. A quick glance at the clock reveals that it's still 120 minutes before the traditional lunching hour, a good four to five hours before our brothers to the south will begin their daily siesta, assuming that reasonable and time-honored practice is still in vogue. Nonetheless, napping I was. Sawing heavy logs and letting them fall where they may.

You're the Governor's son aren't you, says Mr. Wilson, with

that caught-you gleam in his eye that the more eager of my father's constituency are prone to display.

That's right, I say.

I've voted for Governor Degraw every time. Saw your name in the phone book and just figured you had to be some kin.

I smile politely, curse my father, the yellow pages, Alexander Graham Bell.

Well what do you think little governor? Do we have a case?

I smile patiently, oh so patiently, at the one-millionth hearing of that particular diminutive, and decide, all things considered, that homicide really is the only way out.

Well? he asks.

Mr. Wilson, I say, if I'm hearing you right, there are no legal damages to be recovered from a suit like this. Discounting the cost of grass seed that is. It sounds like a simple case of trespassing. Have you called the police?

Night and day, he says, staring at my legal pad, which, if one could read upside down, might look like a long ledger of a night's worth of gambling losses, NBA no less, a phone number for a local barbecue joint, and an unambiguous doodle of my ex-mother-in-law in all her stern glory.

And what do the police say?

They come out twice and told him to stop. The jackass moved his truck both times, then sure enough the next morning he's back in my yard. After that, cops said they got more important things to worry about. But I ain't. I ain't got more important things to worry about.

I can see that, I say. But like I said earlier, there aren't any legal damages to be recovered. Other than two wheels' worth of grass, nothing's been damaged.

My mind has been damaged Mr. Degraw, he says, leaning

fervently over the desk, his injured blue eyes meeting my red ones, itchy and furtive. I can't sleep at night.

So your neighbor parking two wheels on your lawn is causing you emotional distress? Is that what you're telling me?

That's it, he says, smacking his hand on my desk. Emotional distress.

But I'm afraid you can't claim emotional distress, emotional trauma, from a simple case of trespassing.

What about loss of consortium then? he asks with a proud and legalistic smile. By god I got him there.

Loss of consortium? You do know what that is?

Well hell yes. My nephew in the pen knows all about the law. Ain't nobody better than a jailhouse lawyer. No offense of course.

No, I say, none taken. So your neighbor parking two wheels on your lawn is affecting your ability to have proper relations with your wife?

You're damn right it is. I can't think of nothing else but his damn truck on my damn grass. Then my wife gets sick of me talking about it and then she gets mad and then my ass is on the couch. And there you have it. Loss of consortium.

I nod again, consider going back to my considered silence pose, very lawyerly when done well, but opt instead for another old reliable, academic puzzlement. A less grave look, less considered, but not bad in a crunch. While I'm arranging the quizzical face of a not-quite-stumped professor, some true puzzlement seeps in to give the pose just the air of authenticity I've been looking for. What I'm puzzling over is how in god's name I came to practice law.

Have you personally asked your neighbor to stop parking on your lawn?

Yes I have Mr. Degraw, he says with a solemnly furtive shake of the brow. I certainly have.

And what did your neighbor say?

Said his driveway's too narrow for him and his wife to both fit their vehicles.

Is it too narrow?

Yeah.

And they can't park vertically?

They work different shifts. He says they'd be pulling in and out all day long and his wife's got a bum foot and he doesn't want her having to go back and forth up and down the stairs.

Why doesn't he just park two wheels in his own yard?

He's got a line of dogwoods all along the driveway. If he'd just cut those things down he could park in his own yard instead of mine. I been after him for a year to cut those trees down.

I nod yet again, but don't bother to put on a particular face. On the far wall I spot my law school diploma, the small pictures, three of them, of my daughter.

Are the dogwoods blooming yet Mr. Wilson, I ask.

Just fixing to.

Are they pretty when they bloom?

Yes they are, he says. I always liked dogwoods.

But you'd rather have the dogwoods down than have your neighbor park two wheels in your grass?

That's right.

And him with a wife who can't get around too well?

That ain't my problem. They could take time about driving whichever vehicle is in back.

Can his wife get in the truck with her foot?

Nobody's making him drive a truck his wife can't get in and out of.

I forgo the ritual of the nod and stare in the vicinity of

Mr. Wilson, wondering about the things we do to distract us from the things we ought to do.

I'm afraid I can't take your case Mr. Wilson.

Well why not.

I just don't think it's a case for a court of law.

I want that man's truck off my lawn.

I know you do, I say. But you're going to have to find another attorney to help you. Frankly, I'm on the side of the dogwoods and the lady's bad foot.

Well I never.

Well you have now. So if you'll kindly let yourself out, I'll be getting back to my nap now.

Mr. Wilson stands up to leave and to wag a litigious finger. You can just bet your bottom dollar, he says, that I won't be voting for that daddy of yours come November.

That might make two of us Mr. Wilson, I say. Now don't let the door hit you on the ass on your way out.

After he's gone, I take off my suit and shirt and tie and lie on the leather couch in my office. The couch was what drew me to the office in the first place, awakened at the apartment as I daily am by the yipping wiener dogs of my downstairs neighbor. Now that, my friends, daily screeching yipdom, is grounds for a lawsuit against a neighbor.

I'm snoozing away when Sheila comes in with a bag of ice and a picnic basket of assorted bottles. She runs a cool hand across my forehead, hands over a breath mint, and goes to the desk to mix drinks. It turns out she'd just run out for supplies when Mr. Wilson arrived, else my blissful two-month streak of no clients would have continued unabated. Across the room, she stands as if accustomed to having her backside observed for the better part of forty years, the last fifteen of which were spent as my father's personal secretary. When my own former secretary, the esteemed Mrs. Barlow, could no longer handle the withering boredom of the job, not to mention the occasional late-morning cocktail hour, the relatively lax dress code, Sheila decided to call it quits in Montgomery and come on up to Tuscaloosa for a while. Needless to say, we've had an excellent working relationship ever since.

At the moment, she's handing me a Bloody Mary and standing hands on hips to make sure I take my chicken pox medicine like a good boy should.

You're a good secretary, I say.

She smiles at the obviousness of this statement.

Any calls, I say.

Your buddy Chad Kingston, says Sheila.

We're still on for lunch tomorrow?

He lands in Birmingham at nine and hopes to be in Tuscaloosa by noon. Said he'd call from the hotel.

Before I can press for more Chad Kingston details, she takes the Bloody Mary from my hands and downs the last sip. Then my feet are swung around so that I'm again lying on the couch. You looked tired sonny boy, she says.

I guess I'm not sleeping that well, I say.

Still not used to that apartment, she says. Your daddy was exactly the same way after he got divorced the first time. Couldn't sleep a wink. Running the roads at night cause he didn't want to go home. Well, you know.

I nod, trying to picture the young Governor, my young father. Remember, with fondness, the trips for ice cream and pizza, the toys, the ball games and movies on our nights out together before I moved back in with him for good. Then I wonder, considering my present circumstance, why I haven't thought of those nights before now.

Ants in his pants, says Sheila.

Ants in his pants, I agree.

Hard to be away from the kids. Hard on anybody.

To this I don't reply.

It gets better Dev. You just got to get used to a new routine. It'll start to feel more natural when she comes to see you, when it's just the two of you together.

Again I don't reply. What she says is true, I suppose.

I know a couple of things that are good for relaxation, she says, lightly, smiling. Might help you get back on a good sleep pattern.

You think?

I do, she says, pulling her hair back in one of those scrunchy things and lying down beside me.

As we begin the preliminaries, I have the slight urge to ask Sheila how she feels about the potential for social stigmatization that goes along with being a woman who seems to enjoy carnal relations with men. During our discussion, I might touch on the existing double standard regarding gender, desire, and propriety. I might, purely for the sake of argument, even work in a subthesis proposing that perhaps it is this quaintly anachronistic Puritanism, the last vestige of the illicit, that makes the act even halfway worth doing in the first place. Unfortunately, the mood doesn't seem just right for such a weighty sociological discussion. You're a good secretary, I say.

Life ain't all bad, says Sheila, standing up to step out of her dress, one anachronistic, one sympathetic, high heel after another.

Later, I'm walking home from the bar on a crisp night. Unless you've lived in this area, it's hard to describe March in Tuscaloosa.

The air feels clean, like in the fall, just a touch wetter, a touch heavier, and the ground, the soil, is just thumping, ready at any moment to explode into spring. And it's hard to believe that winter has again been so short, so easy. And you wonder, not for the first time, how anyone could live in Cleveland, Ohio.

As I'm enjoying my walk, the sound of my shoes on pavement, my shadow long and mysterious against the backs of apartment buildings, the thought of all those Yankees freezing their asses off, I round a corner and nearly knock into a couple of college kids smoking a joint in the alley. We scare the hell out of each other. Holy shit, the kid with the joint says, I didn't see you sir.

And recognizing me as the adult I sometimes impersonate or perhaps a cop undercover as a drunken lawyer, the little weedhead has quite smoothly pulled the Harry Houdini trick of hiding the joint behind his back.

Sorry fellas, I say. I didn't see you either.

It's cool sir, says the other. Then he points at my suit. Nice suit sir.

Thank you, I say. But about this sir business. Who am I, Peppermint Patty?

Huh?

Peppermint Patty. From Charlie Brown. She's got that friend that always calls her sir.

They shake their little potheads in warm and fuzzy confusion.

Marcie. The girl with the glasses? You guys don't read *Peanuts*?

No sir, they say in unison. And at this point, as an alumnus, I don't think it's just Roll Tide pride that makes me think the University of Alabama has the politest young stoners in the nation.

Well if nothing else, good luck on the snowboard circuit, I say, heading off to my Lions Club meeting, my Eisenhower fund-raiser.

Snowboard circuit, they say, giggling and poking each other in the ribs. Good one sir.

At home, home being a male and stale and vinegar-smelling apartment in a brownstone a couple of blocks from campus, just where a thirty-three-year-old man ought to be living, I head clumping up the rickety stairs to the stinkatorium. Flipping through the mail, I find the inevitable, a bill from my wife's lawyer, old Matlock himself, the wizened Perry Mason, and Frisbee it confidently in front of me, a good toss actually, sailing in a wide and steady arc across the room and behind the stereo, where it settles in a small atomic explosion of dust. This same explosion, or else the delicious aroma of my vinegary pheromones wafting through the ductwork, sets the dogs downstairs into an orgy of yipping and dashing, dashing and yipping. Relaxing? Absolutely.

Back in the bedroom, the light on the answering machine flashes two feeble times. I press play and sit down on the bed. The first message is from my daughter, Katie. Hello, she says, this is Katie. Hello Daddy I mean. Hello hello hello hello. Bye-bye. Uh? What Mommy? I can't hear you.

Then the sound of the phone being dropped. And then free fall dangle sounds, muffled female voices, television, the scoot of a chair. Click.

I lie down on the bed. Hello Daddy, the second message begins, I forgot what I was supposed to tell you. What Mommy? I know. But that wasn't why I called. What? I will tell him. I love you Daddy. Mommy wants to know if you can watch me Friday night. We can have pizza. Bye-bye.

And again the phone is dangling, banging and spinning softly against the kitchen counter. And Mommy wants to know if you can watch me while she gets ridden like a horse by Clark McClatchey. Mommy wants to know if you know she's stroking a male cheerleader for god's sake. A male cheerleader who smokes cigars and drinks single-malt scotch and votes Republican. Who is megaphoning his ass off at this very moment.

Then soft steps, small manicured hands, a nice woman, a good woman, hanging up the phone.

I lie on the bed and fight off introspection.

I lie on the bed and wonder how I got here. I had not wanted the divorce. I thought it would blow over, my funk, our funk. So how did I get here? Here exactly. This apartment. Across town my five-year-old daughter is sound asleep. My ex-wife is watching the news. My old house, a nice house, one you could live in for a while, have another kid or two in, is softly aglow through the front-door window, the blue light of the television flickering in reflection off the mirror in the den. But you hate practicing law, she said.

Yes, I said. I do hate the practice of law.

Then do something else, she said.

Like what, I said.

You could run for office.

No, I said. You know that's out of the question.

You'd win. You'd be good at it.

No. That's not for me. I don't want that life. They own you. They got their hands all over you.

You'd be good at it. You're honest.

I'm reasonably honest.

You love this state.

I have profound ambivalence for this state.

Dev, I can't stand the way we are. You are so bored. You are so unhappy.

I'm not unhappy.

You're not happy.

No, I said. But I'm not unhappy.

See, there, she said. There. Right there you have it. You don't care one way or another.

It was then that I shrugged my shoulders or checked my fingernails, I forget which. It was, I must admit, a considered move, neither happy nor unhappy, a move to validate what she needed validating. Namely that I was the source of her unhappiness.

And not too long after this conversation, we agreed that we were better off apart. Though what we should have agreed to was the fact that I didn't understand what she meant by happy, and she didn't understand what I meant by not unhappy, and that despite the good times, and the good things, specifically our daughter whom we created and loved, we were not, and had never been, particularly suited for each other. Under oath that night, the night of the final big talk, we might have agreed as well that her mother had been right, damnit, after all, when she'd warned us about getting married right out of college. But only under oath. Only sworn-in and under oath and hands forced down on the good book.

So I moved out, and I found this apartment, and I embarked on my current path. Which is not a recommended path, nor a permanent one, but one which seems to do the trick at present. But this question, the one about happiness, modern surely, quintessentially American perhaps, would seem to be a question that a thirty-three-year-old man living alone would have time to ponder on a Tuesday night in Tuscaloosa, Alabama. Would seem, would seem, would seem. Instead I walk to the den, turn off all the lights, and lie down on the couch to watch the kinetic blue of the silent television spinning one hundred miles an hour but never, not ever, coming to a stop.

· · ·

I'm at the office the next day with the echo of early-morning wiener dog dash and yip still ringing in my ears when Sheila comes in to tell me that Chad Kingston is on the line.

Degraw, he says, by god put it back in your pants. Ah god hell that secretary sounds like a peachy one, bring her along, hell where we eating, that sonofabitching Thor was something else wasn't he? Godawmightiest dog there ever was, beat Lassie up one side and down another, beat her like a rented mule. Hell that was a good show, a fine show.

Chad, I say, you're on the speakerphone. I can hear you fine. No need to shout.

I say where we eating? Big man's gotta eat. Still put you over my knee Degraw. Eat you up like a watermelon. Make you cry Momma. Make you cry in front of that little kitty cat you got answering the phone. Meow meow meow. Woof! goes the big dog.

What time?

Right goddam now.

Give me thirty minutes.

Right. Goddam. Now. Degraw. Got shit to do. Opening up that new minimall tomorrow. Kick em in the ass, sign an autograph, cash that check, adios amigos.

Yall could go to Plute's, Sheila says. That's easy to find.

Oh hell, well, excuse me maam, says Chad Kingston, I didn't know there was a lady present. You'll have to pardon my French.

Sheila smiles at the suddenly hat-in-hand bullshitting one.

I'll see you at Plute's, I say. Down on the Strip. Just follow the coeds.

As I hang up the phone, Sheila is smiling and shaking her head. He's a mess, she says.

He is a mess, I agree.

You do remember that you're wanted in Montgomery tonight?

I have a vague recollection, I say.

You ought to go, she says. Be good to get out of town for a night.

You do remember fund-raisers don't you? Big fish? Small ponds? Butts being kissed here and yon? No, I'll sit tight until the family man needs to trot me out in November.

That gal you're sweet on will be there, Sheila says, grinning.

I ignore the merit of this comment and rifle through some dusty bills on the desk.

So what did you think of Chad Kingston's plan? she asks.

What plan is that?

He said he's throwing a reunion of all the actors from the show sometime next month. A public reunion.

What? I say. No. Seriously?

He sounded serious.

The old boy fell off one too many horses I'm afraid. Too many cracks to his stuntman head. What did he say really?

Said he was going to get you, him, Candy Lake, and the dog. Hopes the reunion will get the ball rolling on a movie deal or a TV special or something.

I twirl index finger at temple in the universal sign of the hatter gone mad, then ask if she'd like to come along to lunch before Chad's inevitable and long-overdue institutionalization.

Can't honey, she says. Got me an early date tonight.

I'm suddenly smelling a June wedding, I say.

Twice bit three times shy sonny boy, she says. Not this gal.

Driving through town to meet Chad Kingston, I cruise along Bear Bryant Drive, and pass by Bryant-Denny Stadium, and recall, for the first time in a long time, my days as a student here. Good times to be sure. All the football games on Saturday, all the nice-looking women, and, it seemed, friends at every restaurant, record store, and bar. And as I head down Bear Bryant Drive, I conjure the image that stays with me more than any other of the old coach. It's before a game, any game, every game, and the Bear has walked out last, after his team, after his assistants, and is now leaning casually against a goalpost and watching, nonchalantly, as his team runs through their drills. Knowing full well that every eye in the house, every opposing fan, every opposing coach, is looking at him. The big bad Bear with his houndstooth hat pulled low over his eyes, leaning ever so casually against the goalpost, the casual, imperial symbolism lost on no one. Mine. This goalpost is mine. And what I think now, pulling into a parking spot on the strip, the strip where I had so many good times with so many good friends, think now without irony or self-consciousness, is Roll Tide. Roll Tide indeed.

And it is perhaps this odd and infrequent visit into my past that forces me to recall that I was once, a very long time ago, a life ago, a child actor on a television show that no one's ever heard of called *Bayou Dog*. It's a bit of a long story about how I got the job, having as I did no prior acting experience and most assuredly none since. At the time, my father had just been bumped up from lieutenant governor, another long story involving his predecessor, tax evasion, and multiple indictments, and when a production company seemed dead set on shooting a series in Mobile Bay, well his still-developing but natural instincts for demagoguery kicked in. Yes, the new Governor would love for you kind Hollywood folks to shoot your TV show in Alabama. Yes he would. So long as the Governor's multi-talented son has a starring role.

So it's fair to say that both my marks of distinction, both my small caveats against a life relentlessly mundane, being the son of the Governor and starring, to use the word liberally, as Billy Tucker in the short-lived and forgotten television show *Bayou Dog,* are direct results of a little thing called deoxyribonucleic acid. Chad Kingston, cast against type after two decades of willful and rollicking B-movie cowpoke thuggery, played the role of my kindly father, Sheriff Tucker.

Now Chad Kingston/Sheriff Tucker is somehow confusing the moderately stoned sophomore who will be our waitress for the day. Seeing his long-lost son walk through the door, the old cattle rustler hops up and offers an unrestrained Rebel yell, followed up shortly after with a suffocating bear hug. Then much slapping of back. How's it going, how's it going, how in the hell is it going Degraw?

I give the waitress my drink order and she heads off in the direction of the bar, a look of disgust for the pornographic roughhousing Chad is laying on me.

Properly titillated, we sit down to have a long look, TV father to TV son. Across from me it's a craggy-faced sea captain, bad sport poolhall loser, first-hanged bank robber, and, for one incredibly vapid year, my soft-spoken, soft-maned, too-old-to-have-an-eight-year-old daddy. Across the table, his misting eyes can't believe how grown-up little Billy Tucker is, how he's changed, all dressed up as is for Easter Sunday at the plywood church.

You've gotten tall old partner, says Chad Kingston. You as big as the Governor?

Not quite, I say.

And not as good-looking neither.

Now that's a matter of opinion.

Some young fellows do get handsomer later on you know. Try not to fret it.

Thank you Chad. And that reminds me. I definitely want the name of your nip and tuck man before we get out of here.

I don't know what you're implying.

I have no idea. Now why don't you tell me about this minimall you're opening up tomorrow?

Damnedest thing, says Chad Kingston. Two thousand dollars for cutting a ribbon, waving my hand, and kissing whatever little redneck babies they throw in my face. You ought go down there with me. Little prelude to our *Bayou Dog* reunion.

When is the big reunion anyway?

Three weeks. First Saturday in April. I can count on you now can't I?

No, I say. I'm afraid not.

Why not?

I was horrible, the show was horrible, there will be no one there. No, I'm sorry, you're on your own.

Hell that was a good show, he says. I still get letters about that show.

Odelle Bailey from Opp, Alabama. Who else?

Writes you too huh? Got in them lead paint chips as a baby I reckon. She send you any pictures?

Oh yes, I say, I'm afraid so.

Some of them lately, shew. How old you reckon she is? You'd think she'd have some shame.

You'd think.

That one out by the tractor is that a melon or something in her hand?

I believe it's a member of the gourd family if I had to guess. What I want to know is who's taking the pictures.

The old sheriff shakes his head, he doesn't know Billy, there's no telling Billy, have some more pie Billy.

Our waitress, who just moments before looked to be negotiating a minor narcotics transaction with the unwashed bartender, arrives and hands Chad my beer, me his double whiskey. I'm about to quiz her on her GPA and long-term career goals, just to set a certain tone, when Chad slides a ten-dollar tip into her disbelieving hands and says, thank you sugar, you're doing a fine job.

Cute as a bug that one, says Chad Kingston, as she heads back to the bar to upgrade from a nickel to a dime bag.

I bet you could get her granny's phone number if you asked.

Son, don't make me take this belt off.

By the way, I say, I saw you in some old Western the other night. You looked about fifteen and were just getting the shit kicked out of you by John Wayne.

Was I wearing one of those upturned floppy cowboy hats? Kind of looks like you're wearing your hat sideways?

Yep.

And spitting tobacco on the floor, then grinning like a crazy man?

Yep.

That was *El Paso Sundown*. I was twenty-three. I accuse the Duke of cheating at cards, and he doesn't take too kindly to it.

For the record, I say, did they ever let you be the good guy or was it just suckerpunching Steve McQueen one minute, shooting Gary Cooper in the back the next?

You mean besides *Bayou Dog*?

Yes, other than that tour de force.

I was a priest once in a war movie. Got shot pretty quick though. Played a grocer who got beat up by Lee Marvin another time. In that one, I smile and say, may I help you sir, and Marvin just knocks the hell out of me for no reason. If there was ever anyone could make you look nice by comparison it was Marvin. Other than that, I can't think of any. Typecasting, you know.

Has nothing to do with the punchability of your face?

Well that may be, says Chad Kingston. Might be something to that. Had a barmaid in England when I was in the service tell me I had a cheeky look about me, and hell that was before I was ever in pictures.

Your face just kind of says welcome to Palookaville.

With this, the barroom bullyboy smiles his irritatingly winning grin, the smile that launched a thousand haymakers. Yours, he says, now that we're on the subject, has a kind of antagonizing quality I hadn't noticed when you were a kid. Kind of a hickweed shiteating grin mixed in with a dose of smart-ass prep-school mama's boy.

Quite punchable in its own right I've been told.

I'd like to pop you one now just for luck.

Before the antiquated lawman can teach his impertinent son some manners, Old West–style, the waitress comes back for our food order. For me, it's a Reuben and fries. For he of the stone colon, a sirloin, rare, and a second RedEye.

So tell me about you, says Chad Kingston. Miss acting?

Are you having a go?

No I'm dead serious.

Worst child actor of all time. Potentially worst actor of all time no age limit.

Naw you were all right.

I told you I'm not doing the reunion.

I didn't say anything else about it. I'll get you there one way or another, you can bet on that, but I ain't saying another word. I just thought, as a little fellow, that you were a damn good physical actor.

Rock-thrower, tree-climber, near-drowner?

Don't laugh, he says. You'd be surprised how many of them stars out in Hollywood can't run a lick. Like they never have before. Heads flying, arms kibitzing everywhere, grunt-faced and crying and stiff-assed. Stuff's hard to watch. I'm fifty-eight years old and there ain't ten men in all Hollywood can beat me in a footrace. Much less arm wrestling. Ah hell it's all special effects now. They don't need actors like us. Somebody that looks like a damn man with some hair on his ass and a wrinkle or two like he's been up past eight o'clock at least one night in his life and hadn't been eating tofu and drinking fizzy water and plucking his eyebrows and like he might know how to hammer a nail or a woman too for that matter. Can't run can't fight can't act. Shave their chests and stick a cucumber up their ass and call themselves actors. Crying shame.

I'm laughing, and Chad Kingston's laughing, saying, you ever seen a dog like that one? Do long division. Smoked a pipe. I always figured the reason Candy Lake wouldn't give it up was she was waiting for old Thor to come around.

You know I used to see her naked all the time, I say, leaning close for a cloak-and-dagger story of our beloved costar who went on to ten years of bad-girl, wicked-twin, saucy-wench roles on big-time TV. Then the slow slide to infomercials, new boob job, obligatory last gasp *Playboy* pictorial.

No, says Chad Kingston, no. Naked?

Nary a stitch.

No, Chad Kingston says, no.

Played cards with her butt naked I'm telling you.

Both of you?

No, just her.

Too weird otherwise, even for showbiz.

Even for showbiz.

Cards?

Gin rummy.

Oh you're lying.

No I'm not. She'd call me down to her trailer to practice lines. Nothing sexual about it, just didn't like wearing clothes when she

inman majors

didn't have to. I was the next youngest on set and I guess she just felt comfortable around me.

Just didn't like wearing clothes, says Chad Kingston in semi-delirium, shaking his head, near tears at the thought.

Seeing that we're veering close to a convulsive state and having nothing liquid and cold to throw in his face that I hadn't rather drink, I say, how in the hell did they cast her as your wife anyway?

What do you mean, says Chad Kingston, bowed up nicely now.

I mean casting her as your daughter would've been a stretch. I mean you looked about ninety years older than she did and like you were drooling and fumbling in your pockets every time she came back from the store with a loaf of bread. That's what I mean.

By god, he says, I was drooling. Not ashamed to admit it. Like a long whip of cherry licorice.

Candy at an open casting call in Mobile and me on a dare. What was the budget for that show anyway, a buck fifty? Quite possibly the worst show in television history.

Ain't no way. It was bad, I'm not going to lie to you. But Candy had some undeniable assets. And that damn dog was top-notch. Top-notch. Been in the business forty some odd years and never seen a dog like Thor. He'd drive that motorboat.

He did, I say. I know it. Great dog actor. Candy in cutoffs, worth some points. And you had a certain likeable coonass gruffness about you, playing against type and all.

I thank you.

But I was unquestionably the worst child actor ever to have been thrown in front of a camera.

Yeah, says Chad Kingston motioning again for another round, you weren't too spiffy.

. . .

Sometime later that day I'm awakened from a mildly narcoleptic slumber in one of the guest rooms at the governor's mansion. Sam Shade stands in the darkened doorway shaking his head without movement. And if he is not surprised, can he be disappointed? He stands at the door and looks in on all that failed promise, all those practices he drove me to, all those school dances, the only black face in the stands, in the school lobby.

Smells like a damn brewery in here, he says.

He turns on the light and walks on into the room, kicking my clothes along the floor as he comes. Kicks my underwear up on the bed, then my pants and shirt, that look of resigned disgust so practiced, so perfected. I've made a C in spelling again. I didn't run out that grounder.

What time is it Shade?

Time to get up and get downstairs.

Yeah but what's your watch say.

Watch says eight-thirty. I look real hard it's gonna say kick you in the ass.

Then he picks my wallet off the floor, turns it upside down, and shakes. Tumbleweed and more tumbleweed. He chucks the empty wallet up on the bed. Pulls a twenty from his own and tosses it onto the bed with much disdain.

Is that a band? I say.

Yes hell yes it's a band.

I knew I drove up here for something.

I know why you drove up here, he says. Busy young lady that one. Busy busy. I thought you had a little sense when it came to women.

I sit up and grin at my old friend Shade. Were I a young Chad Kingston, I'd spit tobacco on the floor and wait for my well-earned boxing of ears.

Apparently, much like the Duke in *El Paso Sundown,* he cares little for this grin, for he quickly turns and starts out of the room. Pauses in the doorway. Much shaking of head from my old friend Sam Shade, the man behind the Governor, the former janitor at the capitol, former sergeant at arms for Speaker of the House Degraw, current driver, confidant, and primary policy maker in the state. Always behind the scenes, always in the shade. Mythic ability to poll three old ladies at a church bingo and any combination of shade-tree mechanics and one-chair barbers and predict an election. Yes, those in the know know Sam Shade. He looks back at me, a bad breeze across the mind, that faint rumbling sound. Have you lost your pride son?

I don't say anything.

Cause from where I'm standing that's the way it looks. You just can't keep going like you have these last eight, nine months. Drinking, not hardly working, sleeping crazy hours. You ain't the first man to get divorced you know.

Yes, I say. I know that.

Just about pissed away a whole year. I'll ask you again, have you lost your pride?

No, I say.

Well I thought you had some ambition.

I have no idea why you thought that.

You breezed through law school for one thing.

Law school and ambition are mutually exclusive entities, I say.

Ambition or no ambition, he says, I still got plans for you. Sooner rather than later. I'm not going to be around forever.

That you can forget.

He smiles, suddenly and unexpectedly, figures that about the pride was a little below the belt, no matter how right he might be.

Hell son, he says, you were born on third base. Me and the Governor had to work to get this far.

That's why it means something to you, I say. For me the view from third base is less intoxicating. Now first base, first base just intrigues the hell out of me. And the dugout. The dugout just looks like Paris, France from where I stand.

You'd never make it with the press would you?

I never figured to, I say, turning onto my stomach and pulling the pillow over my head.

Guess I'll just have to live to be a hundred and fifty when one of my great-grandbabies can run.

If I'm alive the youngster's got my vote.

The Shade family appreciates that, he says, walking out the door and turning the light off behind him. The Shade family appreciates each and every vote.

The fund-raiser is just an hors d'oeuvres and sweaty hand-shake affair best watched from the safety of the back ballroom bar. An inoffensive rock band and too many Jack and Cokes have a contingent of secretaries, interns, and horny legislators bloody-ing up the dance floor as the black caucus squirms in pain. Against the far wall and on the periphery, red-faced successful men, heavyset and trotting limply one step in front of the gout. Bir-mingham bankers talk with small-town senators who need new shoes and know it. Women of all ages in black cocktail dresses dominate the room with their relative style and minority status. First-term senators, fresh-faced and eager, try to look cynical, talk over each other's heads looking for someone important, don't yet know how to order from the bartender, too much chin-thrusting bass, too obviously don't know they ought to know Sam Shade, and wonder why they can't get a drink, wonder how the bartender knows they're first-term. And the lobbyists red-eyed with worry and boredom, straining to laugh at yet another corny joke.

Meanwhile, my father's press secretary, Shea Bateman, heretofore known as the Queen Bee, has been circling and daintily arm-touching her way around the ballroom. Still, boy, still. A few of the newer drones trail in her wake, factotums of the second order. The old guard, the keepers of the hive, give the Queen room to recruit, but always their eyes are on her, looking for a twitch of eyebrow, a distress signal sweep of hair. And what lovely hair she has, thick and dark, her hand moving rhythmically from your arm to her hair, sweeping it left for European exotic, right for all-business press secretary, two-handed double flip for Dothan farm girl just back from vacation Bible school riding double on Daddy's tractor.

At the moment her hand is on a drone's shoulder that I've never seen before. A new worker bee for the hive. She straightens his tie, lightly brushes his wrist, his hip. She laughs and laughs, looks serious for a moment, much shaking of head, a moment of concern, a biceps caress, a knowing nod, and what must this round-headed drone think, Oliver Cromwell fresh from the battle of Hastings, but that he is going to score despite the breadth and girth of his cranium. Never has he been so funny, so charming, never have his head and body been so proportional. But wait. The Queen holds up one finger, just a minute, won't be a minute my round-headed love. And now Hooper and Dee-Dee Higginbothan, brother and sister twins, the top courtesans, the keepers of the royal bed, the sprayers of perfume, are making their respective moves, brusquely, no time to spare when the Queen beckons. With supersonic speed, team Higginbothan is huddled by the staircase halfway between the Queen and her ultimate destination, the bathroom. And now the

Queen makes her departure with a final biceps squeeze for young Oliver, a nearly imperceptible brush of the hair, a laugh, you really are hilarious Oliver, can you imagine how good I look naked? Can you Oliver? Can you?

She walks nearer to me than she has all night, but no looking. The invisible pill I took earlier seems to have done the trick. Then toward the staircase. A quick word for Hooper, he's brushed off, then into the ladies' room with Dee-Dee on her heels. Game plans must be formulated, strategies discussed. Because tonight, unlike our previous dates out with the hive in jolly group-date fun, good old Dev Degraw has the homecourt advantage. Key crowd noise, megaphones, my ex-wife's boyfriend vaulting into a saucy back handspring.

Hooper Higginbothan, real name Hooper Higginbothan, incomprehensively tan and wearing the smallest glasses short of those made for children I've ever seen, shoots an envious glance toward the smiling Cromwell in the corner, then heads casually my way as if not on obvious reconnaissance for the Queen. As he approaches, I begin a serious meditation on those glasses. Never-before-mentioned-rod-in-spine equals lightest possible load on face equals ridiculously small spectacles? Tan and smart too? Clark Kent masculine? He sticks his hand out and forces out a yawn. Holding up the bar Dev?

Doing my best Hoop.

So what have you been up to, he asks, yawning, stretching, stretching and yawning.

Just got back from a snowboarding trip, I say.

You board?

All the time.

I went kayaking this morning.

You don't say.

Yeah, he says, but I can't wait till it really warms up so I can get back into rock climbing.

Yeah I'm training for a triathlon.

Ran one last year, he says, stretching out a bit at the thought.

Too exhausted to speak, I simply nod a feeble head.

Sore as hell, he says, rolling his neck and pushing here and there on his chest.

Been working out? I say, as the shaking camera records this impromptu and realistic exchange of male pleasantries for the upcoming khakis commercial.

Been working out like mad. Getting ready for lacrosse.

I nod, reluctantly.

It's the only thing that keeps me going these days. Great club. Great bunch of guys. Great guys. Solid guys. Really solid guys.

My mummified face battles not to reveal its quickly implemented course of action. That being the merciless slaying of this alien attempting to perform as human male. Merciful slaying? Put Hooper once and for all out of his misery? Alien impersonation of human male gleaned from television commercials and pregame football shows as painful for Hooper as it is for innocent bystanders? Brief food for thought. Quickly abandoned. No, slain. Sans mercy. Posthaste.

You ever played lacrosse Dev?

Never have Hoop, I say. Never have. But I was wondering if you might like to dance.

What?

May I have this dance?

He looks at me.

Come on man, it's a good song.

Hooper shakes his teeny glasses, sighs with patience, moodily recalls an awesome lacrosse kegger of days of yore.

Next slow one then?

Then he's waving at Oliver C., the newest addition to the hive and shouldering past me, lowering the boom, trying to just muscle on through as we briefly jostle for position. Good to see you Dev, he says, really good to see you.

Great to see you Hoop, I say, cramming shoulders, really great to see you.

One pleasant surprise of the evening has been the absence of my newest stepsibling, Dallas, who is often to be found at these affairs running from knee to knee in an orgy of jujitsu-style kicking. A lovely child, Dallas, a lovely and loving child. Across the room, beneath a massive painting of a singer belting out a number from her first and only album, *Dear Hunting,* stands the mother of dear Dallas, Carter Allbright, C.A. yall, and the good Governor himself. The new Mrs. Degraw looks less coltish, less down-home, good-time, this-is-a-party-yall, than she does in the painting. In fact she seems to be giving the good Governor, smiling boyishly, the what for.

And though taking a certain guilty pleasure in watching the Governor get chewed on, a man in need is a man in need, so I start across the dance floor to give the old boy a breather. Seeing my approach, Carter peels off in search of a mirror or a record deal. The Governor, meanwhile, has a smile at the ready and arm extended. Anticipating the traditional gubernatorial knuckle-cruncher, I get the jump on him, have his ham of a hand in mine and am torquing at maximum pressure before he's fully gripped. Good to see you Dad, I say.

Good to see you son, says the Governor, ever so slightly yanking his hand from my vise of death. Glad you could make it up on such short notice.

You know I love a fund-raiser.

Sure I do, he says. And I know you wouldn't have come all the way down here just to see my press secretary.

I smile, Stonewall Jackson.

She's got em falling out of trees, wrecking cars, joining the circus. Don't know what she does, but she does something.

She treats em like shit.

Yeah, that'll do it, he says. At least for some. I never did go for that though.

I look at him, give the almost-a-complete-smart-ass smile.

I don't, he says, voice briefly high with an attempt at incredulity. Your mother wasn't like that.

No, I say, she wasn't.

And C.A.'s not.

I nod, bite my tongue in half, swallow the severed tip. The bloody nub works crazily against the back of my throat.

Listen, he says, realizing we've veered dangerously close to self-examination, I'm about to hit the sack, but I want to ask you a favor before I do. I'm supposed to have a meeting with Skip Terry in Birmingham on Monday but I'm not going to be able to make it. How'd you feel about going in my place?

No. Absolutely not. Not even for a lot of money.

Now that you've brought up the subject.

I'm okay, I say.

He gives me a look of some skepticism.

Business is a little slow, I say, but I've still got some cash left over from that moving van case.

From back in the fall?

Late fall, I say.

The Governor nods, considers a more formal and probing

query into my personal finances, then decides against it. And how's my granddaughter? he says.

Fine, I say. She enjoyed her birthday party up here. You did too much though.

It was nothing.

Well she loved it.

I'm glad, he says. Now about Skip Terry.

No, I say.

Come on son. I don't often ask. You know Skip. You know how to handle him.

Yes, I do know Skip. That's why I'm not going.

The Governor smiles his charming smile and waves toward a distant bar for his V-8 juice nightcap. The old boy might be slowing down a bit, I think for a moment. Back in the day he'd have just started rolling on the scotch highballs. Son, he says, I don't often ask.

You're still on that lottery loser?

I am for now, he says.

So we get a lottery, I say. Which opens the door to statewide gambling. Which means my old friend Skip Terry can finally get that casino up and going in Mobile. But what's in it for you? Other than you've always wanted to see Josh Wade in the governor's mansion?

One, he says, I'm tired of Alabama being last in education spending behind every state but Mississippi. Two, I'm tired of every hickass politician saying he can solve the budget if we only had a lottery. Well hell I'll give em the lottery, they'll see it's not all it's cracked up to be, and then we'll get around to doing something to address this state's budget problems once and for all.

Why don't you just raid the highway fund like I've been

telling you? Katie's got twenty-eight students in her class and no-body in this state gives a shit. So you take the money from that bloated Highway Department and funnel it into schools. Nobody will even notice until they start losing axles in the potholes up on 59 anyway.

I've told you I don't care if you put Katie in a private school.

No, I say. It doesn't look good to have the Governor's grand-daughter in private school.

I don't care how it looks. You get her out of there if you think it's the right thing to do. Hell, I'll pay her tuition.

I appreciate it, I say. But we'll see how it shakes out for a year or two first. She's not smoking cigarettes in the bathroom yet.

Well that's a start.

All right, so back to this lottery deal. Schools or no schools, you're going to end up with every black leader and every church on your ass. That's a bad combination for a Democrat to buck up against.

The Governor grins. Then he's taking the offered V-8 and thanking the bartender with a cheery smile. You never did care much for Skip did you? That highway fund idea would be money out of his pocket I guess you know.

A lucky coincidence, I say. But no, I never much cared for old Skip. A little of that dumb like a fox yodeling and backslapping goes a long way with me.

He smiles again, looks to be calculating just what percentage of his average day is spent in the company of yodeling backslappers. Skip Terry's a powerful man, he says, smiling at an eighty-year-old woman passing by. I don't carry the middle of the state like I used to.

Before I can reply, Bunny Akins approaches in classic wob-bling form. First instinct? Flight. Room-clearing, hair-tearing, self-immolating dash through the plate-glass window.

Papa Degraw and Baby Degraw, slurs Bunny, wrapping a minuscule arm around both our waists and pulling us into a tight
circle.

Hello gorgeous, says the Governor, smiling at Snake Akins's
widow, the great Snake, the silver-tongued Senate majority leader
who took the young Governor under his wing when the Governor was still an ambitious and ruddy-cheeked first-term senator
from Baker County, then later, in the Governor's first and most
hotly contested statewide election, delivered to him all of Mobile
County, just like he said he would.

Bunny holds up a red cheek for the Governor to kiss. He does
so, the old charmer knowing what side his bread is buttered on,
when to yes maam, when to flirt.

You too Baby Degraw, says Bunny, eyes closed, reeling, flam-
ing red wig plenty askew.

To this request I assume the standard deaf-as-a-doornail facade, Snake Akins's widow or no Snake Akins's widow.

Now Papa, you tell baby how much you love him, says Bunny,
attempting to place my hand in Dad's.

It's all right, I say. Really, seriously.

Baby governor, tell Papa how much you love him. Hold his
hand and tell him.

Papa I love you, I say.

The Governor laughs.

Hold his hand and say it like you mean it, says Bunny.

Bunny pulls the Governor's hand closer to mine. He's laughing, sheepishly.

No, I say. It's all right. We were making out right before you
walked up.

Tell your daddy you love him. I want to see you.

No.

Well why not?

Because you're ordering me to.

He can be a bit stubborn, says the Governor, but I know he loves me Bunny.

Well he should tell you, she says, needing a drink, fresh embalming fluids, a new audience to torment. Then she rallies. Well, let's pray. Let's join hands and pray. You never know how much you love someone until they're gone. I miss Snake so much.

I know you do, says the Governor, taking her hand and nodding good-bye to me. Then he's off, twirling Bunny as he goes, waltzing gracefully through a room of half-ass muckety-mucks, Bunny smiling now, wine-spritzer tears forgotten for the moment, and the Governor's doing a little quick-footed jig before planting a sloppy one on Bunny Akins. Then he grabs his young wife and swings her round and round in his arms, not caring that she wants to be put down, that she looks worried about her hair, about how this looks. For the Governor knows his crowd. And the crowd does love it, man and woman, young and old. And now he sets his wife down and begins shaking a few near hands. And I must admit, it's something to watch, no matter how many times I've seen it, working a room without looking like you're working a room, for if you look around, every eye is on him. Then he's off again, across the room, shaking hands, a wink here for an old crony, a smile there for a smiling lady. The band has stopped playing and spontaneously the cheering begins. A wave for the room from the bottom of the grand staircase, then up the stairs with his flustered beautiful young wife, who will never comprehend that he is the closing act, will always be the closing act. And listen to the crowd chanting, four more years, four more years. And black and rougey tears running down Bunny's face. And now the band has started in with a little Sweet Home Alabama and the crowd cheers louder and louder, because he's still got it, he's still the big man, the Governor, running when you're walking, fucking while you sleep.

    The Governor's departure and subsequent crowd-pleasing rendition of Sweet Home has evolved into a full-blown Lynyrd Skynyrd medley, much to my chagrin. Sweet Home? Yes, of course, turn it up. Gimme Three Steps? Absolutely. But after that, it's not just classic rock, but classic Southern rock, and despite the yee-hiiis and hot damn yodels from the crowd, partners swinging round and round, shotguns fired in air, Lee's heading back to Gettysburg, et cetera, I'm fully prepared for any other musical genre.

    Out on the floor, dancing throughout the whole of the Skynyrd marathon, the Queen and gal-pal Dee-Dee Higginbothan looking refreshed from their skull session, laughing and knocking lightly into each other in good clean girly fun. At the very edge of the dance floor, miniglasses fogged with misty devotion, stands Hooper Higginbothan, the good guy, the solid guy, waiting for an invitation to join the gals in boogie wonderland. Next to him, the proud Puritan, Cromwell himself, smiling his toothy best. But wait, we have a development. The leader of the Roundheads seems to be considering joining the girl fun. Yes, he's thinking about it, very seriously considering it, all those arm touches, all that sweeping of hair, and then, by god, he's out there, dancing badly just outside the feminine circle of nonentry. Now the Queen and Dee-Dee tighten rank, and he's on the outside looking in, dancing in place, searching about for any stray on the floor to pick up with, and then, my god, he's muscling in, Oliver Cromwell's muscling in sports fans, give the big-headed kid some points on that one, he's split the atom, but now the Queen's peeling off, motioning with her hand for Oliver and

Dee-Dee to dance, both of them shuffling in place, watching her as she goes.

She strolls past Hooper with nary a sidelong glance and heads straight for the bar where I'm standing. She's standing next to me, has greeted two people she doesn't know, oh hey, hey great to see you, glad you could come, to make sure I see nothing but shoulders and the back of that expensive head of hair. She gets her drink, chardonnay, and starts past me, inches from me, and oops, she's forgotten a napkin, must turn back, why Dev, Dev Degraw, when did you get here?

Just walked in, I say.

The Queen Bee smiles. Did you really?

Yeah. About a minute ago.

I can never tell when you're telling the truth.

Dee-Dee and Hooper Higginbothan.

What?

Dee-Dee and Hooper Higginbothan. I just like saying it.

The Queen shakes her head. And what about Devaney Degraw?

Devaney Degraw? Dev Degraw? Good guy. Solid guy. Hell of a lacrosse player. Hell with the stick.

What about me? says the Queen.

Shea Bateman? The late summer, going off to boarding school, her daddy finally let her wear a bikini, teenage queen of the country club pool?

The Queen smiles, pleased. But why haven't you called me since our last date Dev Degraw? Didn't you have fun?

I have, I say. I have called you.

I didn't get any messages. I think my voice mail must be messed up.

A lie? Absolutely. I've called and left at least five messages. Do

I care? Don't be ridiculous. During our conversation, the Queen's pulled her hair on top of her head and bunched it up in a bouncy little ball. The effect? Sleepy good girl. Ready for bed.

I've been waiting, she says, to see if anyone is going to ask me to the Governor's Ball.

You want to go to that thing?

Yes, she says, touching my arm lightly. And I have to go Dev. Everyone goes. The whole legislature, the interns, the staff. I think I'm the only girl in Montgomery who doesn't have a date.

With this she smiles, letting me know that this datelessness thing is as humorous as it is ridiculous. Ah, the twentieth-century Southern courting ritual. Beauregards and Annabelles and plastic mimosas in the air.

Well, if you get stuck, I'll take you, I say. I'd really hate to see you sitting at home.

Oh would you Dev? she says, stepping closer until our legs touch.

I would. I'd love to.

She leans forward and gives me a nice peck on the lips, her smooth dress and all that goes with it brushing lightly in all the right places. Can you wait right here for a second, she asks, hand on arm, completely insincere and believable. I might need a ride home.

No problem, I say, daddy-oest of the daddios.

The crowd's cleared out some with the Governor's departure, and I stand at the bar waiting for the Queen's return. As I'm enjoying a boy's springtime thoughts turning to the subject of love, that old lottery lover, Skip Terry, comes up to the bar and places a chunky hand on my shoulder.

What say little governor, you causing any trouble?

I put on my yukking-it-up face and say, you damn straight I am.

He rubs my shoulder. Look at all that trim, he says, pointing toward six or seven quite untrim ones on the dance floor, perspiring slightly about their fu manchus.

Yeah boy, I say, throwing in a couple of decadent dog barks in the bargain. Yessireeebob.

I reckon you're a hellcat just like the old man, he says. Reckon the apple don't fall far from the tree. What you reckon little governor?

Resisting a worthwhile impulse to savage the randy old fart where he stands and wondering if someone has slipped Skip Terry a minor dosage of Spanish Fly such is the patting and kneading presently being committed to my shoulder, I nod energetically and say, I reckon. I reckon I reckon.

He motions behind me for a round of drinks, leans close in my ear, and says, we gonna have us a lottery come next year?

That's the million-dollar question.

That's the hundred-million-dollar question little governor, he says. The hundred-million-dollar question. What's your personal take on it by the way, friend to friend?

I don't have a take Mr. Terry, I say. I'm so busy practicing law, I really don't have time to follow politics. Basically, whatever the Governor's backing, I'm backing.

Right smart son, he says, kneading and rubbing till the cows come home. No need for a bright boy like you to get messed up in this business.

You're for the lottery, right? I ask, earnest as a young Billy Tucker trying to pull a burr from Thor's injured paw.

With this little bit of subterfuge, his bloodshot eyes commence a proper twinkle, his ruddy cheeks commence a deeper shade of red. I've got a passing interest in the lottery, little governor, he says. And I think it will be damn good for the state. Damn good source of revenue.

I nod in eager agreement.

I'll see you Monday night in Birmingham, right? I'm thinking we'll talk a little about the lottery, a little about how the Governor's going to whip Josh Wade in November, then just shoot the breeze over a couple of drinks for a spell. We'll be in and out in no time.

Nodding to the bartender for one more, he removes his hand from my shoulder and pulls a hundred-dollar bill from his wallet. Let an old uncle give you a little spending money, he says.

No thank you.

He shoves the bill toward me. Treat yourself to a good bottle of whiskey.

No sir, I say. I don't need it.

Let me give you a little advice little governor. A man offers you something, you take it. He wants you to have it. I don't care what it is. A man offers you a watermelon, and you don't like watermelon, you take it anyway. You may throw it out the window on the way home, but you take it.

Well thank you then Mr. Terry, I say, taking the bill. You're awfully kind.

It's nothing son, he says, turning to leave. Plenty more where that came from.

By now, the ballroom is nearly empty and the bartender has begun to box up leftover whiskey. When he has his back to me, I place the hundred-dollar bill in his tip jar without him seeing me.

Onstage, the band is wrapping up with something that sounds suspiciously like an Aerosmith ballad and still no sight of the Queen. I'm brooding on this turn of events, the kidnapped Queen, the canceled naked chess, when Sam Shade strolls over and orders a beer.

Same old shit, he says, watching the bad dancing, the young turks trying to hook up, the old farts calling loudly for one more drink, and the lobbyists scurrying for the door before someone wants to be taken out on the liquor lobby's, the phone company's, the association of peanut vendors' tab.

Seen it before have you?

Too many times, he says, too many times. So the Governor's got you messing with Skip Terry now?

Hell yes, I say. Monday night. Why's he got me messing with that jackass anyway?

What'd he tell you?

That he was busy and couldn't make it. He laid it on pretty thick about never asking me to do anything.

Shade smiles a little. That's right about him not asking, he says.

I don't deny it, I say. But is he busy?

If he says he's busy, I guess he's busy.

Feels a little like he's passing the buck, I say.

Can't always tell what the Governor's up to sometimes.

No, I say, you can't always tell. Some people think he's a little unpredictable at times. I never have myself though.

Nice and steady like you?

Exactly, I say. Nice and steady. So are you going with me or not?

Unfortunately, he says, taking a sip on his beer and pointing quickly with his elbow toward the dance floor, where Skip Terry has begun moving about in earnest with an intern. It's a lively tune, and what he's doing, I suppose, is meant to be dancing. Picture if you will an amorous and drunken bear with an inner ear imbalance.

There's no need to show me things like that, I say.

Shade shakes a weary head in agreement.

What do you think about this lottery business anyway?

Statewide gambling? In Alabama? Your daddy's either gone crazy or he's bored and just wants to make this election interesting.

I'd bet on the latter, I say. But I'm with you. This lottery referendum is a loser. Why doesn't he just say he'll go with whatever the people want and let that be that.

Skip Terry's putting the heat on. Acting like he'll throw his money and support to Wade if the Governor doesn't go to bat for him.

Who gives a shit? If the Governor can't beat Josh Wade without Skip Terry, he doesn't deserve to win.

I agree, Shade says, taking a beer from the bartender without having to ask for one. But the Governor thinks you'd rather have Skip Terry inside the tent and pissing out, than outside the tent and pissing in.

I say cut him loose. Once the weather gets hot, the Governor will chew Wade up. With or without Skip Terry.

I say cut him loose too, says Shade. But the Governor's in for a race. I'll tell you that right now. That Josh Wade's tougher than he looks.

By the time the Queen comes back, a good hour after she left, it's just the bartender and me and the band loading out. And, it bears noting, she hasn't arrived alone, dragging behind her Oliver

Cromwell in the flesh. He's a little flushed-looking and cat who ate the canary, putting his hand again and again through his helium-filled hair, the Queen's hair fetish and osmosis at work here. If I didn't know better, I'd surmise he's freshly returned from an hour long make-out session, an athletic and well-pantomimed make-out at that.

Sorry I took so long, says the Queen Bee. I couldn't find Dee-Dee and Hooper anywhere, then I ran into Gibson here.

Gibson Smith, says Oliver Cromwell, reaching out a preternaturally hairy hand.

How you doing, I say, calmly going for the old knuckle-busting grip, but sake's alive the young brute's got the jump on me.

Great, he says, grip of death accompanied with a toothy smile, a big floating head of hair. Seriously, tie that float down man, we need more ropes, more ropes, this thing's floating rogue, laying siege to Shriners, Rose Bowl queens, the Tupelo High marching band.

I hate to ask, says the Queen, but can you give me a ride home? We rode out with the Higginbothans and they must have taken off without us.

A quick jag of thumbnail to the index finger saves the day and I'm released from the young primate's clutches. I take a good swig on my drink, rattle the ice calmly, order another. The Queen's switch in pronouns has not gone unnoticed. No problem, I say.

Thanks dude, says the original dude.

I say, no problem dude.

On the ride, the Queen Bee sits in the passenger seat, Oliver Cromwell in the back. He tries to keep the conversation light and lively, inquiring with what seems like sincerity about what you inquire about when you think the guy driving you home is jealous because you're going to sleep with the woman he thought he was going to sleep with just an hour before, the woman he may or may not have a date to a formal ball with in a little more than two weeks. At Cromwell's house, yes here, right here, thanks a lot man, I appreciate it dude, really, I do, really, thanks, he stands in the driveway and waits, as I do, for the Queen to get out with him. He's standing there, smiling, big happy head ready to zeppelin across the lawn, a bit confused now, smile fading, and though it's dark, a pink flush starting to rise on that vast and fleshy horizon.

See you Gibson, says the Queen, cheery but tired. I had a great time.

And then Dev Degraw is saying, take it easy, great to meet you, as he's pulling ever so slowly, gently and cautiously, out of the driveway, thinking, as might be expected, dude.

At the door of the hive, it's low-talking sexy man, not-so-good-old-boy mumble and rap, sugar all the King wants is a fried banana and peanut butter and jelly sandwich, and kiss kiss kiss, ear and neck, and girlish giggles, junior-high coy, just for a minute, seriously Dev, just for a minute.

Inside, no other way to say it, it's honeyed. Clean and sweet. A light musk that tickles a boy's fancy for spring. The Queen Bee, sweet sweet Queen, oh misunderstood Queen, goes to the back to change. I sit on the couch and rehearse our routine. Timing and choreography, vaults and squeals, ride the prancing pony, cowgirl's revenge, chinese basket, pin the tail on the ribald, a cartwheel into a backflip into a flying reverse naked scissors in honor of my wife's new Republican boyfriend.

I'm in something of a trance when the ghost of Dee-Dee Higginbothan walks into the den, dressed in her pajamas. The apparition is rubbing her eyes as if she's dozed off in the haunted attic while waiting for someone to come home.

Oh hi Dev, she says, plopping down, sadly incarnate, on the couch beside me.

Hair standing on end, a series of guttural emissions, heartfelt sobbing, rapid sweep of the room for weapons. Hello Dee-Dee.

Higginbothaned. And not for the first time. Dates one and two with the Queen had Hoopers and Dee-Dees popping out of closets every five minutes or so. The obstacle course to the Queen's inner sanctum continues. Rope swing, tire drill, pushing Dee-Dee in a wheelbarrow. We sit in silence, waiting for the starter's gun, listening to the Queen laughing on the phone in her bedroom. The one drink I didn't have does not go unmourned. I light a cigarette.

Shea really doesn't allow smoking in her house, says Dee-Dee, who has a kind of prudish put-out quality about her that might rouse in the spanking aficionado an overwhelming desire to administer a little bare-bottom justice.

I nod, smile, inhale. Consider the fair but firm hand I would use if of the spanking persuasion.

Seriously, I'm allergic to smoke.

Nod, smile, exhale.

Repeat conversation.

The Queen walks in ready for bed. Favorite outfit imagined and topped. Satin kitten. Ice cream in a champagne glass. Mental note to invent high-heeled bedroom slippers.

Sorry I was so late Dee-Dee, says the Queen, but we had to take Gibson home.

Then she grabs a stuffed bear off the bookcase and sits down on the couch between us. Two women in pajamas and young Dev Degraw with subtitled French music playing in his head.

The television flips around redolently, chitchat is exchanged, Hooper's bought a new house, Dee-Dee has a crush, the merits of

Cromwell's melon-headed sweetness are exclaimed. Every so often the Queen leans forward and I catch Dee-Dee's eyes over a lovely brown shoulder with a strap falling down. Boxful of glares. Consternation unlimited. Yes, sadly, Hef's hot tub won't include Dee-Dee on this night. And for Dee-Dee in return? Kris Kringle merriment and mischief, a winkful of mirth and moxie. Let's girl talk till the cows come home.

Suddenly the television is turned off and the Queen rises, a yawning purr, a stretch, a glimpse of lithe tummy, and what Dev would give for a saucer of milk, a nice ball of yarn.

Still yawning, purring, delaying inexorably the moment of truth, teddy bear hugged and hugged, then hoodwinked and back to the shelf he goes, Dee-Dee sitting halfway up, ready to attend, defend, the Queen saying, night Dee-Dee, I'll see you in the morning, then looking at me, yes you, and walking toward her bedroom, which glows in honeyed splendor.

Night night Dee-Dee, I say, emerging from the horizontal barrel and leaping smoothly across the muddied pit. Great to see you. Really great to see you.

In the Queen's chambers, it's very nice. Two things to fight. Overeagerness and emotional fatigue. An interim period is needed. I lie on the bed with shoes off while the Queen stands in the mirror brushing her hair. She looks fresh, sleepy, every so often looking at me in the mirror and smiling.

She finishes brushing and starts the harlequinade proper by turning off the lamp next to the bureau. Lights candle on bureau, turns off lamp on bedstand, lights candle on said bedstand, pulls hair back into farm-girl fantasy with pink scrunchy thing, faces Dev Degraw, the good boy, the solid guy, the obstacle course winner, and steps ever so lightly out of her nightie, Dev Degraw's eyes for a moment stuck on the thing shed, the old sleight of hand, then making their way slowly, past the must-see spots, back for another visit, then off to the out-of-the-way bistros, then back and then back and then back to the must-sees, and the Queen is smiling, turning just slightly, just ever so slightly, to highlight a point, to inform the viewer, then she is moving toward the bed, still in her unhaste, and then she is on the bed, on top of the covers, in all her grace and glory, and Dev Degraw has caught the rhythm, and moves slowly, lightly, tips of fingertips for the Queen, brushes of lips, the king is dead, long live the king.

Giggles and whispers. And low low low talking man, smoothly, sweetly, lightly. The Queen, I can't Dev. I can't.

And on the way home, on the drive to Tuscaloosa, with the sun a dull dirt clod peeking over the horizon, eyes red and dry sweeping past doe eyes glowing in the woods, clothes smoke-stenched and rumpled and perfumed, head a melon teenagers have busted on a mailbox, and all the beginnings beginnings beginnings and almosts almosts almosts, Dev Degraw, dead man, rotting mummy, gnarled possum stiff on the side of the road, oddly satisfied.

The
Milk
Drinker

It's Friday night at Pizza Fun and shell-shocked adults move skittishly through a cacophony of deranged horns, flash-bulbs, piped-in clown chuckles, video game beeping, zapping, crashing, and florping, manic chipmunk-on-speed nonsense Christmas songs, warbling Old West piano, mechanical monkey accordion minstrel, incessant unseen buzzing, put that down now, you're going to the car Jimmy, I told you it was hot, no more quarters, god I need a drink, and choirs upon choirs of tiny faces, insane, sugar-twisted, cola-gargoyled, splattered and smeared with tomato paste and ice cream and snot, screeching rabid hyena versions of Happy Birthday Brittany, Alex, Shareeka, and Dan.

It's loud in here, Katie says.

It sure is, I say. Would you like to leave?

No, I think it's fun. Don't you think it's fun.

It's really fun, I say, peeling a globule of sausage from my hair and carefully launching a waiter toward the counter for my beer. We should come here every Friday night.

As we're getting out of the car and making our way to the stairs of the apartment, Sunny and Nickel, wiener dogs one and two, nearly knock the door down barking at us, scaring Katie, and not really the greeting my Pizza-Funned nerves are looking for. I check for Mrs. Catching's car. Bingo night. Then kick the hell out of the door. Prompting a maniacal yelping head-butting wiener dog scram.

That was funny, says Katie.

That was, I say, that was funny.

· · ·

The thing about five-year-olds is they need entertaining. They are little interested in watching basketball on television or drinking beer. How to fill five hours with a five-year-old while her mother teaches Clark McClatchey all our old moves, the windmill, pick a number, hi-karate, duck duck gander, and that honeymoon maker, scissors in a drawer?

Pen and yellow legal pad are the best I can come up with, and Katie entertains herself for a while drawing people who look like houses, houses that look like people. On television the game is going my way. The Jazz are waxing the Knicks as I foretold. A hurt to the tune of five bills for the Eggman. A good bookie that Egg, a good egg. Punished he must be nonetheless. And considering I'm down almost, well I stopped strict-accounting practices a month ago, suffice to say a lot, this scrambling of egg is coming not a moment too soon. Every so often Katie shows me a picture of a house with eyes. That's you Daddy.

Very good Katie, I say.

I love kindergarten, says Katie. I mean I really love it.

That's good. I'm glad you like school.

And I really really love my teacher. Miss Marcum is the best.

I nod, smile, try to forget the parent/teacher conference I forgot back in November. I'm glad Katie. I'm glad you've got a nice teacher.

Really really nice, she says. And then she's busily back to work, squinting her eyes, gnawing her tongue, an impressively furrowed brow of concentration. You're very serious Katie, I say.

I am. I am very serious, she says.

I'm in the bedroom considering chopping off my fingers to keep them from dialing the Queen's number, knowing she's out on Friday night, knowing any call this quickly after our rendezvous will reek of horn-dog desperation. Oh but my itchy fingers, my itchy masochistic fingers. I'm searching about for a machete when Katie walks in with a videotape in her hand. Can we watch a movie Daddy?

Where did you find that Katie?

It was under the couch.

What were you doing under the couch?

I dropped my pen.

Oh. Well, I don't think you'd like this movie.

What's it called?

Let me see, I say, reaching for the tape. She hands it over, smiling. There's something funny going on here, something tricky. She's waiting for the punch line. Oh this, I say. This is a movie for grown-ups. I don't think you'd like it.

What's it called?

I look at the title, weigh my options, know my daughter's expert ability to read body language, to screw up her face at any hint of untruth. Not an ounce of Degraw in her moral makeup. It's called *Working Girls*, I say.

Is it funny?

Not intentionally.

What's it about?

Girls who work. Massage therapists and such. Nurses and aerobics instructors and the like.

They give massages?

Yes. That's basically it. They give massages. It's pretty boring. I don't think you'd like it.

When Mommy gets married she's not going to have to work anymore.

Excuse me?

Mommy's going to quit working when she gets married.

Mommy's getting married?

Yes.

Well so Mommy's getting married. That's interesting. Mommy likes to be married doesn't she? And Clark is happy isn't he? Mommy and Clark are very happy.

They're very happy. Clark's funny too. Like you Daddy.

Just like Daddy huh? So he's a good guy?

Yes.

A solid guy?

I don't know what that means. He's nice though. I'm going to be flower girl.

That's great. That's really great. Was this a secret? Were you supposed to tell Daddy about Mommy getting married to the funny man, to Clark?

I think it was a secret, she says. I think I wasn't supposed to say anything.

That's okay. I won't tell. But here's a good idea. Since I don't have any movies, and you're probably tired of drawing, and Mom's getting married to a male cheerleader, why don't we go outside and play knock and run with the funny little wiener dogs? Why don't we see if we can drive them plumb crazy?

We're hiding behind my car in the parking lot when Mrs. Catching drives up. Inside the apartment her dogs are frenzied with incessant whiplash wail. Knock on front door, run to back. Knock on back door, run to front. Mrs. Catching, arms filled with groceries, fumbling with the key, scolding, soothing. Sunny, Nickel, what's got into you? Is it a mouse, have you seen a mouse?

Then the dogs are loose, out the door, wieners for the bun, quadripeds of the cheapest sort, nipping and yipping at my ankles, Katie jumping up in my arms, kick, yelp, scamper back for more.

Sunny, Nickel, Mr. Degraw, says Mrs. Catching, as she tries to corral the frothing squirmdogs who are dangling like hairy Christmas ornaments from either side of my pants.

I set Katie on the hood of the car and walk, carrying a dog on each leg, toward the open apartment door. Sunny, Nickel, Mr. Degraw continue to receive ever-increasing admonitions. Set-toothed growls. Bottoms bounced and scratched on cement whimpers. Ouch ouch sorry, says the stiff-legged Frankenstein lumbering toward the door. Ouch ouch sorry.

Inside, the smell of fresh doo greets the visitor to Mrs. Catching's abode. The lingering guest will soon notice a stronger, commingling, though ultimately overpowering scent of old doo, grey and proud, still vigorous after all these years, as well as an after aroma, inherent, of molded dog hair, and farther, deeper into the recesses of nasal imagination, soaked into the walls, the true characteristic of the apartment itself, pheromones, sexless, claustrophobic, schizophrenic, old manic dog musk. Breath is held. Indian war dance begun. Sunny skid and slide into refrigerator. Oh Sunny goes the shout. Nickel popped-up, soccer-style, and knee-juggled into the sink. No Nickel cries the crowd. Sprint for door. No quarter asked. None given.

In the car, on the way to her house, Katie says, why does Grandma call you Peter Pan?

Grandma calls me that does she?

She said you were Peter Pan to Mom.

It's because sometimes I wear green tights and fly through the air with my eyes all aglitter.

She laughs. No really.

Well, I say, there are some people, like your grandmother, who think that your father is not particularly grown-up. I would argue that there are all types of grown-ups, but some people, like your grandmother, like good old Grandma, they think there is only one kind of grown-up.

What kind?

Oh I don't know. Like Clark and Grandma and your mother.

And you're different than that?

Well I never tried to be intentionally, but I guess I am.

She nods, doesn't say anything for a while. Then she taps me on the leg. Do you like your apartment, she asks.

It's okay, I say. Do you like it?

It's okay, she says. I liked it better when you were at our house.

I did too honey, I did too. But it's like your mother and I said, sometimes grown-ups are better off when they don't live in the same house. Sometimes, as hard as it is for everyone, it's the best thing. Your mother is a very good person. And I think I'm a good person. But we just decided we'd be better off not living in the same house. But us not living in the same house has nothing to do with you. Your mother and I love you just the same. And we're proud of how well you've handled this. We're proud of what a big girl you've been.

She doesn't reply but looks straight ahead at the road.

Would it help, I say, if we kept some toys for you at the apartment? Would that maybe make it more fun?

I have fun at your apartment already, she says. That was funny with the dogs Daddy.

It was, I say. It was funny. But wouldn't a few toys maybe make it even more fun to come to my house?

Yes, she says. Maybe just one or two toys.

. . .

One or two toys has turned into a trunkful, an assload. Suffice to say I was toy-mad, toy-crazed. Hell yes for toys.

When we arrive at the house, Clark's SUV, complete with JOSH WADE FOR GOVERNOR bumper sticker, is still in the driveway. I guess it goes without mentioning that he's a lawyer too. As we're getting out of the car, I'm still flush with my raid on Santa's workshop and a fifteen-minute boy-band sing-along and am thus caught off guard a bit when Katie asks if she can take the wooden train set to her house tonight. I stall before replying, the wooden train set the highlight of our toy spree, large enough to fill the better part of an empty spare bedroom, fill the better part of a boring night at Dad's house.

I thought maybe we'd keep all these toys at Dad's house, I say. That way you'd have some special things to play with when you come to visit.

We'll take the rest to your house, she says. And just take this one to my house.

You don't want to keep the train at my house? You'd have plenty of room to set it up, and you wouldn't have to take it down when you're through.

But I could play with it more here.

Yes, I say. Okay. Sure. I understand. Do you think you can get it set up?

Clark can help me, she says.

Then Polly is opening the door as we walk up the steps, looking tired and happy, the glow of taming an angry one still on her face. Polly comments on the train set with a smile and a quick peek inside the bag, then I set the bag just inside the door without crossing the threshold or looking inside, like a deliveryman well-versed in delivery protocol. Then Katie kisses me good-bye and runs to the den, hollering, hey Clark!

Hey girlfriend! he says from the soft light in the den, and

before I know it the cringes come upon me unawares. Because, if my ears have not deceived me, a grown white man just said, hey girlfriend, to my daughter.

Listen Dev, Polly says, I guess you saw the bumper sticker. Clark's a lifelong Republican. I just didn't want you to think he was trying to show you up or anything.

Could care less. But did he just say, hey girlfriend, to Katie?

Yes. Why?

Oh come on. Clark McClatchey, soul sister? Hey girlfriend? He's whiter than I am. Does he moonwalk? Is Kid Dy-no-mite chillin in the den? Chillin at the crib? I don't want my daughter around that.

Around what?

Poor pathetic attempts at funkydom. You go girl. Does he say you go girl? Just on occasion. You go girl. I mean come on. I bet he can't even dance. Hell I can dance and you'll never hear me hey girlfriending. Go girl. Get off on your bad white funky self.

Polly shakes her head, gives her patented and oh-so-irritating look of patient condescension.

And she's playing sports, I say. She's not going to be jumping up and down on the sidelines. She's not going to be peppy. I won't have her being one of those peppy happy people. Jumping around all the time and yelling hey girlfriend to her friends at the mall.

Good night Dev.

Just so you know. I lack pep. Pep bores me. Pep and zest I have no time for.

Good night Dev. You're as sick as ever.

After dropping Katie off, I'm at The Bear's Den drinking a few casual ones, forgoing introspection and personal analysis, and watching the Utah Jazz breeze along. All over but the crying for the Eggman. Jim, Ph.D. candidate in medieval literature and king of the trivia box, is keeping us in a tight match with Gay Henry and his theoretical girlfriend who play under the pseudonym Menudo, as in the horrific prepubescent Mexican pop band. Camp is the word Henry tries to use on occasion, but in general I frown on its parlance.

You know Jim's carrying you Dev, says Gay Henry. If you played by yourself, you wouldn't win all these games.

But winning I most surely am Henry.

If I've got to listen to you run your mouth all night, he says, you ought to at least buy me a drink.

What I'll give you Henry, is a little free advice. When you're delivering pizzas, get em there hot and get em there fast. That's what the people want.

Jim laughs. Henry pretends to sulk. His imaginary girlfriend maintains her vow of silence. I point at Henry's empty beer without him seeing and motion for Dennis to bring him a new one on my tab. And one for his gal. True love and sportsmanship and all that. Before the beers arrive, Henry turns to me and says, you know Dev, why don't you just go to hell.

I shake my head in disappointment as the beers are set in front of the surprised young lovers. Such language from young people today.

Hot and fast Henry, I say, that really is what the people want.

We're tied up with Menudo after four matches and are wrapping up a close all-sports game, the nightly game that is usually my only chance to contribute to Team Cobra.

What we ought to do, I say, is start up an all-boy country

band. A country Menudo. Just get a bunch of cute blond-headed kids, throw some cute little boots and Wranglers on em, write some bland songs about apple trees and malls and hoping to get a pickup one day so I can kiss you on your freckled ass and make us about a million bucks.

Jim nods his medievalist head. Call them Young Country.

Hell yes, I say. Young Country. That's the name.

Weekly voice and underarm checks.

First hair on the soap and you're out of the band. Hell yes. Young Country. The safest, cutest, blandest kids we can find. Sixty-five yards, I scream, sixty-five yards.

You're sure? asks Jim.

Sixty-five yards. Tom Dempsey. New Orleans Saints.

Jim presses C for sixty-five yards to answer the question, *what is the longest field goal in NFL history?*

The answer, it turns out, is sixty-three yards.

Quick unbalanced expletive string.

That was for the game you know, Jim says.

Maledictions unleashed in steady geometric progression.

Menudo got it, Jim says. They won the game on that question. They're taunting us. Henry's got his arms raised like a referee. He's trying to get you to look. Just look. He's doing an end zone routine. I knew it was sixty-three. I knew it.

And on the television the game has stopped, Utah Jazz and New York Knick players gathered at midcourt as if someone were injured. I ask Dennis what happened.

Referee had a heart attack I think.

Is he dead?

Don't know.

They're going to finish the game though?

Hell if I know, he says, obvious amateur, blatant nongambler.

They'll finish the game, I say. They've got to finish the game. But before you know it, the manager of Young Country, the hottest new band in country music, is having another drink, thinking to himself, still money in the bank, forget it, jack the bet at worst. Not going to lose money. Eggman can kiss my ass. Ref having a heart attack. I'll be damned. Not going to lose money at least. Telling Jim, well if you knew it, why didn't you answer. And Gay Henry across the bar, showing no sportsmanship whatsoever, leading the Menudo chant, ironic, kvitchy, campy as the day is long.

Across the street at McCrae's, the only nonundergraduate bar on the Strip, it's the typical Friday night freak show, an excellent kaleidoscope of semiearthlings. Beards and biker boots, glassy-eyed grad students, raging midlife professors, college misfits, hippie girls, many of our hairier nocturnal cousins. And, steely-eyed at the bar, Dev Degraw buying a round on his tab for the band, for anyone at the bar who needs a drink, trying to reverse his luck, looking without incomprehension, with staid and quiet foreknowledge at the replay on the television of a half-court Knicks basket, the ensuing celebration.

You played the Jazz didn't you, says Ewan, the bartender and only known Aussie in the state.

I did, I did indeed. You had the Knicks I assume.

Afraid so mate.

Ref had a heart attack.

Yep, Ewan says. Stopped the game for thirty minutes. Then the Knicks outscored them twenty to three in the last three minutes. It was like the Globetrotters, dunking and doing circus shit.

I saw, I say. Trust me, I saw.

. . .

I've taken to strong drink. It seems the only way out. A drunk front moved in before I could find cover. Quite a little life I've got going here, if I do say so myself. Quite the go-getter. I'm behind the band with my buddy Jim. The band is rocking bluesy and not bad. It's a tiny bar, dark, jam-packed. To get to the bathroom you have to walk through the band and behind the band there's room enough for regulars and weak bladders and dope smokers to stand.

Squeaky, a mute and ageless sage of indeterminate tribe, scuttling spirit man, has just walked in, making his way through the crowd, shaking hands, touching faces, scaring the hell out of first-timers. How long he's been walking up and down the Strip shaking hands and appeasing the ghosts is anybody's guess.

He makes his way through the band, wide berth given, stops in an attempt to shake the guitar player's hand, touches his shoulder, smiles, moves to the drummer, petting of hair, stroke of confirmation, good luck man, moon chaser.

Hey Squeaky, Jim says, sticking out a hand to be shaken.

Squeaky, I say, also extending a hand. He takes it, shakes, turns it palm over, caress, caress, caress, squeeze. Smiles, moves on through the crowd shaking and touching and out the back door into the good dark night.

I nod at Jim, he at me.

The first woman I've seen out in Tuscaloosa, full-grown woman that is, leans against the bar watching the band. She laughs at something her friend says, thanks Ewan for an ashtray. Her hair's pulled back, and she's wearing a blue jean jacket, currently out-of-style garb. A good sign. Laughing like hell at something her friend says.

I walk to the bar and order a drink. Consider that at this very moment the Queen is brushing the hell out of some drone's arm. Ewan comes over, sets the drink down. Half-court shot, he says. Tough way to lose.

Half-court shot, dead referee, all in a night's work. Who's that woman at the bar?

Nice one that. Never seen her before.

How about sending her a glass of water on me.

Dodgy move. That one never works.

Just do it.

Dev my friend, he says, the repertoire needs some definite work.

It's a short bar, so I can see him tap her on the shoulder, point at me, then set the glass of water down. The gentleman at the end of the bar would like to send you a glass of water.

At this point I tip my drink, suave nod of head, howdy maam, and so on. She looks at Ewan, back at me, laughs ever so slightly, and tips the water glass back at me. Then she's talking to her friend again without a second glance.

Ewan walks back over smiling. Maybe you ought to switch to ashtrays.

Jim has joined me at the bar and to be honest, we're drinking. Potations that is. The band has quit for the night, and the friend of the girl I sent the water to is toward the front talking to the lead singer.

Now's your chance, says Jim.

I can't talk to women. I lack subtlety.

I imagine a blunt instrument crudely wielded.

Good one. Nice one.

Just be yourself.

Are you kidding? I can't be myself. That's impermissible.

Perhaps it's time to find out who Dev Degraw really is.

You think?

Sure, why not?

My precopulatory behavior seems to need some work.

She laughed at first.

She did do that.

She did.

Not a chance in hell is there?

Absolutely not.

She's got her back to me when I walk over, so I have to choose between shoulder tap, always scary, or walk-around, space-invading, full presentation of self. After much deliberation, I choose shoulder tap.

How you doing, I say.

Fine.

That water thing was just a joke.

I know.

Well can I buy you a drink now? Or would you just like the money instead?

She laughs. Slightly. With reservations of the heartfelt variety.

If you would just talk back fast at me we could banter, I say.

That was decent, she says.

Really? That one just there? The banter deal?

Not bad.

I ought to write it down then. I don't get out much you know. But seriously, I'd be glad to buy you a drink. Glass of milk or something. You look like you been drinking milk and eating corn on the cob all day.

That's a compliment?

You just look kind of healthy and happy. Full-grown I mean. Do you like corn on the cob?

Yes.

And you like milk?

Yes.

Well that's all I'm saying. You look like you been drinking milk and eating corn on the cob all day.

She shakes her head, starts to look around for her friend.

Was I even close?

She smiles, shrugs, moves off toward her friend. Good night, she says, good night.

I'm in the back alley behind McCrae's smoking dope with Gay Henry. He has dope, I a bar tab. Together we make beautiful music. Henry is drunk and stoned and has become, as he is sometimes wont to do, effusive. He thinks it unfair that Ewan will run a bar tab for me and not for him. It's not fair, he says. You've got a tab.

I've got money, I say.

No you don't.

One would assume I have money.

What about me?

You deliver pizzas.

You don't know the money I make. Tips, he says, the little alchemist greedily rubbing his fingers together. You'd be surprised.

I'm sure I would, I say, brain zapping in nice and tight, though I could probably do with a slightly improved setting. What we have here is basically alley-trash-bugs-rats-stink-stoned-cops, the pungent smell of urine, asparagus flavored, wafting from behind the brooding Dumpster.

I think it's because he thinks I'm gay.

You?

I think Ewan thinks I'm gay.

No he doesn't. Don't be ridiculous.

Do you think I'm gay?

Of course not. Are you kidding? How could I? No way.

Because I've got a girlfriend.

I know you do.

We broke up though.

It was a tough break, I say. A tough tough break.

The lights are up in McCrae's and only a few people are still about. It's between three and five in the morning. Henry's fallen asleep on the pool table, arms curled lovingly around a beer bottle, one shoe off, a nice steady snore aboard the *Good Ship Lollipop*. Ewan mops the floor, sends yellow cockroaches scurrying, contemplates putting one in Henry's mouth, sings that famous Australian rugby song, Ballad of a Dead Referee, seems to amuse himself. Two women I've never seen before and those men who count themselves among the ambulatory join in.

The Utah Jazz were leading
Dev's bookie was a-pleading
But the referee's favorite pastime
Was five hot dogs at the halftime

And he liked his pints
And he liked his smokes
That running to and fro
Was really quite a joke

As the song plays on, Jim and I are talking to Preacher James. We're buying him drinks and trying to understand even one word that he says. The lockjawed Preacher, hard to cipher in the light of day, drunk, head back, eyes red and crinkled and merry, the old tongue coming out free of English idiom, full of hand signals, cave drawings in air, beavers building dams, the phantom coyote not of this world only.

Jim is laughing and nodding as Preacher James roars, slapping his hand on the bar and repeating himself to the ladies. Then a change in tone. A raised hand to signal an edification of some sort for the ladies. A somber nodding of head. An etiquette breach perhaps. Perhaps not for mixed company. Then immediate reversal to original tone. More roaring. More slapping of bar, of Jim's back, of my back. No one word flying fast and furious from his sealed lips can be sorted from the other. Speech pattern without current mold or brethren. You didn't get a word of that, I say.

Yes I did, says Jim.

What did he say?

He was just telling us about his job. About an asshole boss he's got.

Seriously?

Yes.

Got you an asshole boss huh Preacher, I say.

Light but guttural syntactical incomprehensibility. Quick laugh. Hand signal to indicate it's not all fun and games.

What did he say just then?

Wanted to know if you heard about the dead referee.

And he liked his pints
And he liked his smokes
That running to and fro
Was really quite a joke

That hook shot at the buzzer
Was such a nasty mother
Now Dev can't buy a cookie
Cause he's hiding from his bookie

Preacher James leads repeat of chorus.

I've been drinking and there's no room for denial. Henry continues to snooze behind me on the pool table, cooing and giggling. Jim is with me drink for drink, though showing no ill effects, the rummy, the overactive-endocrine-gland-embarrassment to his leprechaun mother. Ewan sends the satellite dish screaming in search of footie, lamb burgers on the barbie, the latest Men at Work videos. Preacher James has begun to look funny at me when I talk.

The women linger still at the bar.

That was a good-looking woman, I say. That one that was here earlier. The milk drinker.

She was, says Jim, the patronizing son of a Blarney stone kisser.

I can't believe I didn't get her name. I'll probably never see her again.

Do you need some ice? he asks. For the puss? Would some ice help at all?

The Preacher laughs.

When yall do my intervention, I say, I want Preacher there.

Absolutely, says Jim.

I think I might listen to the Preacher when it came to something serious.

Of course, says Jim.

See if them women down there'll come too.

Preacher James nods seriously, puts hand in front of mouth so women can't hear what he says, speaks, laughs knowingly, closes with hell yeah, damn right shaking of head.

What about those women down there Jim my boy. Oh Danny boy, oh Jimmy boy.

Ewan looks over and laughs.

What about the redhead?

Preacher James speaks.

What did he say, I ask, thinking for a moment I actually heard what he said.

He said she might have teeth, says Jim.

What? What Preacher?

The Preacher laughs, leans over to Ewan, begins formulating a preliminary blueprint for my intervention.

What did Preacher say?

I swear, Jim says, I thought he said she might have teeth.

Somebody throw something at Henry, I say.

Ewan pops him in the head with a piece of ice. Henry starts, curses Ewan, curses Jim, curses me, greets Preacher James, falls back to a feathery, tickly sleep.

I'm going to talk to that redhead.

Go ahead, says Jim.

Nah.

That referee didn't die, Ewan says. Look, it's on the news. He had a heart attack but he's going to be all right, the fat, lovely bastard.

It's a sign, Jim says.

Good-natured expletive and pronoun. The vocative case.

It is.

You think so?

Sure. Just be yourself.

· · ·

I walk over when her friend goes to the bathroom, divide and conquer and all that. I'm a good bit drunk. She sees me coming, smiles quickly, stubs her cigarette and fishes for another. Not half bad. I pull up a chair. I light her cigarette. I say the things that need to be said.

There's something about waking up in a strange trailer. An unsettling feeling, as if at any moment you might be mobile. Disconcerting it is for a rootless boy, a boy looking for some roots in this his native land, native country. As a woman in the kitchen sings along with the radio, the master sleuth begins his a posteriori search for clues. Locates heat vent above head. Feels face, sand-blasted by dry air, attempts to summon strength to close vent, fails. Calls for IV go unanswered. Tosses sweat-soaked sheets aside, lies naked on bed, begins body check. Locates rug-burned knees. Abandons body check. Longs for the days of Madame La Guillotine.

The woman in the kitchen is singing with the radio and frying something on a pan. On the bed, radiation treatment continues. Forehead volunteers to microwave bacon. Body check begun subconsciously as breathing through nose proves impossible. Complete olfactory shutdown perhaps a blessing in disguise. Quick-dry cement and Super Glue application seem to have taken. Compliments extended to nose mason.

Around the room, scattered men's clothes and women's clothes and towels and lotions and salves. One square plastic wrapper, intact, giddy and virginal on the nightstand. Next to it, his torn brother. Following the bread crumbs reveals, at the foot of the bed, in decadent hauteur, sad, sagging latex applied and discarded, the old desensitizer foiled again. A bad example for youngsters to be sure.

The twelve-step recovery program begins with the first step, that is, blanket indictment of coconspirators. Second step. More sleep.

When I awaken again, a young woman in a robe has entered the boudoir and is sitting on the edge of the bed looking down at me. She smiles. She has summer teeth. Summer there, some ain't. Preacher James's oracle deciphered too late. Well, so be it. The least of my worries now, seeing as the army ants goose-stepping in my brain have finally bored a tiny passage through the nasal cavity. The result? Fecundity gone south, boiling sour mash, the vinegar factory opens today and the green flies are first in line. You want some water honey, she asks.

Yes. Please.

She goes to the kitchen and rattles around. You need anything else, she hollers back.

Yes, I say.

What?

Yes, I say, louder, really quite quite hungover. All joking aside. Someone has stolen my cheekbones and filled my face to the busting point with expanding balloons and gelatinous goo. My tongue is nothing if not a salt-cured ham in a dusty and abandoned smokehouse.

You'll have to speak up doll.

Bravely now, in actual halting motion, the teenage soldier offering the last shot of morphine to his beloved Sarge, I say, yes. Anything at all you have that I can take would be good.

I got aspirin.

Yes, good.

Hair of that dog that bit you?

Yes. Yes indeed.

She comes in with my drinks, smiling that idiosyncratic smile. I drink slowly, consider asking the nice lady to dip her fingers in the water and dribble it on the slabs of meat I formerly called my lips. Now dog hair, now water. Aspirin not to be rushed. Dry-mouth gag reflex could spell trouble.

Ain't quite so proud as he was last night, she says, pointing at the old troublemaker.

I look down. Poor pitiful hangdog utterly defeated. Ain't quite so proud, I agree.

She's taken off her robe and is wearing a black heavy metal T-shirt that covers just enough to arouse curiosity. Quick memory scan for details proves fruitless.

You're the Governor's son aren't you, she says.

I am that.

My daddy had a dog named Degraw when I was a kid. Said he wanted something to kick in the ass ever now and then.

I laugh. It hurts. How old are you by the way?

Twenty. Twenty-one in March.

You don't live here by yourself do you?

She smiles and to be honest the gaps and chips are beginning to endear themselves to me. I got an old man, she says.

Where's he?

Don't know don't care. Laid up somewheres with one of his whores I reckon.

But he could just walk in here at any moment?

I reckon.

Big man I assume. Likes guns and such.

You're funny. He's bigger an you. Don't know if he's got his gun on him or not. Likely he does.

I best be off then.

I was thinking bout taking a shower, she says, standing up and taking off her T-shirt.

And it's bad to say, really bad to say, just not the kind of thing one ought to say, but a naked redneck twenty-year-old is a naked redneck twenty-year-old.

So you're thinking about taking a shower, I say.

I'm back at my apartment after a good morning's work, and a fine Saturday afternoon it looks to be. Let's begin the afternoon by replaying my one and only message from Friday night, a message from my old television dad, Chad Kingston, which exhibits a race at breakneck speed between volume and incoherence, with incoherence narrowly taking home the prize at the finish line.

Degraw, inaudibility, aw god, something breaking, another thing breaking, a muddled chorus of disconnected oaths, much clearing of throat, Degraw, an increase in volume of an old Western on television with lots of firing of six-shooters, something quaffed greedily from a bottle, by god Degraw, click.

Now on to the mail.

Which includes a week's worth of overdue bills, crisp missives from my wife's attorney, and the like. These as might be expected are thrown harum-scarum across the room. However, amid this formal and uncharitable lot, lurks something out of the ordinary, an envelope without postage from my neighbor downstairs, the ever-vigilant Mrs. Catching. Inside the envelope is a note informing me that her dachshund, Nickel, was taken to the vet for potential whiplash and definitive trauma. The curt closing sentence indicates, in no uncertain terms, that I'll be receiving a call from her lawyer, Nelson Foxx, the first of the week.

Yes. Interesting. To be sued by a dog that is. On manufactured claims no less. Nelson Foxx, dog ambulance chaser, barking and scurrying under the wheels as he goes? Nickel in dog psychiatric ward yipping out his heart to attending physician, Scooby-Doo?

Alas, this pales in comparison to the last item in today's mailbag, a grocery sack stapled haphazardly to form an envelope and addressed to my childhood TV alter ego, Billy Tucker. The sender? One Odelle Bailey of Opp, Alabama. Contents? A letter written on the back of a Xeroxed newspaper clipping announcing the cancellation of *Bayou Dog*. Stylus? Thin purple marker. The hand? Standard maniacal sweep of all rounded letters, textbook madwoman's backward lean on the twiglike up and downs. The message?

Dear Billy,

How are you? Fine I hope. How's Thor? Does he still like to have his ears scratched? I think it's just wonderful that a boy and his dog have such a special relationship. It seems like I don't see as much of that these days. Boys are more interested in video games and the like. And dogs don't seem as interested in people neither. Or so it seems to me.

How's your dad? I've written him lately but haven't received a reply. I guess sheriffing keeps him busy most night and day. I did read in the paper about his recent visit to Tuscaloosa for that mall opening and saw where you all are all getting together for a reunion in April. I just wanted to let you know that I'll be there for sure. Which brings me to the point of my letter.

You'll have to excuse me, for the language I'm about to use. A boy your age ought not have to hear such. But as I've tried and tried to keep up a correspondence with your son of a bitch father, and he has again and again failed to respond to my inquiries, I've no recourse but to tell you myself that you are my bastard child. A child of love. For I did love your asshole father once. But a bastard child nonetheless. Oh Billy how I long to touch your face again. What I would not give to have you on my lap again.

I also hope this Degraw fellow is treating you well. I know this has been a trying year for you, but your father thought it best.

All my best honey and counting the days until we are together again. Give Thor a big ole scratch for me.

Xxxooo

Odelle Bailey (your mother)

p.s. I've enclosed a recent photo

Well, yes, okay. An interesting day in the old mail bag. Not too shabby if I say so myself. I pick up the phone to call the Tarzana cowboy, trying to shake my head clear of the picture of Odelle Bailey, my own mother for goodness sakes, astride a hay baler and, well, the less said the better. After about forty rings the good sheriff picks up sounding a bit fogged, a touch froggy.

This is your bastard son Billy.

Huh, says the celluloid cowpoke.

Your bastard son Billy. I'm missing my daddy.

By god boy, what are you talking about?

That's what I asked myself when I heard your message from last night. What end of the phone were you talking into by the way? The mouthpiece is on the smaller end.

Uh, he says. Oh. I did call you. Yeah that's right. By god I know what end of the phone to talk to. You're over my knee at the reunion Degraw. I promise you that.

Your big reunion. Yes, that's what I'm calling about. I got another letter from Odelle Bailey and frankly she's a little upset about the shabby treatment you've afforded her in the past.

I got a letter myself this week. And just for the record Bastard Billy, I never laid eyes on the woman till she started sending those pictures. Is that modern art she's trying to do out there on that baler? It looks like she's got some kind of pulley to get her leg up over that steering wheel.

It is a pulley.

Well.

Yes well.

Enough about that kook, he says. I remembered what I was calling about. Confirmed yesterday that Thor's great-grandson Comet will be at the reunion. Supposed to look just like him and can do most of them tricks, so I hear. Three weeks and counting my boy. Three weeks and counting.

What about Candy? I say sharply, trying to rain on the old stuntman's parade.

Haven't heard back from her yet. Don't you worry, she'll be there. How bout you? Changed your mind yet?

No. And I'm not going to. Billy's skipped his last rock, shed his last fake tear. Now remind me again why you want to have this ridiculous reunion.

Best work I ever did. That soap company doesn't pull their ads and we're on ten, fifteen years.

No one will come, I say. No one remembers.

That's where you're wrong my fatheaded friend. These damn thirty-year-olds, forty-year-olds, anything that reminds them of their pitiful childhoods they got to have it. Hell you can get a thousand dollars for one of them dolls for boys all the kids used to play with.

G.I. Joe?

That's it.

Where you getting your information on the present nostalgia boom for all things seventies and cheesy?

Saw this lady on TV said all these damn young people got so much money they don't know what to do with it, and they had these kinda pitiful childhoods watching the boob tube day and night. Snatchkey kids. That's what they're called.

Snatchkey? I say. You horny old bastard, it's latchkey. Latchkey kids. Latchkey kids came home from school while their mothers were still at work and had to let themselves in with their latchkey so that they could make a peanut butter sandwich and watch a lecherous old man drooling all over his teenage wife on the worst show in television history.

Latchkey, snatchkey. Hell if my mom hadn't been there when I got home from school, I'll tell you what kind of kid I would've been. They'd follow me home from the playground. Momma'd have to turn the hose on em to get em out of the yard. I was a pretty young man if I say so myself.

My god.

That show wasn't that bad.

We were a horrible rip-off of *Gentle Ben.* Same thing exactly. Had a dog instead of a bear.

Wish we'd of had one of them boats that flies over the water like a plane though. That's where they had us licked.

That, I say, and the fact that we stole their idea two years after they went off the air. Every story line we had was straight from *Lassie, Gentle Ben,* or *Flipper.*

Stole one from *Gunsmoke*. Kid stuck down in the well. Except in *Gunsmoke* it was a midget. I was in that episode.

Torturing the midget somehow?

Tripped him on his way to the bar and got one hell of a jack-slap for my trouble from James Arness.

I was down in that well for eight hours that day.

Price of fame my boy, he says. The price of fame. I lost a tooth and had a slight concussion from that lick from James Arness. He felt so bad, had me back for three more episodes.

About this reunion, I say. I'm serious. I wish you well and all, but you're just going to have to count me out.

I'll be in town next Friday to sew it up. Plan on meeting me for supper around eight.

I've got my daughter on Friday.

Love to meet her. I'll call you. By god boy, if everything works out the way I think it's gonna, I can just smell a made-for-TV reunion special. Hell maybe a motion picture.

Later that day, a long and windy mid-March Saturday, skittery and dragging and undefined after the excitement of the morning and early afternoon, I'm winding my way out of town, heading as I do, as I often do, as I ought to do more, to see my mother, the crazy woman who lives out in the country in a trailer next to a hill next to a cemetery next to nothing else much at all.

I'm forty miles west of Tuscaloosa out in the country, and the road out here is bare and spread-out before me. So far, I've passed two pickups and one tractor heading the other way. All three waved, two with index finger lifted from the wheel in traditional

Southern salutation, the other, the tractor driver, with a tip of his John Deere cap.

The land out here is quietly pretty, groves of hardwoods, then a patch of tall pines, then a freshly plowed field of black soil. The colors today against the grey sky are more muted than usual, more browns and tans and greys, the land still in that in-between state before everything has come fully into bloom. And the wind blows sudden piles of old leaves across the road that swirl about mailboxes on thick posts, the mailboxes varying from small house to small house, some bent and unadorned, others done up in crimson and white with the family name on top in an intricate hand. And it's hard to say what is so beautiful and melancholy about the widely spread mailboxes on a country road, the hawk drafting in circles above the new spring wheat. Or why a brown dog trotting along the road, with only a casual look for a passing car, makes the day seem so lonely and unsettled.

About a mile from her house, I stop at Dawson's Grocery, a ramshackle general store with a tobacco-stained wooden porch and rusted metal signs for soft drinks that no longer exist. Bells and the echo of bells on the door as I enter. Mr. Dawson petting a cat on the counter, humming along to a Roger Miller tune on the radio.

Well hey there Dev, he says, coming around from the counter in a flannel shirt and his still-steady gait.

I shake the extended hand, and say, hello Mr. Dawson, how've you been?

Fine Dev, he says. Fine as can be. Same for Mrs. Dawson. We're getting along better than two old coots have a right to.

I'm glad to hear it, I say. And I'm sorry I haven't been by

sooner to clear up Mom's tab. Guess it's getting on up there by this point.

No, no. Not at all. Don't you worry yourself over it. Go get your groceries and I'll have it worked up when you get through.

When I come up to the front with my things, Mr. Dawson has my tab ready and two cartons of Salem Menthols up on the counter. I reach down and pull up a handful of Goo Goo Clusters from the candy rack and plop them on top of the cigarettes. Mr. Dawson smiles. Won't eat enough to feed a bird, he says, but still likes them Goo Goo bars.

Cigarettes and chocolate, I say.

He shakes his head, smiling.

Did you add in some on my tab for that boy that drives her home? He still work here?

Yes, he says. Van's still here. Works mostly weekends. When your mother walks down during the week, I just lock up for a minute and run her home myself. It's no trouble.

Well I can't thank you enough anyway.

It's nothing. Glad to do it.

I'd like you to add on twenty for the boy who drives.

That's too much, he says.

No sir. It's worth every penny.

If she'd call me, we could pick her up too.

She won't, I say, pulling out my wallet and handing over the money. Behind Mr. Dawson, it's a dusty-looking deer's head, Fishing Rodeo posters of days gone by. Beneath the deer's head, a glass case full of pocketknives. I used to love to look at those knives, I say.

Bought you a couple or three as I recall. You still got those knives?

Somewhere, I say.

He nods, handing over the change. How's the law treating you?

Not like it is on TV.

You ought to run for something, he says. I'd vote for you.

I laugh, but don't say anything, then we're shaking hands, and he's wishing me luck as I'm heading out the door with the groceries.

When I get to the trailer, I park the car in the gravel drive and tromp through the mud to the front door. Out in the ostensible yard, a trash bag some dogs got into weeks past, a cigarette carton, generic, windblown against a couple of dismal trees and sitting soggily now at a jagged angle, tuckered by the wind, the long winter, not the energy to head on down the hill to the small wooded plot that nestles up to the cemetery. Scattered about, an assortment of bottles, their muddied glowing finality catching what's left of a raw sun. Rusted chimes pretty in the breeze. A quagmired rake from two falls past. A tire swing, low-slung and slow, filled with rotting leaves and mosquito larvae, waiting for night and the boy ghost who visits.

Inside there's rattling around, a blaring TV. I knock, softly, through a screen door missing its screen. Coming, coming, says the ragged and scratched voice of the woman who is my mother. She opens the door and stands there in an old satin robe looking at me without surprise. A day has passed, a week, a year. Come in Dev, she says. Why of course come in.

After I put up the groceries, she clears off a place on the couch, scooting off a rangy wild-looking cat, cigarette wrappers, an unopened Christmas card. She sits in the reclining chair and wraps herself in an afghan my grandmother made a long time ago. The TV continues to blare.

So how you getting on Dev?

Fine Mom fine.

And how's your wife?

She's fine too.

Cute as a bug that one.

Yes maam.

She pulls out a cigarette and starts to light it with a long fire match. I reach over with my lighter. Hold her trembling hand still.

I sit back down and look at my smiling crazy mother.

It's so nice to have raised a gentleman, she says. Could I get you a drink?

No maam. Not right now.

She gets up slowly, arthritic, and makes her way to the small kitchen. Around the den are filled ashtrays and old magazines. On an antique whatnot her spoon collection. On the television, pictures of me, wedding, school, a glossy from *Bayou Dog*. On the coffee table a shot of the two of us handing out campaign buttons, Mom looking like the pretty ex-librarian that she was. I pick it up for a closer look. See what is there in the face of the smiling woman who will go from governor's mansion to recluse's trailer. And where is the Governor in the picture? On the grandstand, in a meeting, in a hurry. Perhaps wife number two, the reporter, is just out of camera range, talking to an aide, waiting to see the Governor, who must lunch with his family before they can hotel-motel-backseat it.

My mother comes back from the kitchen with her scotch, her cigarette. She sits in the recliner and smiles at me, her son, who has not come to visit for the last two months, who has spent his time in bars, in wasted time not to be recovered. And outside the tire swing has begun to rock in the breeze through the smoke-stained window, a boy running from the cemetery, shooting an air rifle, throwing rocks, sticks, balls, whittling sticks, running sprints, hopping tombstones, missing his friends in the city, long summer days of boredom, cramped quarters, counting the days, one day down, thirteen to go, and burned macaroni and cheese, vegetables from dusty cans, boxes and boxes of cookies, and hating this, hating these two weeks, how many rides can be taken on a tire swing, how many times down to Dawson's Grocery then chased home by ghosts from the cemetery, what is being missed in town, what games played, girls met, and the unfairness, the bitter unfairness, of that old uncomfortable, nagging, will not will not will not go away, love for the crazy woman who is his mother.

It's a good picture of you, I say, handing it over.

She reaches on the couch for her glasses, can't seem to find them, looks anyway. It is, she says. It is a good picture. Who's this little boy?

It's me.

That's not you. You're much bigger than that.

Yes it is. We were campaigning in Huntsville.

Was it hot that day?

Yes. It was. That's right. It was October but unusually hot.

We won that election, she says smiling.

We did.

He was such an optimistic man.

Yes, I say, he was.

Lucky too. I don't think he thought I was lucky. My father wasn't a lucky man, and your father always seemed afraid, if that's the right word, that I'd maybe inherited that from him. He knew he could count on his own luck. Mine he wasn't so sure about. Life is easier don't you think if you think you're lucky?

I do. I sure do.

Would you like a cookie?

No maam. Not just yet.

My mother smiles, pulls out another cigarette. I stand up to light it. She takes my hand in hers, cool and dry. It's so nice to have raised a gentleman, she says.

Sundayed. All day. Blahhed and blanched. The fiddler's bill. A mist of rain constant. All friends out of town, all phones unplugged. Flickerings of the remote and the patient silent phone. Gloomed. Synapsed into grey. Short journeys started and abandoned. The dull fritter. Antsy inertia. Single cars on the road, sporadic, spare. Sneaking. The quarantined sign aglow.

Bouncing check to the deliveryman. Blue-lawed. Blue-deviled. Grey without blue. Sore and stunted. Third-personned. Dev Degraw.

At 12:01 A.M. Dev Degraw sits at the bar, just opened, another Tuscaloosa oddity, earliest Monday after the long dry day. The walk up the wet empty Strip at midnight not for every man. Past closed-up shops and restaurants, and wet handbills on telephone poles soggy with specials on long necks and last night's band, the odd student out for a pack of cigarettes, his headlights coming briefly to rest on a lone walker, Sunday's widower, head bowed, hands stuffed in pockets, curled up into the dark facades of the closed-down block. No time of night for anything save the cutting of edges, the sad lonely need of a human voice.

And into the bar that smells of last night, last weekend, stale and mildewed and cigarette-scarred. Rotted carpet. Whispery walls. What was missed what was missed. Bartender, old friend. A smile. The great and mighty Dev Degraw. A stout poured into a cold glass, foamed and beading. Fresh pack of smokes.

In they come, those who are coming. Singular for the most part, strays and third shifts and graduate students, shaking off the rain, the shakes, a baker's dozen in total. Tabs and loose change, quarters unrolled, dimes filched from piggy banks, sofa cushions. Stand me one Dev. You're stood. The clack of pool balls breaking.

Footfall and echo in the walk home. A throat cleared. Streetlights on puddles, mist in the light. A rat chattering at the Dumpster. An insomniac bird.

Past neighbors' newspapers still in plastic. A lone bulb in the doorway. Up the musty steps. Squeak of a door. Light switch fumbled and found. Home. The unstaved quiet. Black mute electronics. Blank bachelor walls. A pizza box. A coffee table strewn. Reflection in a window. Dev Degraw.

The Butter Eating Contest

As soon as I get through with whatever I'm supposed to be doing here for the good Governor, I'll be skipping off for a meeting with the Queen Bee, who's driven up from Montgomery for a night on the town with some of the gals. Though it was the worst possible thing I could have done, I broke down and called the Queen only five days after our last vigorous chess match. A horrible gambit. Rookie mistake. And the Queen's distracted manner on the phone, like a wasp were flying in her hair or something. Not a good sign.

In the interim on a cloudy Monday eve, I'm sitting with Shade in Skip Terry's Birmingham office. From here, the headquarters of Terry Construction, the old Skipper makes the call on everything from highway projects to the backwoods gambling joints he runs throughout the state. Mr. Terry, it seems, has his porky fingers in many a pie. Those same porky fingers are now prying cubes from an ice bucket and plonking them into glasses for the three of us. Behind the madcap plonking, two rigid and crew-cutted associates are giving old Dev the once-over just for the sport of it. Large men they are, the associates, large and brooding.

How about this view, says Skip Terry, sloshing a whiskey on rocks before an enormous window. Twenty stories below, Birmingham spiders off in every direction to smokestacks, interstates, the odd bit of grass waiting to be paved.

Splendid, I say.

Shade looks over at me and smiles. He seems to be wondering just how he got stuck with me and Skip Terry on a Monday night.

Then Skip's handing a whiskey to Shade, one to me, and

motioning for the associates to grab their own from the bar. Sitting down beside me and placing a hand on my familiar and irresistible shoulder, he says, here's to the Alabama state lottery.

I smile but don't touch the proffered glass.

Skip looks at Shade, Shade at Skip. No tipping of glass in any direction.

All right, he says. All right. I usually prefer to get the business out of the way first so everybody can relax and have a good time afterward. But if we need some chitchat first about the weather, that's fine. I can see I'm in the company of gentlemen tonight.

With this he gives the young fancy pants a significant look. The old sizer-upper. As if I've forgotten that he and the Governor are old high school chums, teammates and the works, and that he has been a frequent and generous donor to the Governor's many campaigns. I smile at Mr. Terry, give him a reassuring nod of my humble young head. Seeing the modest Southern youth before him seems to do the trick, for he offers a reassuringly paternalistic smile as he again raises his glass for a toast. To old friends and the sons of old friends, he says.

With this, I touch my glass to his. Agricola est bona, I say, draining the whiskey in a gulp.

Skip takes a sip to seal the toast. What's that son?

Latin, I say, nodding toward the hefty barkeeps for another. The farmer is good.

What the hell's that mean, says Skip Terry, forcing out a laugh and looking toward the bar for some rowdy confirmation. Skeptical grunts and harrumphs ensue. Shade, meanwhile, is casually sipping on his drink, every now and then admiring one of the seven watercolor prints of Roll Tide glory that comprise the whole of Mr. Terry's art collection.

I think the sentence, when translated, speaks for itself.

The farmer is good?

Yes, I say. He is.

You calling me a farmer son?

I smile. Shade rattles his drink. The associates take a step toward the table, neither bearing round two for Dev.

You calling me a redneck? You think I'm some kind of hayseed?

I rattle the ice in my glass a bit as a reply.

Mr. Shade, he says, what do you think of the young governor here?

Shade takes a casual sip of his whiskey. I like the young governor, he says.

To this, I nod my damn right head.

Skip Terry sighs, motions for the associates to scram. Well, he says, well, well, well. So the Governor had prior engagements tonight? Is that right? Do I remember that correctly?

He did, Shade says. Otherwise, he'd have been here.

Oh I'm sure, I'm sure, Skip Terry says. But are we going to talk about this lottery or not?

Yes, I say, let's talk about the lottery.

The Governor's in a tight spot, says Shade.

What tight spot? says Skip Terry. I'm the one standing to lose three million on a real estate deal. That swampland ain't worth squat without a casino sitting on it. I thought me and the Governor saw all this the same way. Now here it is crunch time and I hadn't heard the word lottery come out of his mouth in the better part of two months.

Our concern, I say, or at least my concern, is that the lottery is unpopular with the voting public. Folks who are for it may or may not show up election day. Those who are against it, on the other hand, the churches and the black leaders and so forth, well they'll be there come hell or high water.

You got to sell it, Skip Terry says. Sell the idea that the lottery means education, no new taxes. Hell it's a good thing economically for the state.

That's obviously debatable, I say. But economic matters aside, the real question, from a purely Machiavellian angle, is if this lottery business is a hot enough potato to cost the Governor an election.

Machiavellian angle? says Skip Terry, looking first at Shade, then back toward the bar and the moping associates. Then he looks at my empty glass, Shade's empty glass, ignores them both and goes to the bar to pour himself a tall one. He mutters something that looks like Machiavellian angle, then something about Josh Wade being an easier governor to work with. And all the while he's smiling at me without true joy in his heart.

Junior here is wondering, says Skip Terry to no one in particular, if I'm going to cost the Governor an election.

Junior here is wondering, I say, if you can handle your affairs without the Governor's public support. Are you viable on the referendum without us?

Skip Terry doesn't reply to this but strides at a nimble pace to rest a big hand on top of my shoulder. The impression given is that he would like Junior to remain seated during the remainder of our discourse.

Us? he says. Us? I was us before you were a glimmer in your daddy's eye. Back when he was just a skinny hick farm boy like I was. Back when he was hustling insurance out of Sharpsburg trying to scratch his way off the farm for good. I been good to your daddy. Been good to you by god. Put some damn steaks on that table. Kept your daddy in new cars.

Be that as it may, I say, wrenching his hand from my shoulder, we are here to assess this from a certain point of view. A very narrow point of view. And what I must ascertain is if you are or if you are not a political liability. Not you personally of course. You are an old and true friend of my father's. I'm talking exclusively about the lottery issue.

Skip Terry tousles my hair, smiles. Mr. Shade, he says, what do you do with our young friend here?

Shade smiles, doesn't say anything.

Mr. Shade, I say, speaking for some reason like a BBC anchorman, generally tries to dissuade me from my current pursuits, old sport. Mr. Shade, I say, is usually bloody free with his kind counsel.

Shit you say, says Skip Terry.

Out your arse old fruit, say I.

Skip Terry stands there with a wry look on his face. Unperturbed would seem to be the look he's going for. In response to this look, the BBC anchorman suddenly folds his hands together and begins bowing like a humble geisha. To complete the picture, the anchorman half closes his eyes and rocks as if in compulsive servile meditation. Perhaps unsurprisingly, this mixing of cultural metaphors, horrific British accent meeting smartassy Anglo-male-geisha, takes most of the wryness out of Mr. Terry's face.

By god boy, you're crazy as a loon, he says without a trace of huckster in his voice or manner. Mr. Shade, this young fellow is crazy.

I been saying that for years, says Shade.

Well I'll finish up our little conversation with you then Mr. Shade.

I just drove the boy out, he says. You want to talk, you'll have to talk to him.

Just the driver huh Mr. Shade? says Skip Terry, recovering his bearing. I forget that sometimes. Just the driver. Well then my crazy young friend, if you can stop bowing for a moment, perhaps you could tell me what the Governor himself says.

The Governor's a loyal man Mr. Terry, I say, continuing to bow obediently but opening my eyes to give him a contrived Hollywood notion of a rakish redneck wink.

Damn right he is, says Skip Terry. Damn right.

And I know you are too.

Hell yes. Hell yes I am.

So it sounds like neither of you would like to do anything that would hurt the other, I say, bowing still like there's no tomorrow.

That's right. That's exactly right.

Then I don't foresee a problem.

Well goddam hell no there ain't no problem. Round of shots?

Goddam hell yes, I say.

Why were you talking like an Englishman, Shade asks as we get out of the elevator and walk toward our cars in the underground parking lot.

Hell if I know, I say.

Got you a contrary streak, says Shade. That's okay, that's fine. I'm pretty much the same all the time. You're full of shit, I'm gone. The Governor though, especially when he was younger, used to mess with em some. You should have seen the overalls he'd throw on when he got around some of them rich folks. Ain't this and ain't that. And same thing. Get him around the good ole boys and he's using words to make their eyes goggle out. Seen him do Skip Terry that way a couple of times when Skip got a little backslappy with him.

He stops at his car and lights a cigarette. Hands one over to me and lights it. He's smiling and shaking his head. I think you handled yourself pretty good tonight, he says. Crazy as hell, but you made your point. It ain't written in stone that we're behind the lottery.

What's the Governor going to say?

I'd say he had a good guess how this would turn out when he asked you to do it. The Governor does like his wiggle room you know.

He's a sly one, I say.

He ain't all dumb, says Shade.

We shake hands and I start for my car. When I'm only a few feet away, Shade says, you ain't much different from your daddy, but you are different.

I stop and turn back toward him to see what he means by this.

Shit'll stick to baby boy, Shade says, that slides right off the Governor's boot.

When I walk in the door of the bar, The Bistro to be precise, I realize immediately that I'm wearing last year's shoes, a haircut from a prior century. Obviously, the Queen is nowhere to be found. On the bright side, I do see Hooper Higginbothan sitting at the bar and gazing fondly into something imported. To the seasoned Hooper-watcher, the glazed look in his eye is clear indication that he's found the happy spot in his brain and is either a) loping languidly across a lacrosse field or b) droning casually about the hive. Breaking the loping, droning reverie after a few moments, he looks up and smiles, then waves me over as if his glasses weren't a blatant breach of the social contract.

Hooper, I say, how in the hell are you?

Fine Dev, he says, baby genius glasses sparkling in the dim light. I'm fine. Grab a seat big guy.

Suspicions aroused? Yes indeed, yes indeed. Friendly Hooper?

Unperturbed Hooper? General conclusions drawn add up to some-one being tooled upon. Someone a bit Devish, someone slightly Degraw. And questions to be answered? Again yes. Again indeed. First and foremost, when did the term girlfriend as used most re-cently in common vernacular by the Queen Bee cease to delineate the specific gender of the friend in question?

Having swiftly abandoned my first instinct of flight, curiosity and the cat you know, I'm sitting at the bar with Hooper, taking turns putting drinks on our respective tabs, and inquiring with all apparent sincerity about the social and athletic components, his term, of the Birmingham Lacrosse Club. The Queen is only, casu-ally, an hour late at this point. But it's been a good hour. In addi-tion to getting to know Hooper better, I've used the time to take in all that The Bistro has to offer in its understated but bravely masculine way. A cigar bar? But of course. Humidors as far as the eye can see. And more young tousle-haired fatheads in loosened ties just back from Vail than you'd care to shake a stick at. A big stick. A powerful stick. A vengeful stick.

So Hoop, I say, toasting his good health, wishing him a life of excellent stickwork, of blissful stretching, who exactly are we meeting tonight?

My sister and Shea and Gibson and some other people.

You don't say. And how is the warrior Puritan?

What?

Gibson, I say. How is good old Gibson?

He's great. Wouldn't you be if you were dating Shea?

And saying this, my little quidnunc smiles a little, his spec-tacles arrested in twinkly and giddy understatement.

Oh they're dating? I say.

For over three months, says Hooper yawning. Dee-Dee thinks they might get married.

I smile, I laugh, I light a cigarette. Hooper, I say, let's see if I can drink you interesting.

As I'm contemplating the inordinate amount of time I seem to be spending in speakeasies and the pros and cons of escorting an engaged woman to the Governor's Ball, that same engaged woman walks into this same speakeasy. At her side, the recently betrothed Oliver Cromwell, old Gibby himself. Head high, hair sweeping, clothes tasteful and form-fitting, the Queen strides to the bar with a coterie close behind. She sees me, waves enthusiastically, and excuses herself gracefully from her court. As she approaches, the visiting team is being hooted off the court. Hooted, not booed. Derision pure and simple. And now the Queen is hugging my neck, lightly kissing my mouth.

Dev, she says, with her arms still around me, squeezed between my legs and pressing up firmly, moving this way and that. I've missed you.

Have you now, I say, fake-voiced and flustered.

I have. I really have.

Without knowing it I've put my hands around her waist, and would, despite myself, very much like to kiss her, the thick honey-eyed drug of the hive clouding my judgment. She's running her hands through my hair, petting and cooing. Next to us Hooper Higginbothan stares into his drink, not experienced enough to know that this is the tooling he's been waiting for, that as soon as he and Oliver and whichever else of the male girlfriends are worked into a froth, the Queen's off old Dev before he knows what hit him. Poor Hooper, poor tiny glasses Hooper. At the end of the bar nearer the door, Oliver C. is acting fairly nonchalant, considering as we must that his date for the evening looks as if she's about to start making out with another man any minute now.

I turn and smile at the Queen who is smiling at me. We lock eyes. If I kissed her, she would kiss me back. In lieu of a kiss, however, I begin singing the old Andy Griffith standard in a high lonesome cat screech of a yodel.

What's you gonna do when the well runs dry honey
What's you gonna do when the well runs dry babe

The Queen stands there looking at me. You are so weird, she says.

Then I'm hamboning, slapping thigh to chest, the fiddler in my head starting in hot and saucy, and banjo man lighting quick, now the jugs hollow and thin, hollow and thin, and here we go in a full hamboning yodelling twang.

What's you gonna do when the well runs dry honey
What's you gonna do when the well runs dry babe
What's you gonna do when the well runs dry
Sit on a log and cry cry cry
Oh honey oh babe of mine

And then the Queen is off in a huff toward the bathroom, Dee-Dee hot on her heels. I wave at Gibson Smith, the iron-willed Cromwell, and shout across the bar, how you doing Gibson? Looks like you been lifting weights.

He laughs, gives a half Mr. Universe in return. Quick cause for reanalysis? Decent guy caught up in the machinations of the court? Doubtful, skeptical, dubious.

Hooper looks over at me and smiles.

I smile back in return.

He takes a final swig from his drink and stands up with what might pass for authority on some Eastern boarding school playground. Then he stretches, saying, well Dev, it's been real.

You usually yawn when you do that stretch, I say. It usually goes yawn, stretch, yawn. Then you follow that up with a bored look around the room. Then, usually, you see how far you can stick your nose up Shea's ass.

What did you say?

I'm pretty sure you heard me.

You're lucky we're out in public.

The rain in Spain falls mainly on the plains.

What?

Buzz buzz buzz, I say, flapping my elbows like tiny wings.

What are you doing?

Bzzzzzzzzzzzzzzzzzzzz. Bzzzzzzzzzzzzzzzzzz. Bzzzzzzzzzzzzzz

Later, after Hooper strangles me for quite a while and still I buzz, after I head-butt him in the nose, buzzing still, stretching now and buzzing as Hooper lies semiconscious on the floor, buzzing now and stretching, prodding Hooper with my foot, seeing if he stretches in his bloody sleep, and after Shea and Dee-Dee and the other buzzing drones have scolded me, stared at me, shed hysterical crocodile tears and helped Hooper to his feet, still dazed, little bitty oh-so-smart glasses mangled and hanging off one ear, and departed en masse, the bartender, a strapping young buck to be sure, a peripheral drone with good standing in the hive, has me in a pretty decent headlock, not what my tender esophagus requests at the moment having just disengaged the Hoopster, but a headlock nonetheless, as he informs me that my credit card has been denied, and how in the hell am I going to pay my tab because

I will, by god, his words not mine, pay the tab, then my ass is out of there, after that, after all that, I ask to see the credit card, are you sure, let me see it, let me see if I gave you the right one, I'm sorry about all this, I really am, can I see that credit card just for a sec, and then the reluctant release, and I say, boy that was a good headlock, I could barely move, and the credit card is hesitantly, gingerly, handed ever so gently over, and I'm looking at it, hhmn, hhmn, that's weird, and taking off out the door and into the night and back the sixty miles to Tuscaloosa where, if nothing else, my bar credit is still in good standing.

Wednesday morning has crept crisply along, sixty snappy seconds to the minute, sixty full-bodied minutes to the hour. I've been dozing, dreaming sweet dreams of Thursday, that beautiful non-Wednesday of a day. While I was asleep I did miss two calls. The first was from the Governor asking me down to Montgomery for dinner. The second, well the second was from an honest-to-god dog attorney named Nelson Foxx. Yes, it appears that Nickel, my neighbor's wiener dog, has retained counsel. Nelson Foxx, dog attorney-at-law, talks corn liquor sweet and uses such phrases as injured party, the night in question, plaintiffs deposition, bark-bark, woof-woof, and surprise, surprise, potential settlement.

I pace around the office a bit, hoping Sheila will wander in sooner or later and give me some good ideas for retribution, but it seems yet another Wednesday has been declared National Secretary Day. After some careful albeit violent deliberation, I scrounge around the office for some letterhead and once I find it, I sit down to compose. The finished though admittedly hasty result?

Dear Mr. Foxx,

In response to your voice message on this the nineteenth of March, in this the year of our Lord, by reference herein, in support thereof, do hereby acknowledge the grievous pain and anguish of said defendant, i.e., Devaney Degraw, i.e. me, immediately proximate upon the receipt of your voice message.

And, as such, and in sound mind and body so far as the plaintiff's jackleg attorney shall know, do herewith and wheretofor hence request the immediate cessation of any further and future phone calls in regards to said canine plaintiff, i.e. wiener dog, i.e. Nickel Catching, as such said calls do preclude and impair said defendant's ability to think kindly of either the human or the canine race.

And that I do further recommend a nonnegligent silence on the part of said jackleg attorney for said plaintiff wiener dog, and, further still, request that said defendant be discharged from liability to any manufactured claims of trauma, physical, mental, spiritual, or other, and that all costs of said manufactured trauma, i.e. veterinary bills, canine psychotherapist, ad infinitum ad nauseum, do hereby return to said plaintiff, canis hotdoggis.

And that, moreover, if further missives, interrogatories, false claims, and other examples of nonnegligent silence persist past this the nineteenth of March, said defendant will sue said plaintiff attorney for harassment, bringing of a false suit, and irritation beyond the call of duty.

In short, i.e., ergo: Cease and desist dipshit.

Aggressively submitted,

Devaney Degraw

Interestingly, as soon as the envelope is addressed, stamped, and placed in the box, I experience an unexpected onslaught of androgen coursing through my capillaries at breakneck speed. Perhaps it's just a young man's inate love of the law. Perhaps it's just a simple matter of biorhythms. Whichever the case may be, and these situations are nothing if not mysterious, as soon as I received this powerful opening surge of chemicals, my nervous system, specifically the medulla oblongata, put out an all-points bulletin for endorphins before my cerebrum could intercede. And after such a series of unpredictable and inalterable commands, Homo sapien physiology at its finest, it's really no surprise that I've begun to hear the halcyon call of a midafternoon debauch.

Queen and Bee are the words that seem to occur and reoccur without cessation, but there's no chance there in light of Monday's unfortunate series of miscommunications. Yes, young Dev has sunk that ship I'm afraid. And Sheila, well Sheila is more than likely resting up after a big night of her own. Ex-wife? Interesting for a variety of theoretical reasons, not the least of which is that she wouldn't. Which leaves Summer Teeth. Which means riding out to Rolling Acres Trailer Park and a door-to-door search. Which means all manner of ill-tempered well-armed nonhusbands opening doors. Which means no.

At any rate, the nine-month serotonin binge has the troops strung out and sullen and demanding their daily stew. Even now the boys down in the adrenal glands are threatening to storm the trailer park, though if that happens, the steady men of mitochondrion might leave and never come back. The cerebrum is about fully shut down by this point and has taken the cerebellum with it, victims both of low blood sugar and chemical overdose. Mitochondrion gather on one border. Food! they shout. Fats and sugars and protein! Fats and sugars and proteins!

Answering in full, with an antic logorrhea, the mad glad gland boys, clamoring for their pleasure.

I'm finishing up my fast-food burger, quick nod to physical well-being and superior self-discipline, as I pull into the parking lot in front of Mr. Chuck's downtown kiosk. Yes, pornography it is. Pornography I'm afraid it's going to have to be. As I enter the establishment, I'm welcomed by two basset hounds lounging ele-phantinely in my path. The hounds attempt to raise their heads at the ringing of the bells on the door, but are weighted down by the rings of dirt and Twinkie goo around their necks, and eyelids packed full of baloney, and pitiful ears lumped and stuffed with Tootsie Rolls and Slim Jims and assorted decades-old, deviled-grab-bag-guesswork. They're real fat.

I step over the dust wallerers nimble as you please. Woe to the Mr. Chuck's customer who makes them squall, makes them move. Mr. Chuck himself is behind the counter, unshowered and un-shaved, mumbling to himself about candy bars, baseball cards, pornographic magazines. He's wearing dirty plumbing coveralls with the name TIMMY emblazoned on the front and a stained foam baseball hat that states, I KNOW YOU ARE, WHAT AM I? He's disdained the societal norm of a shirt, and his coverall is unzipped nearly to the navel, exposing a fair amount of charcoal grey chest hair, curly and untamed. You'd be safe in assuming he's worn the same ensemble for the duration of the week.

What you say there Mr. Chuck? I say.

Garbledy hell garbledy damn gooblily shit.

I know it. Couldn't agree more. You said it there.

Genghis Khan shallup, says Mr. Chuck, launching an open box of Milk Duds toward the front of the store and the lolling hounds.

Then he heads toward the back storage room for some meditative kicking of empty boxes, and I am alone in an empty magazine store, considering for a moment the complicated nature of man.

Beginning my journey toward the porno proper, I take a cursory look at the sports magazine. Flip, flip, flip, Roll Tide et cetera. Next, the weekly news magazine. Nothing shows the well-rounded man quite like being up-to-date on current events. Moving ever so smoothly to the literary magazine section. Oh to hell with that. Then on to gambling, gaming, games of chance. Win Big Big Big. Bury your bookie. First call is free. And now skipping past the muscle-man, muscle-car, muscle-gun portion and stopping ever so gently in the far right corner of the store, next to what I can only assume is Mr. Chuck's mystery closet of doom.

There are many descriptions of these types of periodicals, and they vary according to consumer predilection, but essentially all contain naked humans inside. I personally prefer the ones featuring fit nude females, over eighteen years of age, tastefully posed, nonpregnant, unaccompanied by those of the male gender, and, as of late, shorn in the nether regions. As for the tastefully posed question, that obviously is a matter of some discernment. In general I am not a fan of implements, aids, splaying of any kind, or as implied earlier, the male appendage. Fruits and vegetables leave me cold, and, bewilderingly, whipped cream seems to have no effect at all. Pictorials that emphasize and showcase the backside of a young woman are particular favorites. And, finally, politically correct modern man that I am, I favor no nude country of origin over another, excepting perhaps a slight bias toward those of the Eastern hemisphere, which could, technically speaking, be more a product of testing methodology than true bias.

This is the most exciting and most important part of the ritual of the debauch, the actual choosing of magazines. It's important here not to rush and go with first instinct, which is almost always, the lewder the better. Alas, the inverse proportion between the ideal feminine form and the female form who will allow herself to be photographed doing the smuttier things in life makes for a delicate balance in the professional debaucher's thought process.

I check the table of contents of a number of magazines, but don't indulge my curiosity for a closer examination. I spend about an hour making my picks, every so often wandering down to the business magazine section to clear my head and get a better perspective of what it is I'm looking for.

During the whole of my decision-making process, the store has been blissfully empty. No ministers, little old ladies, or Cub Scouts to dodge. No fellow attorneys without peccadilloes of their own. Quite nice. Every so often a wallowing cerberus will moan for a treat. Every so often Mr. Chuck will gurgle out a jabberwocky riff or kick something. Really you couldn't ask for much more. Quite nice. Quite relaxing.

I finish up the gnashing-of-teeth phase and rely on instinct and natural feel to parry my potential purchases down to three. With only two you run the risk of complete washout. And let's face it, four is just gluttonous. Three's the number. Decisions complete, I gather them up in a rush and walk with a quick proud step to the counter to pay. Self-loathing, sheep's clothing.

I get to the front and flop the magazines up on the counter. Mr. Chuck is in the storage room karate-chopping, it seems, an old loaf of bread. I shuffle my feet, this is no time to tarry, and in the process nearly step on a dusty Milk Dud treat. At the door, the gobslotchier of the gobslotching hounds gives me a mournful moan and with a slow burst of lewd energy manages to open its mouth. Lining up for the penalty kick, Pelé takes careful aim, Pelé shoots a rifle of a shot, Pelé SCORES! Impromptu jig of celebration,

Brazilian revelry. Taking my bows and looking on the floor for another dud, I catch two teasers on the front page of the *Birmingham News*. The first is a sober announcement for an op-ed piece on the Governor's conspicuous silence on the lottery. Worse still, the author of the op-ed piece is none other than Frederick Batch, the respected mayor of Birmingham and influential leader of the black community, who has been, for as long as I can remember, one of the Governor's staunchest supporters. The second teaser, in a garish blue font, is for Cindy Malloy's gossip column. *Whisper, whisper*, says the headline, *sources tell Cindy bad boy governor's son runs out on bar tab*. Story on D-1.

I'm reaching for a paper to see just how bad the damage is, the damage to me, not my father's well-deserving ass, when a well-dressed and strideful matron walks in the door bearing an uncanny resemblance to my ex-mother-in-law. Simultaneously, one of the dogs begins a hoarse choking cough. Frantic attempts to render myself invisible seem to have failed as the cloned matriarch adjusts her pearl necklace, hurdles the coughing dog, and begins her determined march to the counter. Casually, calmly, subterfuge unlimited, I toss the newspaper toward my collection of monthlies as an impromptu cover and just as planned, right over the counter it goes. Mr. Chuck, hearing the coughing dog, comes cursing from the back. To my left, the unknown illegitimate twin of my ex-mother-in-law. Across from me, spread out in a perfect fantail, a copy of *Best of Penthouse*, always solid, *Asian Queens*, like a trip to a foreign land, and, in a nod to coarser instincts and the latest fad, *Shaved and Oiled*.

Burbly shit dog's choking, says Mr. Chuck.

Well hello, Devaney, says Mrs. Dunlap, ignoring the psychopath leaping across the counter and rushing toward his choking dog as she eyes one, then the other, then yes the other too, of the magazines on the counter. Then she looks at me with an aha, I knew it all along look.

Hello, Mrs. Dunlap, I say, turning completely around and trying to block the counter. How are things?

Oh fine fine, she says.

Good, good, I say, facing now toward another stack of the *Birmingham News* and the smiling, finger-to-lips, Cindy Malloy.

I don't usually come in here, she says, but today's the day the Lions Club hands out their glasses to the blind children.

I nod, fumble behind my back trying to stack my girls. Excellent charity, I say.

Mr. Chuck grunts and tries to lift his choking dog, gets bitten for his trouble, falls to the floor.

I believe that dog is choking, says Mrs. Dunlap.

Hairball probably, I say.

I believe that's cats Devaney. Perhaps you should help that man lift his dog.

She smiles. Yes the blood will tell. Attraction will wane, young love rarely lasts, a mule will never win the Kentucky Derby, and governor's mansion or no governor's mansion, no Degraw will ever pass muster in the Tuscaloosa Yacht Club.

I walk over to Mr. Chuck and help him to his feet. Behind me a well-oiled young lady smooth as you please smiles from the counter at the yacht club, bridge club, Lions Club duchess.

From Mr. Chuck a guttural pastiche of oaths, grunts, and blasphemies, the odd piercing scream. He pushes me toward the hindquarters of the dog while he grabs about the waylaid head. Gunt shit three, he yells, and in unison, a real team we are, we lift the half-dead dog upside down, the old atomic pile driver, me getting the real view, all dangling swollen parts and fleas and clotted hair and corpulent et cetera. The other hound has begun to howl.

Mrs. Dunlap at the counter lightly fingers the sleek glossies. Mr. Chuck jumps up and down and has begun to cry, and though I am not quite to the verge of tears, I too have begun to jump. The jumping doesn't seem to improve my view and in fact has exposed some veins and coagulations and just further overall unkemptness that I hadn't noticed on first viewing. The smell is beyond description.

How-how-howl, cries the nonchoking dog behind me. Blockety blug says Mr. Chuck, tears running down his face. I believe you've got it, says Mrs. Dunlap, pointing to the dislodged Milk Dud with the toe of a very fine shoe. She holds the *Birmingham News* up to me, smiles. I put fifty cents on the counter, she says to Mr. Chuck, who is huddled on the floor bawling and kissing his panting, howling dog.

Then she's walking out the door. So good to see you Devaney. I'll be sure and tell Polly.

I pull into the driveway at the governor's mansion after my busy day of wrestling dogs, buying porn, and getting reacquainted with my ex-mother-in-law. The empty office proved a suitable setting for soloist flights of fancy, and so, relaxed and rejuvenated, I've accepted the Governor's early-afternoon invitation to dinner. At the door, I'm greeted by Juanita, the maid, and my stepnightmare, Dallas. It seems Carter Allbright, C.A. yall, has an undue affection for sprawling Southern metropolises. A fine tacky tart she is. A few longnecks in her and watch the honky-tonk sawdust fly. And the wee one, ah the wee little butterine.

Where's the Governor, I ask.

Outside playing tennis, says Juanita.

Tennis?

You'll have to see for yourself. Have you seen the paper, she asks, handing me a copy of the *Birmingham News*.

Not yet, I say, taking the paper and eyeing the pudgy potato eyeing me.

Dev's in trouble, says the cheeky lad, trying to determine which of my pressure points looks most vulnerable. He chooses knee. But the answer is no. Denied. And quick as you like I drop the newspaper and have him by the foot one-legging him around the foyer. Juanita smiles and walks off.

Is he now, I say. Is Dev really in trouble?

Yes, he says, huffing this way and that. I'm moving him around pretty good.

And why is that, I ask, picking him up by both legs and holding him upside down. Suddenly it's the sound of carnival music.

Do your ears hang low
Do they wobble to and fro
Can you tie em in a knot
Can you tie em in a bow
Can you throw them over your shoulder
Like a continental soldier?

And cheers of delight from the kiddies as the Tornado Twister spins round and round.

Now why is Dev in trouble, I ask, twirling round and round.

Face ruddied and red, tears beginning, chubby arms waving this way and that independent of volition, the bitty blowmaunger says, the newspaper asshole.

Newspaper lasso? asks the Tornado Twister. Well I don't think that would work. I couldn't hold a big boy like you with a newspaper lasso.

Eventually the ride comes to a dizzy, crying stop, and I plop young Dallas down on the marble floor and walk to the steps to regain my fragile equilibrium. He lies there splotched and sweating, whimpering slightly. After a few minutes he attempts to make a mad dash my way, but stumbles dizzily and flops down in a heap. Like a sack of potatoes actually. He cries harder now, frustrated one would surmise. The cries get louder, then the screams kick in pretty steadily. I cock my head and howl at the moon. Now would seem the time to read Cindy Malloy's slanderous column.

> *Whisper whisper. Little birds tell us there was quite a brouhaha down at The Bistro sniff-sniff when a certain Governor's son who shall go nameless found himself in the middle of a regular tug-of-war over a certain va-va-voom Governor's aide. Seems the young gov took exception to this young lady's directing her attentions elsewhere. Oh those feminine wiles. Then temper-temper started a rowdy row with an innocent friend of the mystery lady in question. After the considerable dust had settled, the Gov's son ran out on his formidable bar tab. Tsk-tsk we say. Especially with the still-gaga-for-Carter Governor in the tightest race of his political career. Lesson for the day girls? If they're fighting for you, you must be doing something right. Ta ta.*

The second reading is much like the first, *sniff, whisker, tsk,* but the vengeful hand of Higginbothan Inc. does begin to show itself. And the Queen, the rueful tone of voice she must use when discussing Dev with the hive. Could it have been because I was out with Oliver? Oh what should I do? And me working so closely with the Governor. Surely he wasn't jealous. We're just friends, Dev and me. And Oliver and I, just friends as well. Just good naked friends.

The editorial concerning the Governor's silence on the lottery is a bit heavy-handed, in op-ed fashion, but is, all and all, accurate and about the way I see it. The Governor, if I know the Governor, will be well steamed nonetheless. Biting the hand that feeds, et cetera.

Meanwhile, Dallas has calmed down a bit. He stands up, steadies himself, and makes pretty decent forward progress on his death charge my way. Unfortunately for him, the aged but wily matador still has a spring in his step. Ole, says El Matador, moving gracefully and unhurriedly from the steps with barely a wave of his newspaper cape. This goes on for a few turns around the stadium, but too soon the round little bull runs out of steam, cried out, mushy-legged, badly needing a sugar fix. He sits down in a pitiful pile.

So Dev's in trouble, I say, with a pirouette and flamboyant sweep of the Living section. Is that what you're trying to tell me?

Shade and the Governor look like two old athletic guys who never picked up a racket until they were forty. Country boy hacks would be a simple way of putting it. More time is spent adjusting this, stretching that, than actually attempting to play the game. Fifteen or twenty balls lie scattered across the court, waiting to twist an ankle, wrench an arthritic knee. Claims representatives across the state twitch in unconscious dread.

Glad to see a Degraw can still make the society page, the Governor says on my approach, pulling a white sock up to its rightful position just below the knee.

I walk up to the court, considering a quick comment on both the literary and philosophical merit of Mayor Batch's op-ed, but in the end choose discretion as the greater part of valor. Such is my zenlike state after a relaxing few minutes tormenting Dallas.

Wearing him out Dev, he says, pointing across the net. Then he hustles his boys back into position for about a minute and a half. Properly aligned and with an audience now, he fires an ace past Shade, who never moves the first step in any direction.

Shade keeps a stone face as he moves to the ad court, ignoring the Governor's running commentary on his lack of tennis sophistication and savoir faire. Apparently the first tennis ball Shade ever saw was one he ate at his mother's kitchen table, the family mistaking it for an impressive egg. Apparently Shade fetched lemonade for little white boys down at Montgomery Municipal Park in the hope of stealing another of those delicious bouncing eggs. Apparently Shade doesn't know where to put it, played six-on-six girls' basketball in high school and is a simple sharecropper who can neither read nor write. Apparently were it not for the benevolence of the current Governor of the state of Alabama, he would still be fetching lemonade for little white boys and hunting for eggs and generally just sticking his head up his own black ass.

Shade waits impatiently for the serve, whiteys and crackers and coonasses flying out of his mouth uninterrupted save for the odd choicer and fully inflected multisyllabic oath.

They both, by the way, are wearing white hot pants, socks to their knees, and, were it not so, sweatbands.

You still coming to the Ball, asks the Governor.

Looking doubtful at this point, I say.

Come on now, he says. That's usually a good time. Your old buddy Skip will be there.

I smile, wondering what he heard about the delicate geisha.

A few more minutes of adjustments go on, but eventually he puts the ball in play with a pretty nasty serve. But wonder of wonders a return. Then a return of returns. And before anyone can stop it, an honest-to-god rally has broken out. After an exchange of sixteen or so shots, Shade manages to put the very tip of his racket, the old metal itself, on what had looked to be a winner down the line, sending a dull, looping nubber that just barely clears the net. From the opposite endline, without moving a step, the Governor throws his racket at the ball. The airborne racket, predictably, misses the nubbing shot, which lands in, good, a point winner, and sails just over Shade's grinning head before slamming with a disappointing whimper into the high chain-link fence. Fill in the blank curses from the Governor's side, breathlessly mean-spirited and personal. From Shade's side, the less said the better about the unsightly stroll to catch the geriatric Soul Train.

Dev you see that ugly-ass shot?

Boy saw a winner is what he saw.

Hell I'd rather lose.

Not me, says Shade. No sir. Like a soft little hard-boiled egg. Just like a soft-boiled egg. Just right. Like Momma used to make on the farm.

Shade, the Governor, and I are at the kitchen table after the most hideous display of tennis imaginable. Carter, C.A. yall, and the pudgy little metropolis are in the den eating pizza. Apparently Dallas's fragile metabolism depends on one full pound, no less, of melted cheese per day. Otherwise, his fourteen hours of immobility on the couch can leave him restless and irritable.

The kitchen is a casual room, the most casual in the house, nothing grand or gubernatorial about it. When I did homework, it was usually here, the Governor, if he was in, popping in every so often to see how it was going, occasionally frying up an egg sandwich if I was hungry. Now he's frying up burgers and french fries and asking us how we like ours done. A pretty good bachelor-style cook, truth be known.

Can you believe that damn op-ed? the Governor says, plopping a hamburger on my bun, then standing above me with spatula at the ready.

Hmm, I say. Interpretation of my response for those not in the know? Both the hamburger and your comment about the editorial are delicious.

I mean, says the Governor, spatula flying here and yon, what kind of angle could that horse's ass be playing? How could that editorial do anything but piss me off and make me want to do exactly, I mean exactly, what he doesn't want me to do? And this close to the election? Has he lost his mind? Has that ego of his finally got the best of him?

I take a bite of my burger and wait for Shade to respond, that ego comment ringing ironically and leisurely in my ear.

I done told you what I think, says Shade.

What you told me was you didn't have an opinion one way or the other, says the Governor.

I don't, says Shade, shaking pepper on his fries. Could give a shit one way or the other.

Well my press secretary and a bunch of other folks do give a shit. Lieutenant Governor does. C.A. does. About everybody in my cabinet does.

I'm putting the finishing touches on burger number one, feeling good and safe in the knowledge that noted country music philosopher and wordsmith, Carter Allbright, C.A. yall, has a say in administrative-level decisions in the great state of Alabama.

Well what do you say Dev, asks the Governor, apparently divining the torrent of smart-assy comments that are streaming unmolested and bitterly unspoken through my head.

About what?

The Governor sits down at the table, begins arranging his napkin and silverware. Don't wait on me, he says, pointing at my clean-as-a-whistle plate.

Sorry, I say. You taught me better manners than that.

So I do get credit for doing at least one thing right?

Grudgingly, I say.

The Governor smiles in return, takes a sip from his beer. I'm being advised, he says, and I tend to agree, that we ought to get one of our folks over at the *Birmingham News* to write a response to Mayor Batch's editorial. Our editorial would defend my record in regard to the constituency he accuses me of abandoning. Have you read the article?

I have, I say.

And?

I wouldn't reply.

Why in the hell not? I'll stack my record on helping the poor, helping black folks, against anybody else in this state.

I guess cutting Shade a check once a month doesn't cut it anymore, I say.

Shade laughs. And then the Governor does too.

No, I say, I agree with you. You've got nothing to be ashamed of when it comes to helping the poor.

Then why not do the editorial?

First off, he's right. About the lottery at least. Your silence is surprising. I won't speak for Shade because you always think we're ganging up on you, but I don't understand why you're dragging your feet on this.

The Governor sips from his beer, puts down a french fry. Takes another sip from his beer. For the good, he says, and the bad, I don't just point and fire like I used to. I think I've improved at looking at more than one side of an issue. Then again, maybe that's just an excuse for not trusting my instincts like I used to.

But that's my point, I say. Responding to the editorial is pointing and firing. Makes you look defensive about one of your strongest suits. And he's right also about us taking the vote of his constituency for granted every election. We do take it for granted. I know I pencil it in every year.

The Governor pushes away from the table, saying, by god let em have Wade then. See how I look by comparison.

I don't reply. Shade takes a swig from his beer. Let em have Wade, repeats the Governor. See how Mayor Batch likes our young Republican friend over the long haul.

I look at Shade for a response, but he's deep in contemplation about choice grains and hops. So I'm in this one by myself. The mayor's just doing what he has to do, I say. You, and I, and Mayor Batch, Mayor Batch more than anyone, know who the better alternative is. I think he believes what he's saying. And the mayor's a good guy. He's held up his end of the bargain for a lot of years. You've got to admit that. But he's politicking too. He's up for election in two years and it does him no good if it looks like he's in your hip pocket. Especially with this damn lottery thing.

You're on the record with the lottery, says the Governor. Let's move on.

Moving on then. It's a close election. We need every vote. We'll get the black vote over Wade every time. It's just whether we get 20 percent of Batch's folks to come out. Or 60 percent. We need the man. We need his voters. We gain nothing by showing him up.

Hell he's the one who showed me up, says the Governor.

Yep. And you're going to have to take it.

Well I don't like it.

I don't expect you to. No skin off my back whatever you decide. You been in this business a long time. Go with your gut.

The Governor nods but doesn't reply.

I told you what I'd do if the state needed more money and there's no way to raise taxes. Take it from the damn highway fund first. The only reason you're even considering the lottery is so we can keep funding your K through 12 initiatives. Well hell, just hit up other infrastructure stuff and send it to the schools. People start getting their trash picked up every other week and messing up their SUVs on the roads and they'll start taking this budget mess you've been crying about a little more seriously.

You might have a point, says the Governor, taking a swig of his beer. Now why don't we talk about my granddaughter or football or any other damn thing else you please that doesn't have the word lottery in it.

Shade and I are out in the driveway, talking, leaning against my car and smoking cigs. How well do you know Mayor Batch, I ask.

Well enough, he says.

I was thinking you might meet him for lunch or something. Maybe insinuate the Governor's closer than he's letting on about getting off the lottery. Let him know we got the message.

Fine with me. He'll be wondering why the Governor doesn't tell him himself.

No way the Governor's contacting him after that editorial.

No, says Shade. You're right. But you ought to go with me. We could meet up in Birmingham on Saturday for lunch. Get you a little soul food.

No, I say, I don't think I'll join you.

Might make it a little more official.

No thank you.

Shade takes a sip of his beer and lights a fresh cigarette. It's funny, he says, that Josh Wade's not much older than you.

No, I say, he's exactly the same age. We were in law school together.

And already running for governor. Ambitious young man.

He is, I say. He is an ambitious young man at that.

Was thinking you might get a little ambition one of these days.

I smile, blow smoke his way, curse the young and ambitious Josh Wade.

So other than helping us out when it suits you, when you're not busy getting thrown out of restaurants, you're not really doing shit. Is that what I'm hearing?

I'm involved in a couple of cases right now, I say.

A couple of cases? You used to have a right good practice. Okay, your divorce is one. What's the other?

It involves a friend of mine named Noneya.

Say what?

A little friend of mine, I say, named none ya damn business.

He shakes his head, spits, takes a couple of steps toward his car like he's thinking about leaving. Stops. Much collecting of thoughts.

Is that all you are is a smart-ass?

I laugh.

I'm not kidding.

I know you're not.

Well? Answer the question.

No. That's not all I am.

Cause that's all I'm seeing, he says, looking me in the eyes, looking away in disgust. Then he points at my beer. And that, he says, that right there is going to lick you if you don't watch it. You never used to carry on like this.

I don't say anything. The can feels warm in my hand.

Getting kicked out of restaurants? Nice restaurants with rich folks in there? Getting your name in the paper? Fighting? Running out on a tab? How old are you son?

Old enough, I say.

Your dad joked about it, but let me tell you something. You may understand this and you may not. Your daddy going into a nice restaurant is going in there for all the people who never been to a place like that, never will go to a place like that. Or folks who got a little change in the pocket now but are afraid the poor still shows when they go someplace nice. That's why so many people don't begrudge the Governor his money or the way he spends it. Your daddy doesn't talk about it. I don't know if he's even thought about it. Being able to shake hands with the President, which he's done, and the very same day shake the hand of some local Joe down at the filling station and be the same man on both shakes. Am I right?

You're right.

I'm not saying he's perfect. Not by a long shot. And we both know there's people he hadn't treated right. You know what I'm talking about there?

I nod.

So I understand if you're not rah-rahing every time he walks in the room. But when his only child is getting thrown out of high-class places for fighting and running out on tabs, it don't look good. It looks like you're just another fucked-up rich boy. You're starting to stink of that silver spoon, son. You don't want that.

No, I say. I don't want that.

Listen, I'm not going to stay on you. You're a grown man. You know what you need to do.

I nod in vague agreement.

All right, he says, turning and walking toward his car. I know how it is.

I'll go with you to Birmingham, I say to his back.

He waves a hand okay behind him without bothering to turn around.

Then he's in his car and driving away, and I'm alone in the big circular drive, an adult like any other.

I've driven here straight from the governor's mansion, the prospect of man-stench and introspection waiting for me back at the apartment too much to bear after a heart-to-heart with my old friend Shade. Here is McCrae's, most pungent of bars, most broken in. No antiseptic smell to dissuade the veteran patron, no distracting sheen. A nirvana of smoke and sweat bathes the hunters and gatherers, these anthropoids of the rarest ilk, occupying as they do the shady middle and upper regions of the genus. A blues singer from New Orleans with a Dobro guitar. A good-natured poet scribbling notes on a bar napkin. Next to the poet, my friend Jim explaining one of his graduate school theories on the sexuality of parenthesis.

Haven't you noticed how they look like a woman's hips? he says.

No, I say. No I really haven't.

But now that you think of it?

Maybe, I say. I've never given it my full attention.

Think about it, he says. Parent. Thesis. Whatever is inside is the insertion. Thus the parents give birth to the thesis.

How many years were you home-schooled?

Good one, he says. Solid.

So the insertion is phallic?

Possibly, he says. Embryonic to be sure. The baby thesis, baby argument, if you will.

Conceivable, then, a virgin birth. Hips equal woman, stuff inside equals baby.

Not necessarily. Hips equal woman yes, probably. Stuff inside does or does not equal insertion. Result of insertion into hips equals the germinating or germinated idea.

Well which is it, the stuff inside? Intrusive masculine insertion or incubating fatherless embryo?

Depends on how you look at it.

You're a good candidate for a date, I say. Aren't you my zygotey friend? I mean, as it were, you could use one. I mean, all academic mumbo jumbo aside, when punctuation brings on impure thoughts, it's time for a live one. In other words, I'd like to posit this thought. You are one horny bookworm.

Jim, my buddy of buds, orders us another round, nodding affirmatively, that my thesis, if you will, has a certain arcane and simplistic virtue.

We've walked down to The Spot, late-night haunt of the drunken and unstudious. Picture the place in every college town where solo undergraduate guitarists play Brown Eyed Girl to draft beer soggy singalong girls.

At the door we're greeted by a bouncer who in the past has shown not just a little displeasure at my presence. Something in my countenance seems to disturb his bovinely delicate sensibility. Yes, I love a bouncer.

Two dollars, he says as salutation. And to a stranger unfamiliar with this greeter's subtle charms, the adjective gruff might come to mind. Just a bit on the gruff side. Just a bit. Another adjective? Gormless. Lacking any and all gorm.

How much?

Two dollars.

Do you get a drink with that or anything?

He looks at me without answering, then turns his nuanced gaze on Jim for a while.

Or is the two dollars just for the joy of hearing more of the excellent music I'm hearing right now? That's an Eagles song if I'm not mistaken.

Could care less man, he says. Two dollars.

Do we need a baseball cap to get in?

What? he says, pupils dilating nicely now as the adrenaline rekindles its love affair with the steroid cocktail of this morning.

Can we get in without a hat? Looks like there's a strict dress code. I could run home and get a white T-shirt and a baseball cap if you need me to. Hate to get you in trouble with management for a dress code violation.

The big man smiles, glancing into the future, my smart mouth, his chemically motivated atavistic rage, me as dwarf, he as tosser, a winning combination for sure in The Spot's nightly prize for distance.

You're a funny guy, he says.

Thank you sonny, I say, sliding a fiver into his meaty hand. And keep a dollar for yourself for the trouble.

At the bar awaits the second half of The Spot's dynamic duo, the bartender, Mr. Average himself. Much like his blocky friend at the door, Mr. Average has also displayed indifference at best in my trade. Seems once my elbows hit the bar I turn invisible. That is until closing time when I'm honored with the first mention of last call, the first herding nod to the door.

Mr. Average can't seem to see us, says Jim, motioning toward the barkeep at the far end of the bar, his head swerving every which way but ours for a customer to serve.

He is average at that, I say.

Subtly but surely average, says Jim.

No middling mediocrity here. He is aggressively average, unusually unobtrusive.

Still doubt my invisibility? Search the bar, ye neutral party, ye jury of our peers. See ye anyone else waiting for a drink? But look at the sweep of the head. Searching is he not for thirsty customers? At the ready, subtly, averagely, to hop to, carefully, surely, modestly, but all and all successfully, for that far cooler of beer, that faintly sweating bottle of sweet elixir? Sees he not the waving twenty, the only empty mouth at the trough?

Hey, how you doing? I shout. Seriously, how are you? Just an average night?

At the word, at the word, he walks over, slowly, still looking around as if not wanting to accidentally skip a long-waiting customer in his sure, capable, adequate fairness.

Yeah, he says, with a middling nod.

Any specials tonight? Any really good deals, or is it just a run-of-the-mill night?

No specials, he says.

How's business? Just so-so?

He nods, implacably.

Do you have any just regular old average beers back there? What do you drink by the way? I'll have what you're drinking.

Don't drink on shift.

Good, good, I say, that's good.

Well do you want anything or not?

You pick. Anything. Surprise me. But nothing too crazy now. And nothing too tame. Well, you know.

And on I go, hitting tennis balls against a brick wall, good clean exercise for two average American boys.

So was he rattled? I ask Jim after we've received our beers, domestic, not too hot, not too cold, a porridge just right for the average bear.

Moderately so, says Jim.

Indications?

A perturbation around the mouth when you asked about drink specials.

Perceptible to the human eye?

Nearly.

Yes, I say. Good good. Others?

I can't be sure, Jim says, but when he said he didn't drink on shift, I thought a bit of near color came into his neck.

Just over the collar of the button-down, an inch or two above the white T-shirt?

That was it.

I thought it was the lighting off the stage.

Could be, Jim says. Could have been the lighting.

So all and all a pretty typical performance from the Average One?

Right in the middle of the curve, says Jim. Dead on middle C.

Excellent, I say, excellent.

Jim's playing pool with a couple of local toughs he knows from up at McCrae's. Every so often one of the toughs will holler out, play Free Bird, in a country boy yodel, then laugh like he's the first one ever to do that to a sensitive young folk singer just finishing up his James Taylor medley. Of course it goes without saying that the duo up front could use a little more hairy-assed Skynyrd, a little less ponytailed goatee in the repertoire. Seriously, they are both ponytailed and, were it not so, neatly and primly goateed. They are also, were it not so, brothers, a fact I've futilely resisted hearing lo these many minutes, despite their constant banter about doing it little bro and you go big bro. And unless Mr. Average has spiked my beer, they have exchanged more than one lusty and exuberant high five in public, the incestuous undertones nakedly visible to all, the sorority girls up front lapping it up with a spoon.

Free bird, I scream. Free free free bird.

So why am I here one might ask. Which would be a good question. A fair question. One that requires a textured and nuanced response, something to acquit my presence in the land of Mr. Average, the milquetoast Barkley Brothers. Here is my answer. All the other bars are dead, there are no grown women in this town, and one fine day, if the law of averages is truly a law, one of these sweating, beer-groggy sorority girls, with their inexplicable taste in music, is going to see that old Dev has what it takes and will ask him, politely, to ride her like the fine young pony that she is.

Free bird, I scream. Freeeeee Daaaaamn Biiiiird.

During a respite from the Barkley Brothers, a break to drain the weasel as they chirped so boyishly from the stage, I am confounded by a good-looking woman who seems almost within a decade of my own tender years on the planet. She walks by on her way to the restroom, shaking her head and smiling with a kind of pitying sympathy. I search the vault of my mind for a name or circumstance to put with the face, a shenanigan of bygone days of yore to fit the specificity of the just-received look, but no memory crowds its way through the smoky clutter of dehydrated neurons parched and gasping for breath along the super–information highway that was once my spinal column. Note to self. Your back hurts.

When she comes back from the bathroom, I come up with a gem. Do I know you?

She stands in the aisle as if still in motion. Well, she says, I was going to send you a glass of water earlier, but then I thought, oh, that's been done.

Oh, I say. Oh, oh.

Got to go, she says. I'm just now heading out.

Hey hey hey hey, I say, mouth and mind in perfect synchronicity, a stuttering postponement that leaves her looking through her purse for a spoon to prevent the swallowing of my tongue. After much gulping and a kind of windmill motion like I was bringing a plane into the hangar, I manage to ask what her name is.

Michelle, she says, stepping back a bit, out of range of the hand that she seems to assess as reaching toward her hair, the monster tamed for a minute by the little girl's hair, stammering out a tenderly rough duosyllable. Pretty. Then a little louder. Pretty. Then Pretty!!!! Pretty!!!! Pretty!!!! Then yanking her arm from its socket in a frenzy of love and happiness.

You don't say.

To this masterpiece, she says nothing, but checks the aisle, making sure it's clear. Subject seems slightly put off by phallus growing from interrogator's forehead.

Michelle huh?

Yep. By the way, were you the idiot yelling Free Bird?

I point at Jim. It was him, I say, quietly concerned. He's had a little too much to drink.

I could have sworn it was you.

No, I'm sorry, when the Barkley Brothers are playing, it's awed silence from me.

She laughs, looks at my furrowed brow, the bolts above my ears having inexplicably retracted, seems almost to nod at the speed and dexterity of the pit crew who have just changed the oil and greased the gears.

Seriously, I say. The Barkley Brothers rock. They're not just two guys with ponytails up there, I can assure you that. Quite talented. That version of Hotel California? Blew me away. And that Hootie? Jim and I were back here swaying like there's no tomorrow.

I bet.

How long you been following the band anyway?

First time, she says. My friend has a crush on Adam.

Adam, huh? He is like the first man, somewhat primordial sure, a tad simian, but as far as an abundance of well-placed and well-manicured hair, he's all man. But come on, his brother Chip's no slouch himself.

His name's not Chip.

I know. Dylan's a good guy. Dylan's solid.

It's Cody.

Had a dog named Cody once. Good dog. Solid dog. Well-groomed.

What are you doing anyway? she asks.

What do you mean?

I mean doing here, with all these youngsters.

Good question, I say. A very good question.

She nods. Do you work?

Sometimes. Well not really. I'm a lawyer who doesn't practice law. Let me guess, you're an investigative reporter.

She smiles, a little sheepishly. I guess I'm being nosy, she says.

No, I say. It's all right. I enjoy being pinned down by a hard-pressing Q and A.

I teach kindergarten by the way, she says.

You ought to be at home drinking milk and eating corn on the cob on a school night.

I was wondering if you were going to remember that one, she says.

You don't often forget snappy lines like that one.

She smiles, sort of. Well, she says, I'd best be off. The kiddies will be there bright and early tomorrow.

Can I call you sometime?

I don't think so, she says, walking slowly away.

Hey, I say, remembering what I should have already remembered, I've got a daughter in kindergarten.

Katie's in my class, she says, waving good-bye over her shoulder.

I'm in the middle of the bar discussing with Jim, in what must be excruciating detail, my conversation with the milk-drinking kindergarten teacher. No nuance of idiom goes unexamined, no subtlety of body language unreported.

So, says Jim, a moonlighting kindergarten teacher. Finger-painter by day, bar crawler by night. The mysterious Miss X. So you've got a shot?

Oh yeah, I say. Definitely. She knew who I was.

Deadbeat dad, parent conference no-show?

Hey now.

Sender of water. Band heckler. Southern rock lover. Oldest man in the bar.

And on he goes, the wooden-legged leprechaun, quicker as the night goes on, the ales and stouts and whiskeys mother's milk for the strange lad from the Emerald Isle. His pale face rosy as a Dublin trollop, eyes twinkling a merry Gaelic jig.

Lucky Charms, I say, in the practiced voice of the wee people. They're magically delicious.

He laughs at the red herring meant to get the hound off the trail, asks, faux serious as hell, so, did you get her number?

Seriously?

Yes seriously.

Oh Danny Boy. . . . Oh Jimmy Boy.

When Mr. Average walks up to ask us to start moving toward the front of the bar, I point out that there are probably forty people at the back of the bar and at least fifty in the front. I could not be, he could not have picked a spot, more in the center of the room.

I gave last call, he says, more evenly than one would think possible.

You did. You did give last call. I was just wondering if you always start herding em up from the middle?

So are you going to the front?

I'm still having an average time, I say.

Jim taps me on the arm. We can catch last call at McCrae's, he says.

As we're leaving, Mr. Average pauses in his roundup to watch us walk out the door, face edging imperceptibly toward some ambiguous middle of the road.

. . .

Back at McCrae's, the crowd has thinned considerably. Preacher James talking polygloted code to a couple of girls, a ladies' man that one, Ewan watching highlights of bets won and lost. Hank, the friendly and tattooed bear of a bouncer at The Elephant's Ear, the right kind of dwarf-tosser to be sure, is telling Ewan and the friendly poet how he just drained a bottle of Tabasco in a hundred-dollar dare. Not that hard, he says, in a hoarse whisper. Poured it in a glass first and just chugged it down. Burned a little at first.

Your voice isn't going to stay like that is it, asks the good-natured poet, his pockets stuffed with haikus written on bar napkins.

Oh little zygote
Midnight Momma's mystery
Crazy grad school dream

Don't know dude, says the man-mountain, motioning to Ewan for more beer, more beer, fire to be put out here.

Tattooed thunderstorm
    wash clean the molten lava
        guzzled with a rasp

We're discussing other gastrointestinal feats of daring when Allen Dance, the good-natured poet, announces that he can eat a stick of butter.

No, I say. You can't.

I can eat a stick of butter, repeats the poet, belly full and lacquered with a night's worth of cheap draft beer.

Now?

I didn't say right now.

You can either eat a stick of butter or you can't. I got twenty says you can't.

Let's see the twenty, he says.

Give me a twenty Ewan, I say. Put it on the tab.

Ewan hands me a twenty from the drawer, searching page after page to find the end of my tab, makes his mark. I take the bill and move it slowly in front of the young poetry student's face, more money than he's seen in one spot in years.

Get the butter stick, says Allen Dance.

At the all-night market just down the road, I stand in line behind a bevy of blottoed collegians. Of the fraternity hippie variety. Dude, they say. Dude, says I. They're loaded down with potato chips, Ding Dongs, and beat-the-clock beer. They are also quite stoned, and in the fluorescent glare, the sparkling weirdness of being stoned late at night beneath the unnatural minimart glare, they are slow and skittish as retarded kittens. One pours half a bottle of Visine into his bludgeoned eyes, and stands there, head up, eyes closed against the lights, weaving like a small boat on the waves. When his eyes clear, he shakes off and glances down at my parcel. Oh man, he says to his hacky-sacking crew. Pancakes, man. We got to have pancakes. Pancakes? he asks, pointing at the box.

Butter-eating contest, I say.

Allen Dance, the good-natured poet, in an unusually stylistic move, is eating his solid block of fat globules, air, and water, by folding down the wrapper one dainty bite at a time. The first bite he described as not bad. The second elicited no commentary but did prompt a reach for his draft beer.

No beer, I say. Uninterrupted butter eating, that's what we're here for.

You didn't say that, he says, lips and teeth coated with buttery sheen, face a mixture of grimaces and throat lunges. He's about to laugh or throw up.

Ruling, Ewan? I say.

The bet implied nonaccompaniment mate.

Can I get you a loaf of bread with that, I ask. Would a nice steaming baked potato help at all?

The good-natured poet laughs, gulps down the rest of bite two, peels back the remainder of the wrapper and in a show of sportsmanship and machismo begins licking the congealed stick of cow goo like a pleased child with a delicious Popsicle.

Jim, Hank, and Ewan laugh. Preacher makes a face and averts his eyes. The two girls he was talking to inch closer, pleased, excited looks on their faces. Allen Dance, poet and butter eater, gives them a confident nod.

Bites three and four are more like delicate nibbles. One might surmise that the evening's fifteen draft beers have not proved quite the milk of magnesia that the young poet had hoped for. Sweat has broken out on his forehead, and a greasy glistening dairy moustache drapes his upper lip.

I'm not paying you to rub the butter on your face, I say, pointing at the sticky sheen.

Slowly, deliberately, he tongues the residue.

Wouldn't a nice bowl of chili be good after this, I say. Or a big block of cheese. A big block of cheese washed down with a warm glass of buttermilk.

Allen Dance points at Ewan, looking for a ruling.

Heckling's legal mate, comes the reply.

Allen Dance nods, shrugs at the girls, what can you do, what can you do? Holds just less than half a stick of still-cold butter over his head for all the land to see. Plunges remainder of stick in his mouth and begins chewing slowly, luxuriously, a little profane.

Gross, says one of the girls, smiling. Allen Dance nods apologetically, sorry, sorry, opens his mouth wide to show the clumps of dissolving cholesterol, the yellow islands and archipelagoes upon a greasy pinkish brown ocean. And look, there's a pony. And I see an Indian girl.

Oh gather young poets in sweet Arcadia, where the muse is unwanton and the butter is free.

Allen Dance, the good-natured poet laughing and bug-eyed, works steady as a cow chewing her cud. Begins holding his stomach. Gags. A semiwretch. Steps taken back to give him room. Double over in a guttural moan. Rises up slowly, mouth open and clean as a whistle. The old fake vomit, what a ruse, late-night charade. Bows to the cheering crowd. Takes butter wrapper and licks it clean from end to end in a final defiant display of showmanship. Some in the crowd seem slightly put off with hotdogging move. Says, aahhhhhh. Delicious. That'll be twenty Dev.

Walking down the Strip, toward The Spot at the corner, where Jim will begin walking toward his apartment, I mine, I stop and say, that was a pretty good night.

Not bad, he says.

Seeing the milk-drinking kindergarten teacher, the butter boy. Pretty good night.

Better than average? he asks.

Yes, I say. Better than fucking average.

Sheriff
Tucker

On Friday, Sheila's at the office when I arrive, looking a little pale and peaked from her Wednesday and Thursday off. How've you been, she asks.

Fine. No complaints. Messages?

That young guy from the dog track, she says. Eightball or whatever he calls himself.

Oh hell, I say. I been waiting for that. I missed that hearing on the failure to prosecute. The case was dismissed.

Sheila nods.

Did he seem particularly angry or just run-of-the-mill?

He was pretty hot, she says. Says you owe him the money he would have won in the suit. Says he'll take it out of your ass like the dog took it out of his if he doesn't get it.

That's not good, I say.

Doesn't sound good, she agrees.

Man I blew that case.

Yep.

Never should have taken it the shape I was in.

Nope.

We look at each other for a moment, recalling, or at least I am, the young black man with a patch over one eye who came limping into the office with his pitiful case. Leading a dog out that had been somehow, I forget, mistreated by its owner, trying to hustle the dog into the box, the vicious bite on the ass, the owner and track refusing to pay medical bills or leave. A simple case. Asking a flat $1900 and a letter of apology. If I do what I'm supposed to, namely collect evidence, serve interrogatories, and so on, or, short of that, at least show up for the hearing to explain why I was not going forward with the discovery phase within the required 120 days, then Mr. Eightball, a.k.a. Louis Taylor, is $1900 richer and a whole lot happier.

That's bad, I say. That's really bad.

Just pay him the money he would have won, Sheila says. That ought to do it.

That's a good idea, I say. That's a very good idea. I'm just a little short at the moment. If he calls again, just try to stall him a bit. Tell him I'm working on it.

I'll do my best, she says.

How much do I owe you by the way?

You're just a month behind. Don't sweat it. Your daddy gave me a nice severance pay when I left up there. I got plenty to live on till you get caught up.

Okay, I say, I'm sorry. I've been a little distracted lately.

That's all right, Dev, she says. I know you're good for it. Don't sweat it. By the way, Chad Kingston made it in.

Good, I say. I've been looking forward to seeing the old boy.

He's a flirty thing, she says laughing. Wants me to come up to Carmel with him sometime.

Carmel? I say. Seriously, Carmel?

Carmel.

My God his Clint Eastwood fixation knows no bounds. No bounds. All this over one movie back in the sixties.

He was in a movie with Clint Eastwood, asks Sheila, running a hand through her hair.

First fake Mexican killed in *For a Few Dollars More*. Then worked as his stunt double for the rest of the movie.

Does he look like Clint Eastwood, she asks, a little color coming mysteriously into her face.

He's tall, I say. And I guess kind of rawboned and craggy. He's rangy. Wears the cowboy boots and the whole nine yards.

Really, she says, really.

Really, I say, lawyer, noncowboy, non-pretend-cowboy.

Well he wants you to call him over at the Marriott when you get the chance, she says, looking me over, thin-boned and uncraggy. The smooth bloated face of a drunken baby. Bags under eyes like sleeping Dobermans. Hair matted and unprompted to symmetry, unfortunate repercussion of a return to the land of Nod after my morning shower. Sheila begins to smile.

What, I say, what?

Nothing. You just tickle me sometimes.

Why? I say, less than ticklish.

Oh forget it. Just reminded me of this boy I used to know. You kind of look like you been bear hunting with a switch for about a month.

I check my zipper to make sure I'm not missing an obvious reference.

Are you growing a goatee? she asks.

Not that I'm aware. I just forgot to shave this morning.

Seems like lots of young guys are wearing em these days. Rock stars and actors and such. I kind of like em if they're not too wild and wooly, if they're kind of kept trim. Especially if the boy's got a pretty mouth.

Hhhm, I say, picturing myself with a goatee, wondering if I too have a pretty mouth. Unfortunately, the image conjured reveals a swollen vanilla Moon Pie pocked and marred with infrequent sprigs of reddish brown hair.

Looks like you might need to take a little edge off, she says.

Not right now, I say, tongue with a mind of its own.

· · ·

As a precaution against homicidal clients, I've asked Sheila to take no calls and thus am free to enjoy a quiet afternoon drinking coffee, contemplating the pros and cons of growing a goatee, and thumbing sentimentally through familiar and fondly recalled naked women magazines. The Office Collection, by the way, varies subtly but profoundly from the glossies of the domicile. Office equals good clean daytime fun. Girls next door, good-natured, fun-loving nurses and the like, the quaintly provocative, the richly lingeried, the accidentally, whoops, exposed. Take them to meet good old mom and no one is the wiser. But those bad girls waiting at home, those naughty things that follow me home from the office. Well, now, that's another story, another dirty little story to be sure.

First dumb but true thought of the day. A man's well-trimmed goatee and the tightly clipped plots of nude female models bear an uncanny resemblance. Outer rimming highlighting and showcasing small inner protrusion. Which begs the question. Do men grow goatees in subconscious homage to the opposite gender's nether regions? Or is, perhaps, the goatee a latent homosexual subliminal invitation, man to man, who needs them, et cetera. And what of women who kiss men with goatees? What of that? Yes, what what what of that?

First smart but true thought of the day. Don't look at dirty magazines before you've ingested your day's ration of caffeine.

Second smart but true, et cetera. Don't grow a goatee.

Third. Sheila, what were you suggesting earlier?

I'm sprawled on the floor like a middleweight champ who's just received the asskicking he needed to rejuvenate a promising career he'd grown bored with when Chad Kingston calls. Sheila's sitting in my chair thumbing through a girlie magazine and pushes the button to put Chad on the speakerphone.

You're on the speakerphone, I say, so watch the language.

Is your lovely secretary in the room perhaps, asks the dainty hairy bullshitting one.

Hello Chad, says Sheila.

Well hello Miss Sheila, he says. You're even sweeter-sounding over the speakerphone. Like a smooth rich cabernet wine. You know Carmel's in the wine country?

I did know that, says Sheila.

I'm sorry, Chad, I say, but you're obviously drunk on that muscatel you like to drink over ice with Sundrop. Or is it still rye whiskey straight from the sweaty boot? The only Carmel you ever had was on a candied apple at the Opelika County Fair. Before you had your teeth capped.

By god Degraw, I'll beat you like a redheaded stepchild.

Sheila gets up to leave, steps over my still-prone body, and says, good-bye Chad, you call me at home sometime. Dev's got the number.

Symbolically, Chad Kingston removes his ten-gallon hat over the phone, begins politely kissing the mouthpiece as if it were Sheila's gloved hand. I'll do that, Miss Sheila, he says, I'll sure do that.

She's gone, I say.

By god she's a peach. Been years since I've had me a nice Southern gal. These ones out here. Shit, hell, can't stop jazzercizing long enough to give a poor boy a piece. Not a one of em's over about nineteen. Hell, I'm tired of these young ones. Roller-skating here and yon, eating a half a jar of yogurt per week. Weigh about sixty-eight pounds soaking wet and with their titties pumped full of fresh petroleum jelly.

I laugh.

Hell I used to love them caramel apples at the fair.

I laugh more.

I did. Chipped a tooth every summer. And cotton candy. Mother's milk. I'd shine shoes down at the square for weeks waiting on the fair. And the bellyaches I'd have. One year this old man working the carousel give me a plug of chewing tobacco, said it'd cure a bellyache. I'm fifty-eight years old and I'm here to tell you I ain't never had a buzz like that. Caramel-apple, cotton-candy, Beechnut buzz. Hell I was hallucinating in front of the freak show tent. Had visions and premonitions of an amazing dickless boy named Degraw.

I leave the slightly buzzed Chad Kingston in the Nissan when I go to the door for Katie. It seems the large magnet in the hotel bar has snared another man wearing steel-tipped boots for no practical reason. In the driveway of my old house, Clark McClatchey's sporty SUV and another virtually identical vehicle, spanking new, the color of lightly dewed strawberries, pink bow and all. Like Clark's own ride, this new vehicle looks ready to ford a river, cart all manner of cross-country skis and rappelling harnesses, the odd toddler or two fastened to the roof with brightly colored bungie cords.

Awareness of unjustifiable rage notwithstanding, I best not hear the word girlfriend in the next sixty seconds.

The boy cheerleader himself opens the door when I ring the bell and steps out with friendly hand extended. Katie's not quite ready, he says.

To this I give a gruff and meaningful, oh.

Listen, Dev, he says, earnest blue eyes bearing in on mine, I just wanted you to know that who I'm voting for in the election is nothing personal. I have a lot of respect for the Governor. It's purely an issues thing with me.

Clark, I say, I could care less. I don't even know what the issues are. Frankly, I'm thinking about voting for Wade myself. I like a man who's not afraid to wear suspenders.

Dev, he says laughing, you are a character.

And then Polly joins us on the porch to make a jolly three-some. However, I am on my best behavior and question neither the sports nor the utility of the new vehicle parked in the driveway.

Who's in the car Daddy? Katie asks.

That's my friend Chad Kingston.

From *Bayou Dog*? Polly says.

Yep.

Red ears burning, Chad Kingston acknowledges his fans with a practiced wave of his movie star hand.

No kidding, says Clark. I think I saw that show when I was a kid. You've had quite a life Dev.

It's been a happy life, I say. I've always tried my best to be happy.

Polly rolls her eyes, begins looking around the living room for a cross-country ski to bash me over the head with. Dev, she says, patiently, ever patiently, I was wondering if you could go to a parent-teacher conference for me first week in April.

Absolutely, I say. I'd love to.

Polly gives me a look, hard to describe. Suffice to say it's irritating.

Seriously, I say. I'll be there. I guarantee you I'll be there.

We've landed, barely, at a place called Goony Goofy Golf, having narrowly escaped with our lives at that *Lord of the Flies* cheese jungle across the street known as Pizza Fun. Chad Kingston has seen better days, is perhaps regretting this outing. He seems to have shrunk and his once broad shoulders sag with the weight of chipmunk music, boogery-looking pizza and draft-only beer. That's right sir, no liquor. No sir, no schnapps either. We don't have bottled beer sir. Draft only. Will that be light beer sir? Sir, don't cry, don't cry sir.

Just now, returning from the restroom and his nip on the just-purchased bottle of RedEye, he looks a bit better for wear, nodding at a woman, nodding yes maam I'm him, I'm him, though she has no clue whatsoever who he is. We're presently on the third hole of our eighteen-hole tournament and I'm kicking Katie's ass by two strokes and am looking for some stiffer competition. Plus, no daughter of mine, she refuses to wager even with the generous strokes I'm offering.

When did kids get so loud, the weary sheriff asks, face flushing into fine ruddy red form.

Too much MTV, I say, not enough *Bayou Dog*.

You laugh. But that show had morals. Heck if Billy Tucker starting acting up, I'd just warm that fanny a bit.

You never spanked Billy once on the show.

The threat was implied. Viewers knew that. Why if Billy Tucker kept hollering trying to have his way all the time, trying to run the house, he'd of had another thing coming.

Whatever you say Sheriff. But how bout it, you ready for a little wager.

Oh I ain't into these sporty little games, he says, looking about for his home on the range. I wasn't one of them snot-nosed cry-babies all the time driving down to the country club with a bunch of pals named Scott.

If you're scared, just say so.

I'll take three strokes per side. Hundred dollars a side.

Two strokes, I say. Five a side.

Done. Young lady, have you ever seen your daddy cry?

No sir.

Well you're fixing to.

I'm whipping Chad Kingston like the California cowboy he is. He plays as if he's never held a putter in his hand, wielding the club with the dexterity of an untrained bear. And Katie, showing a bit of Degraw at long last, has begun to egg on the erstwhile adult with a steady stream of subtle taunting. Almost Mr. Kingston, she says as he rams a ball over the hole at warp speed, ricochets it off the leering face of a clown and rolls it back over the same hole and four feet past where he started. And her natural gift for such, the mimicked deadpanned sweetness when rendering a walk tall champ, or good and solid, that swing is good and solid, is enough to bring a tear to a proud papa's eyes. Note to scientific journal. Subject seems to take to competitiveness and questionable sportsmanship like a fish to water. Nonplussed by antics of the male gender. For the moment all traces of you-go-girlfriend cheerleader pep seem to have vanished. Hope yet for wayward progeny.

To summarize the golf match as it now stands, I handily swept the front nine with a combination of raw power and sheer will, earning a cool fiver for the effort. At the turn, Chad Kingston bothered not to go to the restroom for his liquid fortification, opting instead for the surreptitious swig and aahhh behind a bespectacled dinosaur on the ninth hole. Fortunately, only one or two children bore witness. And though revived enough by his brain lubricant to double the bet on the back nine, his game has shown little improvement. He trails by seven strokes going into the fourteenth hole, a nasty little loop-t-loop through the mocking mouth of what looks to be a decapitated and morphine-addled wood gnome.

What in the world is that, asks Chad Kingston.

A decapitated wood gnome would be my guess.

It's one of the seven dwarfs, says Katie.

Iggy? I ask.

There's not a dwarf named Iggy.

What's an Iggy? says Chad Kingston.

Don't you worry about it long knocker, I say.

Yeah long knocker, says Katie.

Same order on this hole, I say. Katie first, then Nicklaus, then last but certainly not least, the Buzzed Ranger. Heigh ho, Silver, keep your chin up Buzzed Ranger.

Yeah, Buzzed Ranger, keep your chin up, says Katie.

The wearied ranch hand smiles a weary smile, laughs a bit. Katie, he says gently, where'd your mommy get that pretty red truck?

We're on the eighteenth hole, tie score. Since stumbling upon a suitable line of taunting, Chad has kept up a steady stream of questions for Katie regarding her mother's new means of transportation, her mother's new boyfriend, a typical night around the house, Clark's favorite outfits for a night on the town, toys assembled or tree houses built, peppering in such comments as necessary to elicit one compliment after another for the new man in Mommy's life.

Compounding the weirdness of Chad Kingston striking an unusual rich vein of comedic torment, the erstwhile cowboy has begun pulling shots out of his rangy and doubtlessly craggy ass.

He tees off first and miraculously navigates the minuscule opening of the Tin Man's inverted oil funnel head, sending his ball rocketing through a non sequitur of a loop in the Tin Man's back where his heart should be and out a grey tin leg, three feet from the hole. Wallacaballa Wallacaballa Wallacaballa, he says, bringing the putter up to his mouth and planting what can only be described as a pornographically lubricious kiss. Worse still, the mere mention of the nonsensical Wallacaballa has begun to send my daughter, former confidante, sidekick, and apple of Daddy's eye, into wild spasms of snorting laughter.

As I'm lining up for my attempt at shooting the gap in the Tin Man's head, knowing all is lost if I fail, Chad says to Katie, does Clark ever dance in the den?

Good god Black Bart, I say. That's below the belt.

He does, Katie says. But in the kitchen. We dance all the time. He taught me the Funky Chicken. He likes the same music Mommy does.

Chad Kingston nods, smiles, encourages Katie to demonstrate Clark's version of the Funky Chicken.

Clark sure is fun, I say.

He is, says Katie.

Sure sounds like fun, says Chad Kingston, flapping his old wings and leering at me over Katie's head like a fevered and gargantuan Cowboy Bob split seconds after gangster-slapping Howdy Doody's head into the front row of a crowd of screeching kids.

Hoss Cartwright here's funny too isn't he Katie?

He is Daddy. But not as funny as you.

Kookamalooka, I say.

Wallamakala, says the tanned from a bottle Grizzly Adams.

Kookamalooka, I say, stepping back to line up the putt.

Wallamakala, says Jock Ewing, facedown drunk and drooling

after another successful day of ogling his daughters-in-law by the pool.

Kookamalooka, says I, training a laser eye on the ever-widening breadth of the Tin Man's glowing silver funnel.

Kookamalooka, says Katie, showing the Degraw's inherent disdain for the cheap shenanigans of suddenly front-running octogenarian cattle punchers with lemon juice highlights in their grossly and pubescently thick hair.

I raise a furrowed brow, signaling quiet in the gallery please. Somewhere in another galaxy a whispering British announcer is commenting on the capricious winds here at Goony Goofy Golf, the diabolically narrow funnel of the Tin Man's jaunty chapeau, the steadfast and steely and sibilant look in young Degraw's eye as he rams the ball through at warp speed, loop-t-looping as she goes, slamming into the corner banker, ricocheting off the opposing banker, ricocheting off the original banker, and coming finally, a hard day's night to be sure, faint British chuckle echoing galactically, to a gentle baby's rest six inches to the left of the stupefied ball of the drunken gringo. Si senor.

And the crowd chants, Kookamalooka, Kookamalooka, Kookamalooka.

Without being dramatic, I can say that all the marbles are riding on this last shot of mine. Katie has knocked her ball down the final chute, and the plastic faced El Cid, after much knocking of knee, much shaking of hands, has manipulated his facsimile of a putting stroke into actual contact with the ball, and further yet has guided said pitifully stroked ball into the far lip of the cup where it has dropped with a self-satisfied gurgle into the incredulous hole for an even par two.

In other words, I can't win. Jacking the bet is the most I can hope for. I step off the distance to the hole, three feet. I judge the slope of the green as it relates to pin placement and find, interestingly enough, that from all angles of vision, the grade is 0 degrees, like every other hole on the course. I lick a finger and test the wind.

Just hit it Daddy, Katie says.

Kookamalooka, I say, with ever-furrowing brow, the British announcer crisp and fey in my ear, awed by this great lion of a champion, this bastion of American grit and can-do.

Bet you a thousand dollars you miss it, says Chad Kingston.

I step away from the ball with this little bit of braggadocio. Katie stands there with a wide-eyed look on her face. It seems obvious that her beloved grandmother has mentioned the words Dev and dead broke in the same sentence recently.

I can't bet that, I say. I'll make this putt, and I don't want to take your money.

You let me worry about my money, he says. *Gunsmoke* reruns are being played every minute of the day somewhere in the world. I got residuals coming in hand over fist.

Well, I can't anyway. If, by some rare chance, I miss this, I couldn't afford to pay you.

Okay, he says, looking kindly down at Katie. Okay, I can understand that. How about this then. I'll give you a thousand dollars if you make the putt.

Katie's eyes get wider. With that kind of money she and her mother could eat something more substantive than the cold porridge they've been forced to subsist on lo these many months.

Fine, I say. Sounds good. I'll take it.

If you miss, he says, you do the *Bayou Dog* reunion and no crying about it. Signing autographs, posing for pictures. Hanging out with Odelle Bailey and her vegetable stand.

No way. Billy Tucker has flown the coop. He's climbed his last tree, tossed his last stick.

It's a three-foot putt. I just made mine piece of cake.

A thousand dollars?

I spent a thousand dollars getting my boots shined last week.

Behind us, the only family not scared off the course by the tribal chanting, the cowboy with a bad bottle of RedEye screams, and the fact that two outlaws have kidnapped a cute little girl and are torturing her via a round of miniature golf, have arrived behind us and are waiting patiently, quietly, for me to hit this three-footer and clear the hole.

You're serious? I say.

Yessir.

All right, you're on, I say with a confident wink for Katie.

The course seems to draw in its breath as I stand over the putt. Overhead the moths beat less frantically across the lights, the wind stills. Somewhere a whippoorwill awaits the new morn. I get the bead of the putt, it's straight in, not too hard, not too soft. I take the club back slowly, and just as I'm about to make contact, Chad Kingston's voice. So Katie, he says, when's Mommy getting married?

It's quiet in the car on the way home. Katie sits up front so Sheriff Tucker and Billy don't have to make eye contact. She seems to be handling it well, the primordial and eternal howl, one long low inarticulate malediction, sweeping and haphazard, the putter flung across six lanes of traffic and landing skidding and clanking on the roof of the Pizza Fun, the family behind slinking off toward their minivan without finishing the last hole, the quick awkward bribe to the teenage putting pro by Chad Kingston, the harried loading of the getaway car, the echo of the final and barely audible cry on the eighteenth green. Wallamacalla.

We're about a mile from the house when Katie says, Miss Marcum said she met you.

Who?

Miss Marcum. My teacher.

Oh yeah, I did meet her.

She wanted me to ask you something about a bird. Some song or something.

Free Bird, I say. It's a song. Daddy requested it a few times at a concert but they didn't play it.

She said you were nice.

Really?

Really.

And she's nice you say?

Very. All the kids like her. Some of the boys are in love with her.

Billy Tucker nods, recalls an episode of *Bayou Dog* where he had a crush on a fetching young teacher. Sheriff Tucker had to put him on a knee and explain, in the vaguest of seventies TV terms, the ways of birds and bees and all due time. Some reference being made to the kettle needing time to boil.

The kettle needs time to boil? Billy Tucker asks the seemingly dozing sheriff in the rearview.

That's right boy.

But what does that mean?

Water's ready when the water's ready.

But what does that mean?

Means some things can't be rushed. Can't rush a man. A man's a man when he's a man.

Who wrote that?

Nobody wrote it. My daddy used to say it. Said it to me when

I was fixing to go to California and everybody else in town said I was chasing pie in the sky, said I ought to be off at the mill making a living.

So he didn't try to talk you out of it?

No. He never did. Said Bedford would be there when I got back. I don't reckon he ever got out of the state except a honeymoon in Gatlinburg. Never even went to high school. But he knew the world, knew people better anybody I ever seen.

You just worked it into the script?

No, it just come to me. We professional actors like to call that improvisation. Those damn writers would have had us eating bagels and saying youse guys if I hadn't stepped in.

No matter how big the field, the horse's always sniffing at the fence?

Freedom, says Chad Kingston, looking out the window at the passing darkness. That's one of Daddy's. I'm telling you he was a philosopher.

When we get to the house, Chad Kingston makes his goodbyes to the newest member of his tribe, makes her promise to come to the reunion and see the great-grandson of the imperial Thor. At the door, a light comes on in the living room, but no one comes out. Katie gives me a kiss and starts to open the door but stops before she does. I won't tell Mommy about you throwing the golf club, she says.

No. You tell if you want to. You're allowed to tell.

Okay, she says. But I probably won't.

No you can. Daddy shouldn't lose his temper like that. He knows better.

Okay.

Okay then.

I think Miss Marcum likes you.

I doubt it.

And then Polly opens the door on cue, and a thick warm glow from the house spills onto the porch and the smell of candles? dinner? incense? bubble bath? kid's laundry? kid's toys strewn about? And I say, I love you honey and Katie says, I love you too and Polly says, bye Dev and I say, bye and turn quickly and walk from the porch to my car.

At the hotel bar, we've grown nostalgic. And for an extra fifty dollars the DJ has stacked up Hag, Johnny, and George in the agreed-upon order, moving from adrenal and meditative and somewhat combative to combative and adrenal and somewhat meditative to purely and simply meditative, as it should be, as it must be, when one is drinking in the early-morning hours of a hotel bar in Tuscaloosa, Alabama.

Do you remember that one where I was visiting the undertaker? I ask. I think he was my uncle. It was before church and I didn't know how to tie a tie, you'd always done it for me before, so I asked this uncle mortician to help me and he had me to lie down on the sofa and fold my arms over my chest so he could tie it.

I do, says Chad Kingston. I do remember that one.

I think that was my favorite episode, my favorite scene. That crazy-eyed guy. He looked like a mortician.

Willie Bledsoe, says Chad Kingston. He started out about the same time I did out there. Was always the undertaker, the crazed deacon, the crazy man on the street the kids were scared of. Told me once down in Mobile, must have been that episode, that he played Ichabod Crane in a school play and got a bunch of laughs and his first lay and never looked back. Got three kids now, two of em doctors.

But who wrote that scene? I say. That was funny. A kid lying down to let a mortician tie his tie.

I wrote it.

What?

I wrote the damn scene. We needed some excuse to get Billy out of the house. Candy was having a tough time then and needed a vacation from the show. So we just said that Candy's gone to visit her sick mother and I'm going hunting with Doc Baker and we'll just send Billy to visit his cousins in Lafayette.

You wrote that scene?

Well I told it to em. My granddaddy was a mortician. Whenever I went to stay with him, that's how he tied my tie.

No kidding.

No, he says. No kidding. I knew you'd like that scene.

I did, I say. I did like it. I liked most all of it except for the fake crying.

I know you did son, I know you did. I liked it too.

At home, after being dropped off by the taxi, I glance about the place for a while. It looks dandy. I pick up the phone book and begin searching. After forgetting once or twice who I was looking for, I find it. Degraw Devaney, 1104 Riverside Dr. 555-2354. I look at the name and the number for quite some time. No thoughts seem to register, nor do I seem to recall who exactly this Degraw fellow is or why I was looking up his number. I dial the number. Busy. I hit redial, still busy. I continue this for a while but never get through. The number below this one is Degraw Polly, 167 Blue Meadow Lane 555-1423. I pick up the phone again and dial.

A man's voice answers, sounding sleeping and confused. Hello, he says. Hello.

This is Clark McClatchey, I say. Is my wife there?

What?

This is Josh Wade, Republican candidate for governor.

Go to bed Dev, he says, hanging up the phone.

It's Saturday, high noon, and I'll not go into issues of personal appearance or my overall sense of well-being. I've just arrived at The Elbow Room, well-known soul food joint deep in the heart of North Birmingham, and seem to be the only white face, if that's the word for the hue I've got working, for about a ten-square-mile radius. Note to self. Save break dance moves for later.

I'm getting the well-deserved greenish-white-guy-in-a-suit eyeful from a couple of young toughs in the parking lot, so I nod, and they approximate a nod in return. Addendum to note to self. Bring wife's new fiancé to Elbow Room, encourage him to talk funk to friendly black men in parking lot.

Shade's already at the table with an iced tea when I walk in, but Mayor Batch has yet to arrive. The plan we agreed on Thursday was to keep Mayor Batch in the dark about my appearance and to keep the Governor in the dark about the meeting in general. When in doubt, subterfuge. But back to the point at hand. Iced tea. Yes. Iced tea. Iced tea is not the whole answer, but it is the first step, the most important step, to solving a complicated equation. I gently tackle a passing waitress and put in a heartfelt request for iced tea.

I take a seat and look forward to Shade's gentle touch to see me through another day.

Why you so dressed up? he says. It's Saturday for god's sake.

Funeral, I say.

Oh, says Shade. Sorry about that. Who died?

My innocence, Shade, my lovely girlish innocence.

Did somebody die or not?

As far as you and Batch are concerned it's a distant cousin on my mom's side.

Shade makes his patented look of irritated but probable comprehension, then nods at an old-timer across the way. The place is not as packed as it is during the week, but still a decent crowd. And John Lee Hooker on the stereo. Bad like Jesse James indeed. Once the waitress arrives with my half-gallon glass of iced tea, I rate the ambience as, not bad, with points deducted, obviously, for the dearth of fatheads in baseball caps and fraternity T-shirts with whom I've grown accustomed to dining.

So, son, again, the suit, I'm not following you.

One, I say, I look like hell. So it's a bit of camouflage for this damn meeting you've guilted me into.

I didn't guilt you into shit.

Two, I'm probably going to lower the boom on his ass and don't want to look like some punk in jeans when I do.

Lower the boom you say?

I'm thinking bull in a china shop. Just follow me or keep quiet or side with him. I could care less. I'm making it up as I go. Do you mind?

No. Not at all. Have at it. I'll probably be devil's advocate just to keep you honest.

You're not going to gang up on me and start doing a bunch of handshakes and shit I can't understand are you?

Shade smiles, comes as close to laughing as you'll ever see. Here's our man now, he says, nodding toward the door. Try not to screw this up.

Mayor Batch approaches with a bemused look in his eyes.

We've met on a few occasions and he knows who I am. He's wearing dress slacks, a sports coat, and some sleek Italian loafers with no socks. Shade and I stand up to greet him, but several tables flag him down before he gets to us, so he takes his time with handshakes and a quip or two for the population at large. The end result is that Shade and I are left standing at our table like idiots or valets for a couple of minutes, waiting as he meets and greets and just generally establishes who is and who is not on home turf.

Mr. Shade and young Mr. Degraw, he says when he gets to our table. Then it's handshakes all around, the modified soul for Shade, the standard pasty white for yours truly.

Pleasantly surprised to see you Dev, says Mayor Batch, sitting down.

Same here, I say.

You're looking sharp. Wedding?

Funeral.

I'm sorry to hear that.

Thank you, I say. I appreciate it.

Quite a few, most actually, of the tables are looking our way, and waitresses are buzzing around slapping drinks and baskets of rolls and condiments on our table. One of the waitresses stops and asks the mayor if he wants to move over to his regular table in the corner, but he shakes her off and says where we are is fine. Not here for business today, he says with a smile.

Then the orders are placed and I go with pintos, greens, fried okra, and creamed corn. An excellent order if I say so myself. Though the back-and-forth regarding my starch of choice, mashed taters or creamed corn, did prove a dizzying one, corn taking home the prize only after I'd ogled some in the flesh on a neighboring patron's unsuspecting plate.

We're small-talking about sports primarily and the weather

intermittently and the food arrives in a flash. Then it's chow time, serious chow time, and the talk is minimal as we concentrate on our speedy and mechanical intake of nutrients. Seriously, it's good food.

We finish in a virtual dead heat, with Shade, the eldest among us, perhaps a forkful or two behind. But a worthy effort by the old lion, worthy indeed. So now it's toothpick time, pushing chair back time, deciding about dessert time.

Young Mr. Degraw, says Mayor Batch with a smile, I thought you'd be running for Congress by now.

Politics must skip a generation, I say. Don't believe I've got what it takes.

Nonsense, he says. Move up to Birmingham and Mr. Shade and I will get you elected to whatever you want to run for. Ain't that right Mr. Shade?

Shade looks deep in thought for a moment. I think Dev might be right about that generation thing, he says. I'm not sure we'd get him elected only white boy in the room.

We're all laughing at that one when the waitress comes by and takes dessert orders. When the mayor says the peach cobbler is hard to beat, we take him at his word, and the order is unanimous.

I'm having such a good time, says Mayor Batch with a professionally unforeseeable change of tone, that I almost hate to ask how my editorial went over down in Montgomery.

There's a long moment afterward when no one says anything, and only the sound of quiet conversation and utensils scraping plates at other tables can be heard. And for someone not used to this kind of casual lunch, the term awkward silence might be appropriate.

Didn't bother me none, says Shade. I know where you're coming from. I've been trying to get the Governor off the lottery for months now.

Lottery's no good for my constituents, says Mayor Batch. I hated writing that piece. The Governor and I have always worked well together. And I know I put the wood to him pretty good. But that lottery, we just can't have it. It's bad for poor folks everywhere. But for metropolitan Birmingham, it's the worst thing that could possibly happen.

Wouldn't be good, agrees Shade with a sincere nod.

What did the Governor have to say about the editorial? says Batch. And more importantly, what's he going to do on the lottery?

Hadn't talked to him too much about it lately, says Shade. He's been busy. I just thought it'd be a good idea for you and me to get together and see where everything stands.

Then the waitress arrives with our desserts and coffees. As she's placing the items on the table, Mayor Batch tells her that the coffee smells good and the cobbler smells better and to pass it on to Miss Kate in the kitchen that his wife's blaming her cobbler for all the weight he's gained over the winter. The waitress laughs and heads back to the kitchen and almost immediately Mayor Batch is turning to me and saying, what do you think young Mr. Degraw? If you don't mind my asking. About the editorial. Did you happen to read my little piece?

Yes, I say. I read it.

And? I mean if you don't mind. I'd be curious to know what you thought. Just give me your honest opinion.

I take a bite of my cobbler. It's delicious. Just as Mayor Batch said. At this juncture, I'm ranking it in my top three all-time peach cobblers. I take a sip of my coffee. Nice as well. A fresh pot. Then I look to the expectant Mayor Batch. I thought, I say, that if the Governor's so bad for your constituency, if the Governor is taking your constituency so much for granted, then why in the hell don't you just go ahead and throw in your lot with Wade. That's what I thought.

Is that right? says Mayor Batch.

That's exactly right, I say.

I haven't supported your father? I don't get my folks out to the vote? I'm wrong for being against this lottery and wrong for asking your father once and for all to come out against it?

Vote for Wade then.

Are you saying I haven't earned the right to challenge the Governor when I think he's out of line? And I mean way-way-way out of line.

I'm saying then vote for fucking Wade. And that's all I'm saying. Vote for Wade?

Vote for fucking Wade, yes. See how you like it then. Wade's against the lottery, that's true. Let's see how he is on school vouchers, and welfare, and gun control, and planned parenthood, and the minimum wage, and tax breaks for the wealthy. Should I go on?

That's enough Dev, says Shade, grabbing me by the elbow. And I'm sorry about this Mayor Batch. Dev's out of line.

You ought to vote for Wade too, I say, taking another bite of pie. Seriously Shade, vote for Wade. I've always thought you were a closet Republican anyway.

Mayor Batch laughs a rueful, a scornful, laugh and stands up quickly from the table. He grabs our waitress when she walks by and hands her a wad of bills. I got the tab today, he says, I got it.

Thank you for lunch Mayor Batch, I say.

Mess with a tiger young man, and you're going to catch a fang, he says.

If I were you I'd vote for Wade.

Then he's laughing again, dismissively, and heading out the door with a curtailed nod to Shade.

Shade takes a bite of his pie, a sip of coffee. I do the same. Several of the tables and most of the waitstaff seem to be looking at us with fairly frank hostility, the mayor leaving so abruptly, the untouched cobbler where he was sitting, the full cup of coffee. Shade reaches for a toothpick, begins digging in earnest. Well, he says, I guess I need to have the Governor call Mayor Batch tonight and apologize for his jackass son.

Might be a good idea, I say.

Bull in a china shop, says Shade, reaching for a fresh toothpick and shooting me the sly beginnings of a near smile. Young bull raising all kinds of hell.

It's still Saturday, interminable Saturday, and back in good old Tuscaloosa, I've walked down to the Strip for a cool afternoon beverage and a game or two of trivia. On the walk down, through the back streets and alleys, past featureless block student apartment buildings, past Dempster Dumpsters teeming with spent student debauchery, I had a brief fit of worrying about canine dog bite victims who might or might not be lurking in the shadows. But all and all it seemed a little early in the day for a homicidal assault, and the weather, crisp and early-springy, just didn't seem right either. Yes, I decided with a definitive bounce in my step, if I'm to be assaulted, it will be on a day more atmospheric than this present one.

It was then that I made the important decision to continue forgoing introspection. As a corollary, I also chanced upon the notion of postponing any and all taking of stock, evaluation of present conditions, and consideration of long-range goals for the future. Additionally, after giving the matter some thought, I banned until further notice any attempts by the Superego to join the rocking good time being had in that great soup of my subconscious, leaving all future decisions, major and minor, in the good hands of the irrepressible Id. Ego, meanwhile, is to be kept on retainer for the moments when he is feeling unusually large and masterful.

Dennis is working the bar at The Bear's Den, and the only other patrons are Gay Henry and his former simulacrum of a girl-friend, Deli. They're playing trivia at opposite ends of the bar. When I order my beer, Henry asks me to stand him one.

Now why would I buy you a beer?

Because you usually do.

Not good enough, I say. And I'm broke. By the way Dennis, is my tab still good?

You still getting my Auburn tickets?

You know it.

Good as new rope then.

In that case, I say, give Henry a good talking to. Just put it on my tab.

I've talked Dennis into letting me put a long-distance call on my tab and have enlisted Henry's assistance on a harmless prank to the hive. At the moment, I'm torn on the best alias for Henry. Should he go with mystery cousin from Ducktown just in for the 4-H convention? Or Cindy Malloy's society page assistant inquir-ing if the Queen would be interested in a fashion in politics spread for the Sunday paper? Let's hear your country cousin, I say.

Is Shea Bateman there? This is her cousin from Ducktown.

That's horrible, I say. You don't sound like a friendly country cousin. There's not a bit of agriculture in your voice. Try it again.

Hey yall, this is Shea's cousin. Where's she at?

That's worse. Not friendly. Not even Southern. Like someone

from Michigan trying to do a Southern accent. She'd peg you.

Let me do that radio DJ bit.

Phrase of the day?

Yeah. That one you did on Jim. Warm and breezy? Oh good guess. Good guess sir. But we're sorry. The WEPZ phrase of the day is Jim's pussy hurts.

Yeah yeah that was good, I say. But you've got to sound like a DJ though. You know how they sound, kind of puffed-up and smooth. You sound like a slightly drunk pizza delivery guy.

That's not funny.

Well it sort of is.

If you don't want me to help, just forget it.

Okay, I say. Okay. You don't have a dime to your name and I'm the only one in this town who will stand you a beer, but okay. I almost take it back. I nearly apologize.

Go to hell. I don't know why I put up with this.

I don't either Henry. I don't think you have a masochistic bone in your body.

I'm leaving.

Aw come on. I'll stop. I can see you're acting like you're actually going to leave.

I will leave, he says. I am leaving.

I know you are. You're halfway out the door, you're nearly home. Maybe we can do the society page assistant. Saw his name in the paper. Robert Montegue.

Why don't you just do it yourself?

Well I may. I may do a Josh Wade, Republican candidate for governor, demanding a debate here in a second. But first I want so see if she's answering the phone before I waste a good fake voice on the machine.

What do I have to do?

Can you sound kind of you know like a fashion guy would sound? Sort of proper and refined.

And gay?

Well not necessarily.

I'm not gay.

No one has ever said you were. I've never heard a single person say that.

I screwed the hell out of Deli.

I'm sure you did, I say, I'm sure you did. Everyone knows yall were very serious. We all thought you really had something special going.

We did. I loved her man.

Okay but can you do the prank or not?

Three more beers, he says. Imports.

Fine. Just say what I told you. That about the fashion in politics and getting her to meet the photographer on the Capitol steps early as hell next Sunday. Photographer's got an afternoon wedding or something. Say you're quite taken with her style and panache.

Got it, he says. No sweat. What should she wear?

Good, now you're thinking.

Business-slash-monkey business?

Good. Perfect. Business-slash-monkey business.

What's her name again?

Shea Bateman.

And what's my name?

Robert Montegue, I say.

Rob Montegue, says Henry.

Rob it is.

I have Dennis turn down the stereo and signal Deli across the bar to keep it down. I give Henry a firm shake of the shoulder. He motions for his first import, picks up the receiver, and with a solemn yet sophisticated nod of his fashion guy head indicates he's ready for me to dial the number.

May I speak to Shea Bateman please? he says. Well hey Shea, this is Rob from the *Birmingham News*. Rob Montegue. We met last summer at the Swan Ball.

With this opening, he motions for a cigarette, gives me a rakish wink of confidence, accompanied, unfortunately, with the I-got-you-covered-kiddo pistol motion, a combination of gestures that leaves little doubt to his fans in the bar that he's about to butcher this prank and give up my name in the process. And what in the world was I thinking, placing such a commando raid in the sweatily squirming hands of the drunken innocent?

Now you remember, he says, tipping a phantom fedora in my direction.

Well listen, Shea, he continues, we're doing a piece on fashion and politics. I'm the new assistant fashion-slash-style editor, and everyone here just thinks you're the most glamorous thing in the state.

As the Queen modestly deflects the compliment, Henry takes a casual sip of his beer, crooks the phone on his neck, and gives the fisherman reeling in a catch sign. And gone now is all pizza stain residue.

Bring him a cognac, I say to Dennis.

Rob Montegue yawns casually into the phone, says, now modesty doesn't become you. Surely, darling, you know you're the most beautiful flower in the greenhouse, and I won't hear a word of argument.

Yes, well, yes, she is pretty too, says the cognac sipper, the intrepid yawner, but so common, just a little common wouldn't you say? But you, my swan, you are just so European. So tres this and tres that.

Rob Montegue gently twirls his cognac, tut-tuts a bit, says, but just because you've never been to Europe doesn't mean you're not European.

Dothan, Alabama, you say? Well knock me down with a feather.

Oh yes, well, that boarding school sounds top-notch. I've never heard of it of course, I'm more familiar with the New York girls' schools, but yes, I've been told that there are some schools of distinction in North Carolina as well.

Ha-ha, so Daddy couldn't have his little darling too far away. Oh Daddy Daddy Daddy. I just know Daddy bought you a horse named Butterscotch.

Well, my Shea, can I get you for a shoot next Sunday? I've lined up our best photographer, promise he'll make you look like a star. I was thinking the Capitol steps, say around . . .

I hold up eight fingers.

Around seven. Best light you know. Just wear what you would for work. On a day when you're meeting that special guy for lunch. Smart sexy. Business-slash-monkey business. Seven it is then? Fantastic. Until then. Chow love.

He hangs up and begins blowing discreet and discriminate kisses to his audience and bowing at the waist in all directions until Dennis holds the soda gun in front of his face and says, enough Montegue.

Meanwhile I'm in a state of blissful shock, kicking myself for not playing the vanity angle during prior skirmishes. For months that flank has been vulnerable. Like candy from a baby and none in the hive the wiser.

I shake the good Montegue's hand, am filled with much need to slap back, jostle, and hoot. I motion for a round on the house, all four of us, and begin formulations for phase two of the siege.

What in the hell do you know about girls' boarding schools, I ask.

Nothing, says Henry, lighting one of my cigarettes. Just figured there had to be some in New York, and North Carolina's got to be about as hick as we are. Daddy Daddy Daddy Daddy Daddy.

We drink well into the afternoon celebrating with much good cheer and not a little braggadocio. Finally, at dusk, with the birds flitting and chirping in the last faint moments of the gentle day, a quiet time to be sure, though I can't really see what the weather's like outside because of the dark windows, and truthfully there may not be a bird flying in the entirety of the county and I can't remember the last time I noticed a bird, all of which is beside the point, because it is the time of day when those who work, those who fly, are wrapping up their business for the day and are a bit tired, a bit off their game, especially those who have whiled away the afternoon deciding on outfits for pictorials, and at any rate what I was going to say before all this weather jumped in, is that I am at the point where I have drunk enough and wrung the last bit of celebration out of the successful espionage and have decided to risk all earlier success with another call to the Queen.

Don't do it man, says Henry. You're going to ruin my good work. It's too fishy if you call. I'm telling you she's going to be at the Capitol at seven next Sunday morning dressed up sexy as hell.

Smart-sexy, I say. That was nice.

Thank you. Now don't blow it. Save the call for another day.

No can do, I say. Josh Wade, Republican candidate for governor, demands a debate of the pertinent issues.

He wouldn't call her at home.

Home, work, it doesn't matter. Josh Wade's home is with the people. The white people, the rich people, to be sure. But the people nonetheless. Josh Wade is people people.

You're pressing your luck.

Nah, I say. She won't answer. No way she answers her phone twice in the same day.

As foretold, the answering machine picks up on the second ring. Uh, yes, I say, making my voice a butter-smooth reflection of New South sheen, this is Josh Wade, I'm calling for Miss Shea Bateman, the Governor's press secretary.

The Queen picks up as I'm about to outline my plan for a series of debates. Hello, she says, this is Shea, and the sound of a human voice, a regal one at that, throws me for a bit of a loop.

Yes, well, I say, suddenly going into my standard pranking voice of the gap-toothed country boy with a cord of firewood to sell. Henry begins shaking his head vigorously to this voice. Switching quickly to what might be mistaken for the stuttering mumble of Dev Degraw, attorney-at-law, I say, sorry to call you at home, I hope you're not eating supper.

Who is this? says the Queen.

Josh Wade, I say, in the voice of the assistant fashion-slash-style editor of the *Birmingham News* as interpreted by Gay Henry. Henry shakes his head violently. Dennis goes to the other end of the bar laughing.

Is this Dev?

What?

Is this Dev?

I look at Henry, who has both hands wrapped around his neck in the universal sign of the choke. Across the way Deli is smiling and looks on the verge of attempting human speech, mouthing what would look to a professional lip-reader like the phrase, hang up dumb-ass.

Excuse me? I say.

Is this Devaney Degraw trying to pull my leg?

That obvious huh?

Not at first, she says. But I was wondering why Josh Wade would call my house.

I can't do pranks. My voice is too recognizable. I just get too nervous.

Henry shakes his head. Deli, trivia box in hand, reaffirms her vow of silence.

I can't either, says the Queen, laughing a bit.

What are you up to?

Just waiting for you to call. I tried to call you so many times. And you never call me.

I didn't get any messages, I say.

Oh I never leave messages. I heard my voice on one of those machines one time and said never again. Especially if I'm calling a boy I like.

Really? I say, amazed as always by her facile and strangely titillating unacquaintance with the truth.

So, she says, are you or are you not going to take me to the Governor's Ball next Saturday like you promised?

Well.

Didn't you have fun the last time you came to my house?

Yes, I say, I had fun.

So you'll take me?

Sure.

Great. I've been dying to see you. Eight o'clock then? My house?

Sounds good.

But I'm warning you Josh Wade, I'll try anything I know to get your campaign secrets.

I've been at home for about an hour now after the excellent day of politics and prank calls and am relaxing in front of the television.

However, after so much stimulation, Id that hairy gorilla has fallen asleep. And our good friend Ego has that headachy kind of semi-buzz after a good afternoon in the cups going and has begun to listen to that Pat Boone of a Superego of mine who has noticed for the first time ever, after twenty-plus amiable and entertaining viewings, that on the set of *Working Girls,* in the first and pivotal scene when the first working girl, a gym teacher or aerobics instructor or leotard salesman of some distinction, gets friendly with the gardener, a friendly sort himself and not the least bit shy, not self-conscious in the least about being hired help, and what Super-ego had noticed is that, inexplicably, there is a set of bongos on the glass table next to the pool. And never any bongo playing, nor the first musician in the movie. No naked bongoist to show up and beat the three-headed drum. No working girl who is a working girl by day, bongo player by night. And as the first leotard salesman is about to go into her high-karate pose, Id, that half-ass bouncer, is asleep in the back of my brain, just sleeping on the hard floor like an animal, slobbering and sated on beer, nuzzling some furry thing that's just crept up moist and warm and covered in dust balls from the corner, snoring to wake the dead, and now that other ninny has Ego's ear all to himself and is saying, but why bongos? Why not a harp? Or a ukulele? What do bongos have to do with anything? What kind of plot twist could there ever have been with bongos? Or maybe the director plays the bongos? Can you imagine a porno director who plays the bongos? Some hairy-backed guy playing bongos for a bunch of naked drug-addled girls who were abused as children by some uncle in a shed and are just doing all this nasty stuff to get enough cocaine to numb their minds to the disgusting memory? And you know those girls are somebody's daughter. You've got a daughter. Bongos? My god, why not a trombone out by the pool? Why not a Jew's harp? Is that a pimple on her ass?

And it's not that good, this time, *Working Girls.* Not that good at all. I turn the television off and as soon as I do, he starts in like I knew he was going to. Boy, things sure did go smoothly with the Queen Bee today. Almost too smoothly if you ask me. Oh it's probably nothing. But still.

And now they're drinking hot chocolate together and analyzing the phone conversation like a couple of middle school girls, talking badly about Id, his lack of hygiene, his loud voice, his blue-collar love of tall boy beers, and as they begin popping popcorn and planning Friday night's outfit and discussing what Oprah would advise in such and such situation, Id cries out once in his sleep, then rolls out of the den, off the porch, and falls without waking ten feet down, landing with a grunting thump on Mrs. Catching's prickly bushes below.

And as the gals talk, I'm left to ponder what life could have been like in another time. A time more certain and sure for the likes of me, for a man of my particular talents. Surely I could have been cannon fodder of the first order, well suited to be skewered by a lance. And I have little doubt that I would have been a more than capable bubonic plague victim. And there are certain confident moments when I feel I could have been, and with not a little style, stomped to death by a wounded mastodon early one day of a fine spring morn.

The Governor's Ball

On Saturday, the day of the Governor's Ball, I wake up looking like a big hunk of meat loaf, grey and dried out and stuck for three days to the chipped plate in the sink. It's been a full week, filled with all sorts of goal fulfillment that modesty prevents my detailing in full.

When I get out of the shower, I notice an oddly manic blinking light on my answering machine. I circle the machine for a few minutes, pacing and toweling, lost in a quizzical wonderland, the tension building slowly, manic red beep by manic red beep. Who all could it be? But who all could it be?

The first call, early bird gets the worm, is a rather perfunctory threat from my client, as it were, the enigmatic Eightball. Other than the excitement of his now having my home number, there's nothing new to report. Money owed. Bodily harm. Et cetera. A run-of-the-mill semistalking.

The second call is from Chad Kingston informing me that he's officially in town to begin his reunion promotion whirlwind and that if we don't catch up tonight, he'll catch me tomorrow.

The third call is from the Queen.

Oh hey Dev, she says, pauses, twists hair into next month's *Cosmo* cover, wonders how this strange plastic gizmo has come to be attached to her ear and mouth. Sorry, I was just, well listen, I'm just so busy today you wouldn't believe. I'm running all over town with this and that. Is it okay if we just meet at the governor's mansion? I hope so. I'm really looking forward to tonight. Love ya. Call me if there's a problem.

. . .

Problem? No. Other than arriving alone to a formal party at the governor's mansion, I've made my way to a temporary bar without the first tuxedoed moment of self-awareness. The usual suspects mill about, looking like they never actually went home from the last party. Some have aged a decade or two in the last month, have added an extra wobble, an addendum of teeter, to their step. The Republicans are here as well on this night, lively and gaily dressed as ever. A few of them are Caucasian. By the staircase, the Governor chats with a few of his lobbyist buddies while Carter Allbright, C.A. yall, looks over their heads to see if anyone in the room is offering a new record deal or to adopt a lardish lad from the Lone Star State.

You'd think that with my perch here in the farthest corner of the ballroom, I'd have all the angles covered and would prove a most elusive target. Unfortunately, the anti-Dev missiles of one Bunny Akins, widow of the Governor's first and only mentor and current friend of all liquids poured or guzzled from the bottle, seem to have snuck in under the radar, and I am one dead duck when she sees me as she's coming out of the bathroom. Having but little time, I quickly search about for materials with which to assemble a crude flying machine. Thinks I, I'm fucked.

Give me a big hug baby governor boy.

So midlilting Bunny step, we hug, a quick and forced and keening one, then break crisply as from a boxing clinch.

So, she says, I hear you and C.A. are sharing the stage. Honey, I can't wait.

Excuse me?

Bayou Dog reunion next Saturday, she says. Oh child, don't tell me I spoilt a surprise. Daddy Governor saw them posters all over town and called your friend Mr. Kingston to see if he wanted a musical guest for the show. Oh law, I can't wait, I just can't wait.

And your daddy is proud as a peacock with a fresh coat of paint. It'll be like our own special family reunion.

Stunned speechless by the deafening cries in my brain from the long-ago and permanently institutionalized Billy Tucker, I smile politely and nod in a jerky circular motion, the fishing bobber being taunted and teased by the finicky catfish of fortune.

You've seen the posters haven't you? she asks. They're all over town. Everybody's talking about it. Ads in the paper, on the radio. And it couldn't come at a better time with the race and all. I told Daddy Governor he'd have to make a speech, but he said this was your special day, and Carter's too. He wouldn't dare do a thing to steal your thunder. You know that don't you? Give me your hand baby boy governor.

And I do. I give the wizened widow of Snake my hand, brain of the supersleuth kicking into methodical overdrive now, working out the possible progressions. Snake. Garden of Eden. Equals widow of Satan himself. Equals I am officially roasting in hell.

You do know that? she says again. The Governor loves you more than anything. There's not a thing he wouldn't do for you. Have you told him you loved him? Have you just hugged him and kissed him on the mouth and told him how much you loved him lately?

I think I'll do that right now, I say, attempting to disengage a sweat-slick and nervous hand that is being squeezed and patted and just generally bullied into submission.

Apparently she's slipped a little Super Glue into her palm, oldest trick in the book, and wants to be dragged across the dance floor chirping about the love of father and son and C.A.'s concert and how she wouldn't miss it for the world, not for all the tea in China.

Before I can karate-toss Bunny over my shoulder and into the back of my father's head, who is to blame, is absolutely to blame, for this pestilence of tiny rabbits being loosed on the innocent people of the land, she's in full voice and demanding the Governor get C.A. up there singing with the band. Shade, a few feet behind and drinking a beer by himself, sees me and smiles the shiteater of shiteating grins.

If I may be so bold, if I may be so bold, if I may be so bold, Bunny says until all heads within earshot, all heads not fleeing like rats from a burning ship, are turned toward her and waiting for whatever boldness she is about to spring.

You may be so bold, says the Governor. What is it?

I was just telling baby boy governor about the great news, the fantastic news, about Carter's show at the *Bayou Dog* reunion.

That is great news, I say. Great news.

The Governor forces a smile, some long-forgotten bell in his head detecting that someone in his presence might actually be giving him a tad of shit. And then a buzzer, soft and insistent, powering somehow through the melange of tired but defiant testosterone and habitual vanity and thirty years of getting his ass kissed by every sycophant under the sun, which heralds the five minutes a year he allows for circumspection and reflection.

Now Daddy Governor, Bunny says, give baby boy governor a hug.

But before he can move, before Bunny can get even bolder and propose we strip down and leapfrog each other across the room, I break forcefully from her Chinese handcuffs and engage the Governor in a roughhousing bear hug, a kiss on the mouth, then grabbing his oddly tired face in my hands, I say, I love you I love you I love you.

Bunny claps and jumps up and down. The Governor forces another smile. Carter Allbright, C.A. yall, checks her reflection in a punch bowl. Shade waves, already in motion, moving slowly and deliberately away. I think to myself, I can neither confirm nor deny that I have a father.

Without warning Bunny begins gathering hands for a prayer. But before she can begin instructing the flock in earnest, a waiter with a tray of champagne glasses arrives just in the nick of time. Yes, saved, most assuredly saved, am I. For once the glasses have been grabbed, Bunny is off on a tangent to C.A. about how champagne always makes her giggly and a little talkative and more than a little frisky if you know what she means. As she's jabbering away, I shoot an ambiguous glance to the man responsible for my relationship with one Bunny Akins, a.k.a. the worst person in the history of the world.

The Governor smiles another tired smile then, showing the deft moves of a former player in the post, takes two small steps to the side and seals off Bunny in a classic box-out move. I hear tell, he says, that you had some frank words recently for our mayor friend.

Just thought I'd remind him of his voting options, I say.

Shade said you were a right jackass.

I'd say that's a fair assessment.

Well I called the mayor to apologize. Usually I like to let a man take care of his own apologies. But I figured in this case you wouldn't mind.

No, I say, that's fine.

We ended up having a pretty good talk, he says.

I'm glad to hear it, I say. The mayor's a good man.

Smiling and putting a hand on my shoulder, he says, it's fun sometimes, isn't it son?

I'm back at my original post, a good deal more diligent than before, and the Queen has yet to show for the evening. At the moment I'm wondering if there might be just the slightest chance that the Queen has called the *Birmingham News* and discovered, considerably to my chagrin, that Rob Montegue may or may not be able to meet for their early-morning photo shoot. As I'm considering this, Shade walks up, looking as if his planned cavalry strike on a vulnerable flank is all but unstoppable.

Bunny too tired to dance? he asks.

A quick sacrilege and a series of graphic lamentations greet his remark.

Hell I've got thirty years of it, he says.

She doesn't try to get you to kiss Dad all the time.

No, but every other buzz she throws on we're sure as hell holding hands and praying.

About that, I say. Don't you prefer being led in prayer by a reasonably sober member of the clergy?

Still can't believe Snake Akins left a good wife for her, Shade says. But this place'll do funny things to a man. Speaking of funny things, what I take to be your date just walked in.

I turn toward the door and here she comes with the Higginbothans and the wily leader of the Roundheads, Oliver C. himself, looking very much like the double date that they are. Mathematical permutations begin whizzing at a rapid rate. The Queen Bee and Hooper? An impossibility. Oliver Cromwell and Dee-Dee? Beyond irrelevant. Which leads to the only plausible conclusion. The Queen Bee is on a date with all three and all three are on a date with the Queen Bee.

If that shit in your mouth don't taste good, spit it out.

What?

That face you're making.

I didn't make a face.

You ain't got a hair on your ass if you let that one get to you.

I start to point out the obvious, that there isn't necessarily a correlation between my highly evolved state and an outmoded concept of masculinity, but decide against it. Shit, I say. I'm bearskin rug back there.

And look who else just walked in, Shade says pointing at the door. Young Josh Wade. Probably here to measure for drapes, decide where he'll put his chaise lounge at.

Ears and suspenders burning, Josh Wade spots Shade and nods, then he sees me and it's the old heigh ho cheerio tip of the phantom cap.

I bet he wouldn't wander around like a sick puppy every time some crazy rich gal flashed her eyes at him, says Shade. Yep, I bet old Josh boy knows how to work it.

Oh I'm sure.

I'm serious. That boy's smooth. Bet he's got em coming and going.

You're obviously baiting me.

He's got money. He's fixing to be governor. And he ain't bad-looking.

Listen, I say, I'm bad-looking. I'll be the first to admit I'm no prize at the county fair. But Josh Wade is simply repugnant.

Got that golden hair.

He ran for every single office in college. That's all he did. He didn't care about dating.

Those the kind that get it on the back end. Shy and sly.

He wasn't shy. He's just an . . .

Yep, Shade says, work hard early, make their mark, and sit back and let the world come to em. Oh yes, women from twenty-two to fifty-two like a solid young man like young Josh Wade. He's a lawyer ain't he?

Well hell yes.

Got him a good practice, probably looking to settle down, find him a good woman that don't take all her pleasure out of driving him crazy, ready to be a grown man. And ready to do something for the state too.

Do what?

Lead it, says Shade.

He couldn't lead a frat house across the street to the Playboy mansion.

You think you could do better?

Than Josh Wade? Well hell yes if I had to.

Maybe you'll be ready to run against him next time then.

Yeah, I'll do that, I say, turning to the bartender and waving on another. I can't get enough of this scene.

An hour has passed since the mobile hive hit the party, and I've managed to avoid the Queen's circling maneuvers by a stealthy and unpredictable bar rotation. At the moment I'm at the bar just below the grand staircase, draped grandly as it often is with serious-faced drunks. Next to me three young female interns sip cherry-colored mixed drinks and wait for yet another mortician moonlighting as a state representative to offer them a late dinner on a lobbyist's tab. Shade, meanwhile, has been trapped about ten feet away by Skip Terry, beloved lottery proponent and coonass boyhood pal of the Governor from Bugtussle. Every five minutes or so Shade's nodding me over to help out. With each nod, I've smiled politely in return and given Skip the six-shooter getcha-in-a-minute move. The casual onlooker should surmise from my posture and quietly animated body language that though I'm standing by myself, I am, in fact, quite busy.

I've also been watching Gibson Smith, Oliver C. to friends and family, and am having a hard time disliking him as much as I'd really like to. He follows not too closely on the Queen's heels, tripping occasionally over first one Higginbothan, then the other. Then again, I'd still like to cuff his tender bloated head. Shade, I call.

What is it boy? he shouts over the heads of the impressionable young interns.

I think I've found a man with a hairy ass for you.

What? Shade says, laughing and looking over at Skip Terry.

I'm betting that fatheaded fellow there has a hairy ass, I say, pointing at Oliver C. until he turns to look at me. As I'm pointing at the warrior Puritan, I've begun staring at Skip Terry in a crazy cross-eyed manner. He seems not to like this look and begins his way toward me. Oliver and the Queen have begun a fairly lively step in my direction as well. Higginbothans, though officially members of the dramatis personae, should be shunned by cast and crew when playing this scene. Audience should take their cue from same.

With utmost deftness of hand, I swivel toward the bar, receive my next round just as Skip Terry and the cave boy arrive, and turn to the three interns and ask if they'd like to dance en masse. They are, to an intern, disinclined.

Did you need something, the proud Puritan asks.

His posture during the query is affably threatening. He suspects I'm having a bit of go, but no need to be paranoid about such things. And nothing quite as red as fighting while dressed up. A bit Bobby and J.R. to be sure. Shade here was looking for you, I say.

Shit you say, says the poet among us.

Seriously, Cromwell says, do you need something?

No man.

You were pointing at me.

Yeah.

I'm not Hooper if that's what you're wondering, he says, taking a step closer as Shade moves casually between us. Meanwhile, the Queen is in frantic Higginbothan conference at the edge of the dance floor, just missing Dee-Dee in the chops with an elbow as she sweeps her hair from twenty-first-century sex kitten to high school sweetheart crying at the boys fighting over her in the Dairy Dip parking lot.

No, I say, you're not Hooper.

So do you mind if I ask what you said?

I told that man there that I bet you had a hairy ass.

I do have a hairy ass, he says. Hairy as hell.

Told you Shade.

Shade shakes his head, wonders about the strange rituals of white boys in their quest for white pussy.

Is that it? says Oliver C. Is that all you want?

That was it.

All right then, he says.

All right, I say.

As he makes his departure, Skip Terry steps forward and says, what's all that staring about boy?

And, to be fair, Skip has patiently waited his turn, so I cross my eyes and smile and move closer to his ruddy face. What staring?

Skip Terry looks at Shade, looks around for his absent associates, realizes whatever he's going to do he's going to have to do for himself, and says, Mr. Shade, this boy's crazy as a bedbug.

Shade smiles but doesn't say anything. Then Skip Terry is off across the dance floor.

Still with my crazy happy convict's face, I say to Shade, you know, I really might run for governor one of these days.

. . .

Thirty minutes later and I'm in the same lucky spot. During the interim, my eyes have uncrossed and I no longer look like an extra from *Deliverance*. On the other hand, my backdoor is still shamefully devoid of fur. Across the floor, there are two minor developments. The first involves the Governor and Mayor Batch laughing and backslapping like a couple of long-lost army buddies. I consider going over and offering a quick heartfelt apology of my own for my trauma-induced, funeral–et cetera performance up in Birmingham, but figure that the Governor's call probably did the trick and that even before the call the mayor had written the whole thing off as just a hotheaded son defending his father and no harm in that, so I simply toss a wave their way, which is returned, and feel all is well in the lottery/editorial department. The second development reveals that old two-timer Skip Terry with a firm grip on Josh Wade's elbow as he tells him what's what in big stick backwoods politics. Not the least surprising of course. And for those keeping score, the Queen Bee and I are entering hour three of our date. During said date, the Queen has ventured a few halfhearted spins on the dance floor with Hooper, Dee-Dee, Oliver, and, on at least two occasions, the whole of Higginbothan Inc. I need not mention it's been a hair-tossing, fake-laughing night. And I've had dates spend less time rubbing another man's back. However, one phrase has played in my mind throughout the night like a mother's sweetest lullaby. If Momma said it once, she said it a thousand times, Rob Montegue, assistant fashion-slash-style editor for the *Birmingham News*.

As I'm enjoying a brief moment of dateless pleasure, Shade walks up looking as if he might give me some advice for a change of pace. Free o charge too.

You see who Skip Terry's talking to don't you? he says.

Donny Most?

Who?

Donald Most.

Who in the hell is Donald Most?

Ralph Malph.

Son, what in the hell are you talking about?

Josh Wade? I say. Is that Josh Wade he's talking to? By golly, it is. Your old friend Shade. The cherubic apple of your eye. Your newest favoritest white boy, suspenders and all.

You going to be like that all night?

You going to keep up with the Josh Wade fan club and the free advice for young lovers?

Fair enough, he says, ordering a beer. Fair enough. So you still think Skip Terry's irrelevant?

Yes.

Rhino making his last stand is dangerous, old and irrelevant or no. Your buddy Wade don't think he's irrelevant.

Maybe not, I say. But what's Skip Terry bothering with him for anyway? No way he's backing a lottery.

Skip's done switched sides. Man like him ain't got all his eggs in one basket. Shit, there's always highway jobs for a construction man. And he figures he's talking to the next governor of the state.

No way, I say. The Governor hadn't even started campaigning yet.

Governor's going to lose son.

No way. Not to Josh Wade.

Shade doesn't reply to this but simply nods to the dance floor, where the Governor shakes a bad groove thing with his young wife, a picture, in this instance, worth a thousand words.

Following a separate plot string, the Queen Bee has just caught my eye and begun a discreet three-second make-out with the less-than-puritanical Cromwell before walking out the door hand and hand.

Shade points toward the door. Last free advice to young lovers, he says. You best let that one keep walking.

I'm afraid, I say, that I'm my father's son when it comes to minor distractions.

What about when it gets down to the nut-cutting?

When it gets down to the nut-cutting, you eloquent old poet, I got hog legs in one hand and a razor in the other. I'm not going to be a half-ass lawyer all my life.

Back to farming then?

Back to the farm.

As my date for the evening has been gone for the better part of an hour and was last seen stroking the back of another man, I've decided I might as well call it an evening myself. I'm standing in the driveway, waiting for the valet, when I spot Bunny Akins moving vaguely, a small craft in a high wind, toward my vulnerable position. Anticipating a one-on-one sermon or a forced hugging session with the valet, I hightail it around the side of the mansion toward the garage and guesthouse. I'm stumbling about looking for a non-prickly bush in which to roost when I hear voices beyond the big fountain. Fearing Bunny is replicating herself at rapid speed, I make for the guesthouse patio with a barely repressed shiver of spine.

The voices are just this side of the tennis court, and, it turns out, are not an exponentially expanding platoon of drunken lagomorphs but Josh Wade and a young woman who teeters and buzzes beneath a queen's crown of a moon.

Josh, she coos, this is so bad. I work for the other team.

You can be my double agent, he says.

And at this juncture, only the discipline of a Christian martyr throttles the instinctual bloodcurdling scream. Seriously, no one should have to hear a line like that.

What do double agents do? says the Queen, biting a lip, delicate village girl in made-for-TV movie, family just set ablaze by the enemy, tears aplenty, and yet this strange man, so virile and mysterious, so like a Milwaukee sitcom god, who asks, nigh demands, that she give her nubile body to the very tribe who burned her village and family. But first him. First he will teach her in the ways of Republican love. Shot fades to tender sweaty whoopee in backseat of late-model Oldsmobile.

Why don't you use your imagination, says Josh Wade, making a move to take her in his arms. And to be honest, half of me wants to give the guy a little credit. I didn't think he had it in him. The other half, well he's tiptoeing into the guesthouse, feeling about in the dark, unleashing a massive silent oath as he smashes a knee into what must be a leftover sword from the Wallace era, and feverishly grasping about for a telephone. Phone retrieved, I race through the list of possible prank calls.

Montgomery police reporting Oliver Cromwell suicide attempt? Too obvious.

Hooper Higginbothan invitation for late-night popcorn rehash of the night's proceedings?

Too Higginbothan.

Rob Montegue, geeked on cocaine, calling from office wanting to move photo shoot up an hour to catch prime morning sun and cut short vicious grinding of teeth?

Coked-up fashion-slash-style editor voice one of my all-time worsts.

Improvised interruption of unbearable spy dialogue by any means possible?

Si senor.

By straddling what must be the widest love seat in history, I've managed to prop open the door just in time to hear the Queen say, now Josh, I can't come over to your house after just meeting you. I never go to the boy's house until I'm sure.

I'll come to your house.

Now now Josh, says the Queen, I've made a strict pledge to limit my lovers to the fingers of one hand. And I've only got three fingers left.

I'll take all of them, says Josh Wade at about the same time a cell phone begins ringing clear as a bell on a calm cool night.

Let it ring, says Josh Wade.

It might be Momma, says the Queen in a voice giggly with neck being kissed. Hello.

Shea, I say, it's Dev Degraw.

Oh hey.

Listen, I'm sorry I'm running late for our date. I got tied up here in Tuscaloosa. Are you still at the mansion?

What?

Are you still at the mansion?

Yes.

Well I'm just leaving Tuscaloosa. I tried to call earlier, but your cell phone number was at the office. I'm in the car just now leaving the office.

What are you talking about?

I'm sorry I'm late. I was really looking forward to our date to-night.

Where are you?

Just leaving the office. Listen, I'll make it up to you. I'll see you at your house in forty-five minutes. We'll do a late dinner, then dancing if you want.

That's not a good idea.

Be there in forty-five. If you're late, I might be crashed in your driveway.

I'm not sure what you're up to.

Be there in forty-five, I say, waiting in the driveway, sorry to disappoint you, couldn't be helped, know you were looking forward to it, round up Higginbothans and see if they want to join us, see you in a bit, bye-bye now, Higginbothan roundup, bye-bye.

And with this I quietly hang up the phone, crack my knee again against the discarded sword, and tiptoe gentle as a country mouse back out to my perch on the back patio. And from here, looking out on the backyard of the governor's mansion, the sound, nearly audible, of a mysterious circumstance gone not so mysterious, a young gubernatorial candidate bidding adieu to the elusive melody of the humpbacked whale.

Who was that, says Josh Wade.

Just a friend, says the Queen in a voice that suggests the gathering up of things, the distracted moment just after the dreaded just-a-friend phone call.

But one thing remains to be heard by our intrepid eavesdropper, one more thing to cap a dirty night's work.

What's not a good idea? says young Josh.

He's thinking about quitting his job, says the Queen.

And where will you be working this time next year?

Oh I don't know, she says. It's all so confusing. Everything is confusing. I'm just so suddenly tired. I best get going. I've got an early morning ahead of me.

You're leaving?

I've got this newspaper thing tomorrow, she says. It's nothing really, just a silly fashion and style piece for the *News*.

Yes. Oh yes. And now I'm stepping gingerly off the porch of the guesthouse, tiptoeing through the gate, and once in the driveway, commencing a whimsical clog of indeterminate origin. Extraterrestrial funk.

I'm still high-stepping by the time I get to the valet, but he seems to have reparked my car. Feeling quite good about being out in the early-spring air and strangely invigorated, I decide to walk the forty yards to my car rather than wait like I normally would. Yes, I'm feeling sprightly indeed when I come upon Oliver Cromwell sitting in his SUV, door open, smoking a cigarette, and looking peeved. Perhaps a touch higginbothaned.

How's it going man, he says.

Fine bud. Couldn't be better. Yourself?

I'm pissed. Shea left for the bathroom an hour ago. You haven't seen her have you?

I stall around a bit. Tattletale was never really my favorite role.

Not the governor guy? he says. The guy with the suspenders?

The suspenders aren't good, I say.

Fucking hell. Drags me to this damn thing. Well he can give her a ride home then.

He turns and starts the motor, a look of ire across that proud and considerable brow.

By the way, I say, that whole photo shoot thing tomorrow is a crock of shit. I guess she mentioned it.

She did. Several times. Prank call?

Afraid so.

Good one, says Oliver C., sticking out a hand.

Thank you, I say, shaking the offered hand. I kind of liked it myself.

· · ·

Hell yes. Hell damn yes. Back in Tuscaloosa where the women are young and my friends are grizzled, all things queenly and gubernatorial in the rearview. Ewan, patron saint of debtors, has extended an unprecedented ninth straight week of open tab, so we're celebrating. Though, I must say, the celebration has been dimmed a bit from my point of view by the *Bayou Dog* Reunion flyer that Ewan has so graciously posted above the cash register.

BAYOU DOG REUNION: *Meet the stars from the beloved show*
FEATURING: *Chad Kingston (Sheriff Tucker)*
Candy Lake (Suzy Tucker)
Dev Degraw (Billy Tucker)
Comet (great-grandson of the legendary Thor)
SPECIAL MUSICAL GUEST: *Carter Allbright*
FREE: *Popcorn, cokes, autographs, and so much more*
LOCATION: *The Windbreeze Mall*
DATE/TIME: *April 4, 11:00 A.M.–2:00 P.M.*

Believe it or not the guys are razzing me. They've procured a little kid's baseball cap from the lost and found, no telling how it got there, and Gay Henry has been starring as little Billy Tucker for about an hour now. Golly gee Mr. Bartender, could I have another drink on Mr. Degraw's tab. Holy smokes Mr. Degraw, no one's ever heard of this show. Jiminy willikers Mr. Degraw, are autographs really free? Variations of same ad infinitum.

We've pretty much got the bar to ourselves by this point. We being the stinking freeloaders who continue to slaughter my tab. In addition to the erstwhile Billy Tucker, the assorted crew of near humans includes Jim, Preacher James, and the butter-eating poet, Allen Dance. We're about to begin the paper-rock-scissors tournament to see who has to run down to sorority row to pick up our dates when, wonder of wonders, Chad Kingston, Sheriff Tucker himself, walks through the doors of the saloon, bits of tumbleweed and horsehair scattered about his disheveled person. In one hand, a roll of flyers, the other waving unambiguously toward the bar. Cowboy hat pointing skyward as if riding a tough hombre of a pinto in a windstorm. Boots quite simply on the wrong feet.

By god Degraw, I been up and down this here Strip looking for your scrawny ass. Been all over hell and half of Georgia, he says, slapping Gay Henry a hearty one on the back. Baseball cap and Henry fly off in opposing directions.

Can I buy you a drink? I say. You look a little parched.

I'd like a spot of sherry, he says in the worst British accent ever attempted. To celebrate this evidence of his acting range, he applies the old jolly backbreaker to the butter-eating poet. Preacher James nods approvingly, gives what seems to be a Rosetta stone request for another lick to be placed on any other back but his own, then takes a few steps back, motioning Ewan for another round in the process. Chad Kingston laughs, tips his hat at Preacher, and knocks the breath out of me.

Once things have settled down and Chad has stopped his merry injuring of the gang, he puts shot glass to lips, a pause in the action long enough to send the poet scrambling for pen and paper. Slamming the shot glass down, the good sheriff snatches the pen from the poet's hands, unrolls a flyer, and signs with a flourish.

Thank you sir, says the dainty dairy-fed poet.

Chad Kingston Tucker tousles his hair. You're more than welcome son. You are more than welcome.

Solicitous to a fault, the ever-quizzical poet begins asking about the grand *Bayou Dog* Reunion. Chad Kingston answers every query with great garumphing gusto. Hell, he says, I talked to a good twenty-five hundred people today. The word's out, I tell you. We'll have two thousand come Saturday, or I'll eat my hat.

Two thousand? I say. Two thousand? There won't be twenty people there. There won't be four people there. My horny-ass father, that's one. And excellent choice on the music by the way. Excellent choice. And Odelle Bailey and her collection of gourds, that's two. And who else? Seriously who else? Then I let go with a few frank appraisals of Mr. Kingston, his gussied-up tent revival, and an admittedly unnecessary riff on the unsightliness and indigestibility of his gargantuan wide-brimmed chapeau.

Immediately, I'm set upon by the rest of the aberrants. During the whole of which the bloated cowpoke assumes an air of quivering masculine indignation.

You've got to admit Dev, it does have a certain kitsch factor, says Gay Henry, who seems, regretfully, to have regained consciousness after the jarring jolt from Chad.

Ewan, I say, kindly add twenty dollars to my tab and give it to Henry on the condition he never utter that word again.

Ewan pulls a bill out of the register and hands it to Henry.

That includes campy, I say, or any other synonym denoting extreme irony. If at any time you break this agreement, you must reimburse the twenty.

Deal, says Henry.

Then I've got Sheriff Tucker saddled up again. Ten to one, I say, you haven't even talked to Candy.

You'd lose that bet, sonny.

And the assembled rabble cheers and hurrahs their stalwart.

And? What did she say? Eager to daub the dried spittle from your octogenarian chin?

She'll be here Friday afternoon, says Chad. Said she was looking forward to seeing the gang. Wouldn't let me pay for her plane ticket. I was going to see if you'd be willing to pick her up at the airport in fact.

Can-dy, Can-dy, Can-dy, shout the assembled ruffians.

What gang? I say.

But before Chad can answer, Jim, the sly one in the group to be sure, begins a rather brisk inquisition into my relative merits on stage and screen. Not to veer too far from the subject at hand, he says, but Mr. Kingston, what was the worst bit of dialogue ever to come out of Dev's mouth?

Hurry Daddy, Doc Baker's barn's ablaze, says Chad Kingston in his best drunken oil rigger's imitation of a little boy.

Says the hero-worshipping poet, of the many many horrific scenes in which Dev was involved, can you pick the worst?

The gruff one furrows his brow for a moment, then seems to have a moment of near clarity. Oh yes, he says, I've got one. Strange man comes to town, turns out he's my harmless old crazy uncle. Anyway, strange man is skulking around the property. Billy, Dev here, is alone in the house as a storm approaches, racing from window to window trying to keep an eye on the stranger who's behind this tree, coming around that corner, and so on. Just popping out everywhere. Luigi Santermo was way ahead of the game with that pop-out move to build tension and scare the hell out of the audience. Well anyhow, there's this one moment when the stranger is making his way toward the back door, the lock's busted on the door or something, and Billy is on one side of the door, the stranger on the other, and Billy, Dev here, is supposed to have this look of courageous terror, the boy-trying-to-be-a-man lip trembler, and Luigi insists on panning in for a close-up. Hell, I've never seen anything like it. He's wagging his head up and down about a mile a minute and kind of waggling his whole body to try and get his lip to quiver. Luigi, he's Italian you know, he's laughing so hard he can't hold the camera straight, shouting, you are a scared little boy, not a poodle shaking off the rain.

Preacher James shoots out a quick something that may or not have an interrogative somewhere in its syntax.

You're asking if he's the worst actor ever? Now that's a big statement.

Worst you've ever worked with? says Ewan.

Worst child actor ever? asks Gay Henry.

Chad Kingston puts a large arm around my shoulders, begins to slowly and sweetly suffocate me to death. He wasn't a bad physical actor, he says. Pretty good at running and swimming and such. But I will say, that in forty years in the business, working with drunks and folks who can't hardly read and dope heads and people crazy as a bedbug, I ain't never seen anyone any worse at trying to spit out a line of dialogue. Not for one second of one episode was this fellow here ever a boy named Billy Tucker. Were you son?

No.

Just good old Dev Degraw?

Just good old Dev Degraw.

The Governor's son?

The Governor's son. Listen, I couldn't agree more. That's why there's no way in hell I'll be at the reunion on Saturday.

We had a deal, says Chad Kingston.

Tough shit.

You're not going to welsh are you now? I wouldn't have put your picture on the flyer if I'd of known you were going to welsh. Our fans are expecting the whole gang.

Tough luck.

Unfortunately, my response and generally sour disposition prompt the inaugural recitation of a recently composed poem by the wordsmith in the group, a poem that on second reading quickly morphs into a rousing and unsightly jig by the drunken rabble, The Ballad of Dev Degraw.

Who hadn't any balls
Whose life was full of flaws
Who always flubbed his line
And said it out of time
The governor's firstborn child
An actor meek and mild.
And when the bet was done
He'd take off on the run.

After twenty or so renditions of this, Gay Henry dons his miniature baseball cap to lead the group in call and response.

Golly gee
BILLY T!
Aw shucks
BILL TUCK!

And on to the inevitable fifteen minutes of rhyming permutations. During this session the piping pixie continues to besmirch the good character of Billy Tucker with pornographic shrillness, leading the swarthy inebriates in verse after verse of the dreaded song. I, for one, am hoping that all this prancing about will soon send the gathered lechers abrawling over his boyish wares, but that may just be the wishful thinking of a sentimental dreamer.

Actually the gang is in good voice and I've begun to sing along when through the door comes Squeaky, the mute and inscrutable prophet of Tuscaloosa. He stands in the doorway, radiating under the dim beer lights in his Roll Tide T-shirt, Roll Tide gym shorts, and through the open door the full moon a hazy pink in the sky. He looks peacefully up the bar for a hand to shake, an arm to pat, the song dying down as he approaches. He walks slowly, inscrutably, his head moving amiably about. Some of the crew have begun to holler, hey Squeaky, what's going on Squeaky. To this, he smiles without showing teeth, sends line upon line of face into peaceful motion. When he reaches me, his rough hand clasps mine. Hey Squeaky, I say. He rubs my arm. Shakes my hand. Rubs arm. Then he is in motion again, heading back out the door and toward his next destination.

Sitting at the bar, I have a brief discomfiting moment of what can only be described as goodwill. I try to shake it off, try to laugh off the nagging earnestness, the awful self-consciousness of being, but it's no use.

All right, I say, I'll do it.

I knew you would son, says Chad Kingston, mauling my hair.

Preacher, I ask, is Kitty Cat Taylor still running that all-night craps game out in Bollenger?

I turn to Jim for interpretation. Yep, says Jim, him and his brother Ground Squirrel.

Can we just show up? Or do we need to call first? I haven't been out there in five years or so.

Preacher James frowns, shakes his head, doesn't like the idea of it, speaks more forcefully than usual.

He says we need to stay put, says Jim. Gets rough out there sometimes on Saturday night. He's not going. He's got church in the morning.

Got to go, I say. Just got the double arm squeeze from Squeaky under a full moon.

I can see that then, says Preacher James.

I nod aggressively to the clearest thing I've ever heard him say. Ewan, I say, can I get a hundred on the tab?

A hundred mate? Is that all?

Clear up Monday one way or another. I'll sell my car, whatever. Come Monday, we're level.

Do you want the damage now?

Well hell no of course not.

Is a hundred enough? he asks, grinning.

If it's all the same, make it two while you got your hand in the till.

He hands over the cash in crumpled twenties, grimy and moist to the touch.

I'm winning by the way, I say.

Whatever you say Dev, grins the wanker footie fan, whatever you say.

It takes us a while to find the house. It's out in the middle of a whole bunch of nothing, black country roads and pine trees, then suddenly a random and sullen congregation of brick ranchers in a strip-cleared field. Perfect for that afternoon picnic with the old gang from the militia. Yessir, gun city. Second Amendment, by god, Second Amendment. Of course the Founding Fathers themselves loved stuffing their fat asses in camo and playing army men in the woods. And damn right a few of their kids accidentally shot each other out in the shed. But freedom ain't free now is it?

Kitty Cat's house is at the end of a cul-de-sac, then down a long driveway shrouded with trees and overgrown bushes. A NO TRESPASSING sign, THIS MEANS YOU, then a clearing where about seven trucks are parked in the front yard. The three pansies not driving pick-em-ups have arrived in SUVs, big ones. Nonetheless, my Asian economy strikes quite a formidable pose as we pull into the yard, and I, for one, am brooking no guff from the farm boys inside.

Gay Henry is the first out of the car, drunk and bouncy and one would guess never having seen the squeal-like-a-pig scene from *Deliverance*. The word kitschy almost makes its way out of his mouth but I silence him with a cold stare. Then it's Jim, who looks forward to practicing the defense of his dissertation regarding the pregnant parenthesis, and finally the butter-eating poet, Allen Dance, ready at a moment's notice to cry me a river over the retroactive giant steps backward the New Formalists are making, should anyone care to ask. Chad Kingston, the one of us who might, through physical presence, down-home whimsy, and behind-the-scenes dirt from *Cannonball Run IV*, be able to save us from the beating we so richly deserve, has his face plastered against the window, idiot's smile just where you'd expect it, dreaming sweet dreams of the mudbuggy bayou. Seriously, we're dead men.

Are you sure about this, says Jim, the chronicler of all things parenthetical.

No problem, I say. I've been here before. As long as you've got money, they could care less.

When were you here? says the poet.

With a few of my dad's friends a couple of years ago, I say, making a mental note to advise him against using the word craft at any cost. By the way, I say, you're not a carpenter or something are you?

No, he says, I'm not a carpenter.

Because I keep reading about these poets who are carpenters and lumberjacks and deckhands and enough is enough. There's not a chance in hell of any of us winning money in there if we've got a poet with us who is any kind of artisan or tradesmen or back-to-nature sawmill something or another. You don't make knapsacks out of fresh papyrus do you?

No.

I'm serious. I need to know that before we go in.

I don't.

Because if you're building birdhouses in your time away from verse, I just don't think I could stand it. I'd rather you take martial arts if it came to that.

I'm not an artisan, he says, and I don't take martial arts.

Just a regular poet who's lazy and likes to drink?

Yes, exactly.

Because I don't know you that well. And if you suddenly start talking about the discipline inherent in poetry and the craft of tae kwon do, and all the while you're carrying numb chucks and a chapbook in a lovingly handcrafted from fresh papaya shoulder bag, I don't know what I'd do with myself. I know I couldn't roll dice.

Are you nervous or something?

No poetry boy, I say. Henry, are you going to wear that Cub Scout hat inside?

Yes.

Is it lucky?

Golly gee Billy T, absolutely.

Are you fearless or stupid?

I am a bad motherfucker is what I am.

All right, I say. All right. Good. That's good. But can we all agree that Jim is the most morose-looking piece of shit we've ever seen, and that there's no way in hell any of us wins any money if he goes in looking like that?

I'll wait in the car, I'll wait in the car.

Oh good god. Are you ready to win some money or not?

I'll do whatever the group wants me to do.

That makes no sense. Gobbily gook gobbily gook gobbily gook. There's one question on your oral exam. Do you want to win some money or not?

It's not as simple as that, he says.

Do you feel lucky?

Define luck.

I will kill you where you stand.

I feel lucky just hanging out with you guys. Is that what you mean? We could discuss rhetorically the whole concept of luck.

I will kill you where you stand.

Mathematical, cultural, sociopolitical? We could begin with a derivation of the word.

I will kill you where you stand if you don't tell me whether you do or do not feel lucky.

Within the limited parameters of a word you refuse to define. . . .

Stay in the fucking car then. Henry, Juzitsu, let's go.

I turn and head with my skeleton crew through the waist-high weeds toward the door. It's just a standard rancher with basement. Muffled music coming from downstairs through the open window, David Allan Coe, that bad bad man. Penned-up dogs in the back yipping coyote-style. On the front porch, a beer sign busted from days of yore, a lily ready to bloom in a pot stuffed with cigarette butts, and moths popping around a naked bulb.

Let's roll them bones, says Jim, rushing up behind.

I give him a fierce hell-yes nod and knock on the door and abracadraba it's opened the moment I do. A Mrs. Kitty Cat or Mrs. Ground Squirrel serving as greeter.

Can I help you boys? she asks, looking about the yard for the bikes the young Mormons have ditched just moments before.

I'm about to answer when a malevolent cumulus nimbus of smoke drifts up from the open door leading down to the basement, bringing with it a pit bull whose head would not look out of place on Oliver Cromwell's shoulders. A low growl begins deep in the throat of the great beast. Then excited pant. Then growl. Then pant. Behind me someone moans.

We'd like to join your dice game if we can, I say.

Roy, she shouts, then turns to walk back into a darkened den, the wood paneling and a photo of someone's granny glowing blue in the flickering light of the television. She's kindly left the dog behind. Who, to his credit, is admirably unselfconscious about his foaming at the mouth problem. Roy, for what it's worth, hasn't heard his name called.

Down the stairs it's country boy jubilation one second, Appomattox the next. Then someone behind me, through clenched and chattering teeth, makes the not unreasonable suggestion that we leave. I would like to respond that to make a movement of any sort at this particular impasse would lead to a maiming of the first order, namely of me. Instead, while smiling at the dog, I say, nnnnnn.

What? says Gay Henry in his normal voice.

Nnn, I say, toning down the negation, stressing the abject neutrality, the complete lack of volition that I feel in the presence of the nice doggy before me.

Again in a normal speaking voice, Henry says, Chad's waking up. He's thrashing around in the car or something. What's he doing? Seriously, look you guys. Look Dev. He's having a nightmare. He looks like King Kong swatting at the planes.

The dog has gone from alternating growls and pants to what could only be called a continual stony-eyed stare of disdain. Mentally, I am berating Gay Henry until the cows come home. Nn, I say aloud.

I think he's getting out, says Henry, in a shrill, dog-torturing, whistle of a voice. The pit bull's ears cock. A car door slams shut.

n, I say.

A string of unrelated words rings through the still country night, profane, nonsensical, something from an Italian menu.

, I say.

Then I can hear Chad Kingston tromping up the steps. He pauses for a moment to introduce himself to Jim, Henry, and the poet. Smiles warmly at the just-met strangers. Comes up behind and tousles my hair. Takes a knee and begins rubbing the pit bull's belly in a delicate, soft-porn way. Hitler or Nascar or whatever the dog's name is flops on his side, legs spread and tongue lolling. Chad Kingston looks over his shoulder with what I have to admit is a winning sly fox of a smile. Dogs and old ladies, he says. Dogs and old ladies.

Then he's tromping down the stairs with faithful Fido quick on his heels. The rest of us timidly fall in behind. I must say, and I'm a smoker, that they've really got the dry ice going tonight. Completing the Night with Dante prom theme of the place, they've forgone air-conditioning in favor of a retrospective means of air circulation, something along the lines of the boiler room of the *Dixie Queen* as it circumnavigates the magma sea of the Earth's sun. I get to the bottom of the stairs and round the corner where a tiny rodentish man is frisking Chad Kingston. He fishes out a flask from one boot, a sheath of rolled-up flyers from the other.

Two-drink minimum, says the bouncer, setting the flask on an early-model electronic poker machine. We got setups two bucks a pop. So that'll be four just for the glass.

Suit me just to nip from the flask, says Chad.

We ain't Mississippi. You'll drink from a glass round here.

Well do you mind if I put a flyer up?

Knock yourself out, says the tiniest bouncer in the world, pointing to a clear space on the wood paneling. The rest of the wall is covered in true gentlemen's club fashion with race car and Roll Tide memorabilia, buzzing electric beer signs, and about twenty posters of thonged-oiled-tanned butts leaning over muscle cars, choppers, F-16s, and what have you. Shiny butts all in a row. Not a face to be seen.

Cheeky, Jim says, leaning up to whisper in my ear.

I'm about to banish him to the car for breaking the rule that strictly forbids the use of wordplay, specifically that of a horny-ass Ph.D. nature, in a redneck gaming house when I'm called forward for my pat-down. You carrying a gun, he asks, holding a bucket beside me filled with all manner of easy-to-hide weaponry jabbed and jutted and stacked against one another like metal crabs. Guns go in the bucket.

Forgot mine at home, I say.

He begins his unseemly procedure. As he's working my thighs, I can't help myself and ask him to move a little higher and to apply a little less pressure.

Kitty Cat don't like smart-asses, he says.

Are you Kitty Cat? I say.

He stops the minimassage to look at the idiot who knows people who refer to themselves in the third person.

That's Kitty Cat, he says, nodding a head toward another infinitesimal man who is serving as croupier.

So you're Ground Squirrel?

That's right, he says, spinning me around for the back-of-ankle check.

And how does Ground Squirrel like smart-asses?

He don't like em neither. Next.

. . .

We're gambling in the basement rumpus room of a standard brick rancher out in the sticks. Suffice to say, it's classic Southern rock or its close cousin Southern classic rock or nothing at all twanging from the hi-fi. Suffice to say as well that my fondness for the closely connected genres has never been higher. Of the five of us, two, Gay Henry and the butter-quaffing poet, are passed out under a row of poker machines, victims of Kitty Cat's two-mason-jar minimum, the house vintage being a jug of paint thinner disguised as moonshine. Jim, meanwhile, is resting one foot on Henry's tender fair head and the other on the knee of the poet as he pumps quarter after quarter into a poker machine. As for Chad Kingston, the moonshine has either awakened a misty-eyed nostalgia for the many liquids he drank as a youth that were first filtered through a rusty radiator or it has canceled out the keg of bonded whiskey he chugged earlier in the evening in a fermented yin and yang kind of way, for he's doing a fair impersonation of a sober man. At any rate, forecasters predict an unusually turbulent and restive night for liver organ donors across this great nation of ours.

Besides Chad and me, there are six other men of international intrigue about the gaming table, in various degrees of drunkenness and undress. A quick tally of dice-throwing sartorial splendor reveals two tank tops, one half-length net-style jersey, two shirt-optional overall ensembles, and three men free of any sort of upper garment. I and the croupier fall in the last category. Chad, meanwhile, is splendid in old-timey sleeveless T-shirt.

To be sure, I'm losing. But it's a slow-grinding mode of losing. Winning one shooter, losing the next. To give the game its due, we are blissfully free of no-passers, those black cats of dice who bet with the house and against the thrower. Unfortunately, I've yet to make a number and seem to be viewed as something of a jinx by my fellow gamblers. And though steadfast Chad Kingston continues to pump me with standard and fatherly dicing exhortation, he, like everyone else, keeps his chips off the table as I prepare for my next roll.

But before I can throw and get it over with, footsteps are heard on the stairs. Then four large men are joshing and backslapping with Ground Squirrel, who, true to his name, has yet to perch atop anything above floor level during the whole of my visit. The first and joshiest backslapper of the bunch turns out to be that old raconteur and man about town, Skip Terry. Followed of course by his two beefy associates. And, just now sheepishly rounding the corner, dressed still in his suit, tie, and suspenders, the Republican candidate for governor, the make-out king himself, Josh Wade.

We all got guns and we're keeping em too, Skip Terry shouts, picking up the Ground Squirrel and spinning him around.

Aw Mr. Terry, says Ground Squirrel, adrift and abashed above terra firma as he is.

Got the next governor of the state with me tonight, says Skip Terry, turning his back to the room to buddy-buddy-elbow Josh Wade. You heard me little Degraw, he says. I seen your crazy ass.

Kitty Cat looks at me. You the Governor's son?

Only for the time being it seems.

I take a swig of warm moonshine from a discolored fruit jar and wipe my mouth on a sweaty and nicotine-grimed bare shoulder. Then I adjust the tuxedo shirt I've tied sheik-style over my head for a more rakish Omar Sharif effect. All the while Josh Wade is looking at me and smiling a bit of an irritating smile. I return the smile, warm as you please, then roll.

Snake eyes, says the Kitty Cat, a little louder than necessary.

Chad Kingston leans over to me and says, there's the house money right there.

I know the man, I say, the dice moving across the table toward the shirtless farmers gently awakening from my roll of the dice.

No friend of yours, I reckon, says Chad Kingston, smiling and nodding at Skip Terry and talking out of the side of his mouth. There's any trouble, I can handle two of them goons with him. Our gang any good in a brawl?

I look behind us, Gay Henry asleep and nuzzling his empty mason jar like a teddy bear, the artisan poet grinning comatosely beneath the blinking, buzzing poker machines, Jim obsessively pulling the lever, face fixed in concentration, working up a solid thesis regarding gaming, the end of Southern agrarianism, and the inequity of the culturally elite getting all the decent trim. Oh, in a brawl, I say, we're set. These guys are all kinds of hell.

Good, says Chad Kingston, stuntman twinkle in eye, a nostalgic scar twitching eagerly beneath his lip, anarchical grin for the group as a whole. I can't remember the last time I cracked any head.

The silent sallow gamblers have made way for Skip Terry, Josh Wade, and the rest of the merry gang, so we're squeezed in pretty tight around the table. At this point the basement smells like a subtle mixture of dead man's toes, cheese fondue, and a barrelful of monkey ear wax set aflame.

When the dice come my way again, my end of the table keeps the pass line free and clear of chip clutter. And, as might be expected, Skip Terry is betting No Pass and showing Josh Wade the finer points of ruining hoo-ju for the table as a whole. I take my next-to-last five-dollar chip and place it on the Pass line. On the other end, Skip has a mountain of chips piled up on the No Pass and is loudly encouraging the rest of the flunkies to load up as well. The boy's cold, he hoots. As ice. As the morgue. As a witch's tit.

You do look a little cold Dev, says Josh Wade with a clean-cut and irritating smile as he loads a modest pile of chips on the No Pass.

I'm close to telling the Josher what he looks like in those suspenders. Ever so close. But opting to lose the battle to win the war, I decide instead on a quick cleansing of the mind. Begone, ye negative distractions. Git ye the fuck out of here. The old instant catharsis. Oldest trick in the book. Becoming one with the dice and the universe and the gambling farmer within. Take the rock, grasshopper, take the rock.

I come out with a four, Little Joe from Kokomo. More chips added to the No Pass backup. None in support of the dicer. I send a serene and knowing look in the direction of the bloated Big Daddy and the Howdy Doody Party candidate, then throw the dice in a wide looping arc, the release perfect, athletic and good vibey, followed up with a first-time idiosyncratic snap of the fingers, the dice nearly scraping the ceiling, curling defiantly within half an inch of Skip's pocked nose and fat cigar, a seriously perfect toss and release, and settling quiet and comfy as a basketful of sleeping kittens on my good friend Joe. From Kokomo, that is.

Five dollars for me. The easy way. Kitty Cat scrapes up the huge mound of No Pass chips with quick apologetic swipes. Blind hog finds the acorn every now and then, says Skip Terry.

I turn to Chad Kingston and ask for a five-hundred-dollar loan.

Son, he says, that's all I got left with me of the reunion fund. I got to pay the concession guy with that.

I'm one with the universe, I say.

One with the universe? says Chad Kingston.

Well most of it. But I've definitely found the inner gambling farmer within.

Huh? What?

I've got my throw down now. That's all you need to know. I needed that little snap thing.

I didn't much care for that snap thing.

Neither will those assholes. I'll drive em snapping fucking crazy. You sure?

The worm has turned, I say. The worm has most assuredly turned.

About time, says Chad Kingston, throwing the bills on the table, I been betting the come ought sixty years now.

I've been rolling for well over an hour now, and either dawn is preparing to break or the roosters are getting a jump on the day. Four men remain at the table, Skip Terry, Josh Wade, Chad Kingston, and the Tuscaloosa Kid. The associates have long since gone bust. The old farmers from earlier got in halfway through my roll, recouped their earlier losses plus a bunch, and are now en route to the all-night all-coverall store for a parcel of brand-new ones. For those keeping score, the sheriff without a liver and his gap-toothed son are up approximately nine grand each. And the Useless Friends Fund, a little-known charity for horndog Ph.D.s, butter-eating poets, and pizza delivery boys, has topped the thousand-dollar mark as well.

Skip Terry's face is quite red. Quite.

Hey there Governor, I holler across the table to Josh Wade for the fortieth time. What do you say Governor, Governor, Governor.

Then that exquisite toss, that oh-so-familiar Rat Packing snap of fingers, the gentle dice breeze wafting by smoldering cigar, Chad Kingston exhortation, Kitty Cat's weak call of winner.

Skip Terry throws more bills on the table, more chips on No Pass. He sees that Josh Wade has decided to take my advice and sit this one out and pushes a sizable stack in front of him. Consider it a campaign donation, he says.

Mr. Terry, I say. Do you mind if I call you Mr. Terry?

Well you crazy damn fool, that's what you've always called me.

And Governor, I say. Governor, do you mind if I call you Governor?

Josh Wade smiles the smile of a man who'd rather be waking up in a warm bowl of honey.

And Chad, I say, tossing the dice, snapping snappy as you please, do you mind if I call you . . .

Winner, says the Kitty Cat, with, I'll have to give him credit, a fine flair for the dramatic.

That's it, that's it, cries Skip Terry, pushing his chips in a clattering heap. Game's over, game's over. I'm not going to sit here and watch this smug shit anymore. Cash him out and throw him out.

Immediately, the associates spring into action, one clambering up behind me, the other to the side of the ever-grinning Chad. All this action seems to break Jim's video poker reverie, a harsh blow indeed, daydreaming as he was about the upright provocative melons that comprise the number eight, for he is suddenly and earnestly kicking our two sleeping beauties into consciousness. Then, as the accounting commences, the McCrae's crowd can be heard tiptoeing up the stairs, slamming a screen door, and making Three Stooges scaredy-cat noises as they serpentine toward the nearest pick-em-up truck loaded down with alfalfa and heading to town.

Cash him out first, says Skip Terry, throw him out second. I pay my debts. Even to punks with nothing going for em but a fading name.

Ground Squirrel finishes stacking our chips, big tall stacks and lots of them, then begins counting out the money.

Chad, I say, I believe I'd have owned this gaming establishment and the Governor there's suspenders too if they hadn't quit on me.

Chad Kingston laughs, shakes his head, godawmighty.

Skip Terry forces out a little smile. Mr. Degraw, he says, I don't believe you're long for this world. Come November, your daddy's going to lose. Hell he wants to lose. And young Wade here, who's sticking to his guns about the lottery, sticking to his guns the way he ought to, he might remember me when a university construction job comes up. But even if he don't, even if this is the last I ever see him, I'll still be here. I ain't going away. But you son, come November, you ain't the Governor's son no more. You're just a Degraw. Just a half-ass Degraw.

That's right, I say, taking a final swig of warm moonshine. I'll just be a half-ass Degraw. But you'll always be a country-clubbing, deer-hunting, Hilton-Head-visiting, football-boostering, fat-ass redneck with money, now won't you Mr. Terry?

With this, the associates take a step closer and wait for Skip Terry with eager looks in their eyes.

Whatever happens out in the yard is yall's business, says Skip Terry, turning toward the bar. I've washed my hands of the Degraw family.

In the front yard, the sun is rising like a bloody soggy beet over the mist-shrouded hills. Roosters are crowing, tree frogs still in full song. In the distance a church bell sounds seven sweet times. During my brief time here in the great outdoors, I've been trying to ingest the lovely and unfamiliar early-morning ambience as my personal escort continually pushes me down and picks me up like a cat tossing a mouse before going to the decapitation proper. Beside us, beneath a lush and foggy weeping willow, Chad Kingston and his friend are simply duking it out like actual men.

Hey Beefy-T, I say during the interim after I am tossed and before I am picked up again, aren't you getting tired yet? A beefy boy like you ought not overexert that beefy heart of yours.

Unfortunately, the big fellow seems a little sensitive about his hulking manner, something I should have considered before expressing concern for his precarious health. At any rate, this triple use of beefy has him in a state of high rancor, for when he picks me up this time, he squeezes me about the thorax with discernible finality. As I'm trying to calm the fellow and simultaneously avoid asphyxiation, there's a reasonably loud crash and a subsequent slumping of the crazed and sensitive beef boy. I've slumped back as well and am attempting to extricate myself from his gooey clutches when I realize, dizzy and winded, that Gay Henry is helping me to my feet while simultaneously kicking the supine bear to a lively and staccato flamenco beat.

After I'm up, Beefy-T rouses himself from a bed of mason jar glass and moves in a stumbling waltz toward Henry and me, light-headed one would assume and unsure which of us to kill first. I'm standing there a bit light-headed myself as Henry makes like the artful dodger, moving and kicking at the groggy bear's wobbly legs. Just as Beefy-T is about to get Henry corralled once and for all, out of the woods comes the butter-eating poet with a practiced and primordial scream. Beefy-T turns into the scream at almost exactly the same time a roundhouse jujitsu-style kick is making its choreographed way toward his smoked ham of a chin. Crack goes shoe on chin. Down for the count goes Beefy-T.

I'm standing in the lawn shaky and surreal as in a dream as Chad Kingston is placing the traditional, and finishing, power left hook to the formerly symmetrical jaw of the other associate. Hot diggety dog, says Chad Kingston, bleeding from the mouth and grinning over his fallen foe. Hot damn diggety dog.

And then it's Jim ripping the car around in a cloud of post-modern dust. And then we're barreling down the drive and back toward civilization.

Boys now that's what I'm talking about, says Chad Kingston. You boys were all kinds of hell all right. All kinds of hell. Dev, you weren't much, but I wasn't expecting much. But the rest of you boys, well I'll take you in a scrap any day of the week and like my odds.

I thought you didn't know martial arts, I say, turning to the backseat.

I might have had a lesson or two, says the butter-eating poet.

That was a nice roundhouse.

A well-crafted roundhouse.

Yes, I say, well crafted. And Henry, my god, that was pretty spectacular back there.

Gay Henry nods modestly. I am a bad motherfucker is what I am.

We're halfway back to Tuscaloosa and the sun has come up near to full on a delightful Sunday morn. The car, smelling of vinegar-flavored unfiltered cigarettes and stale moonshine, is tooling along at a casual eighty miles an hour. Obviously, it's a perfect time for Rob Montegue to call the Queen.

I brief Henry on the previous night's episodes, explain that if things went according to plan, the Queen should just be returning from a good hour, a solid hour, on the Capitol steps, and has called Higginbothan Inc. on at least two occasions to send them scrambling for phone numbers of newspaper employees and to prepare them for the soothing and coaxing that will be their lot for the remainder of the day. I explain as well that she should be experiencing strange feelings of profound impatience, unfamiliar exasperation, and a vague gnawing sensation that for once in her blessed life, something has not gone the way she planned.

Henry and I come up with a rough outline, greeting, excuse, i.e. miscommunication regarding appointed meeting time, profuse apology, attempt at reschedule. Henry begins to insist on a few ad-libs but I thwart this frivolity at once by reminding him of the money he's yet to receive from the Useless Friends Fund I started back at the Mirage. This shushes him appropriately, and he agrees to stick to the approved script. I borrow Chad's cell phone and dial the Queen's number.

She answers on the third ring, a crisp tight hello that displays little of her usual distracted languor. To a stranger she might sound as if she were already awake at this early hour and expecting an important phone call. To the untrained ear, she might, indeed, sound peeved.

I hand the phone hot-potato-style over the seat to Gay Henry but as the preliminaries are exchanged, he drops into something akin to a New Orleans drag queen in midproposition to a young pizza delivery boy from Alabama. I grab the wheel from Jim and veer us suddenly toward a tractor heading the opposite direction and hiss, fashion-slash-style editor, and by the time I've got us back in the correct lane, he's the rakish and urbane Rob Montegue of old, apologizing away about the unfortunate miscommunication.

Oh Shea honey, he says, I just can't imagine my saying seven in the morning. Seven in the morning I'm just going to bed girl-friend.

As could be expected, I nearly jump out the window at this most inexcusable of usages. And, predictably, the witty Mr. Montegue seems to pick up on my clinching of teeth, for he begins to use the dreaded term of affection every other word.

Maybe I did girlfriend, he says. Had I been drinking that day? One day last week I took a little funny blue pill after a margarita grande lunch. Girlfriend, most days I refuse to win the lottery before nine A.M.

No more girlfriends, I say through a clenched jaw.

Oh girl, he continues, smiling. What do I know about catching the morning light? It's just one of those snap-snap deals, then a champagne brunch down at Rico's. That's where I'm heading in about two shakes.

Now he could have played Billy Tucker, says Chad Kingston, nodding at Henry, who is whipping his cigarette around in exaggerated fashion, inches on either side from igniting a small eyebrow fire.

I'm at the Capitol right now girl, he says. Been up all night. Don't ask. If you ask, I'll have to tell you. But can you come down, girlfriend? Camera's set up. We're in and out slam-bam—peanut butter and jam. Then it's next Sunday's spread of the beautiful Shea Bateman classing up the joint down at the Cap-I-Tol. Great. You're gorgeous. Brunch on me wherever you like. Fantastic. Great. Purina Cat Chow girlfriend. You know. Chow chow chow.

He hangs up and it's a rousing round of applause from the gallery. I hand Henry and the poet their cut from the craps game and put that for Jim in the seat between us. Then I turn again to the backseat with tears forming in my eyes. Henry, I say, I just want you to know that from this day forward you are my one and only American hero.

With this, Gay Henry puts the finishing touches on a twenty-dollar-bill paper airplane. Dev, he says, sailing the airplane neatly past my ear and out the open window, I'd like to thank you for a kitschy kitschy kitschy evening.

· · ·

When I get home the apartment looks like an unlucky dying man has been doing his unlucky and stale and stinky business here for about nine months now. The den is a macabre collage of empty containers, smoking paraphernalia and accoutrements, loose change of the smallest denominations, plant fungi, yard-sale furniture, leftover odors from the last dead unfound thing I thought had stopped stinking, ransacked and used-up naked magazines, a small pyramid of menus, scraps of paper containing the hieroglyphics of a two-month-long stretch of horrific, NBA for god's sake, gambling, and approximately five hundred scattered and caseless CDs of the bleeding ear punk or high lonesome bluegrass variety. A tough spot to find beauty on a fine Sunday morn. Though, in the interest of full disclosure, the sun through the porch window is shooting octangled beams of soft light across the dusty hardwood floor. And over the couch, where Chad Kingston is sleeping with cowboy hat tipped over eyes sombrero-style, the shadows of trees move like slow-motion shakers at a football game. All up and down the street, in fact, it couldn't be quieter, wiener dogs strangely at bay, wiener dogs having eaten own vocal cords, and Chad Kingston riding that A-lot range with a steady cloppity clop of the nose. Yes, all and all, I've had worse Sundays.

I wake up at seven that evening feeling nothing so much as a craving for fried whole elephant. Rousing myself heroically and meandering to the den with a body, ribs specifically, that feels as if it were beaten soundly by disgruntled primates of an unspecified genus, a big dumb genus to be sure, I happen upon Chad Kingston, sheepish on the couch, showered, groomed, and freshly face-lifted half an hour ago. The den itself is unrecognizable.

I don't recall you playing the fussy old cook in any of your movies, I say.

He doesn't reply but instead feigns interest in an animal show on television. Man, he says, I'd hate for that rhino to get after me with that hooker of his.

I ignore this attempted redirection of the conversation. The old ninny bitch cook, I say. Cowboy movie, army movie, they all got the grouchy old gelding ladling soup and sprucing up the place.

Get your ass kicked one time and wake up whining like a baby, says the fussy cowpoke.

Are you or are you not Uncle Charley from *My Three Sons?*

Hey I knew Bill Demarest, he says. He'd of whipped you black-and-blue. Hell, I was up for that part. That was a good part.

If you say tough and sensitive.

You'd think all that money on that table there would make a man feel a little better about what's left of the day.

I disregard the obvious merit of this point and reach to pick up a crusty tube sock Chad missed behind the stereo. I pick up said sock, smell it, jerk head back quickly as if recently shot in the forehead from close range. Smell this sock Chad, I say, tell me if you think it's dirty.

He bothers not with a reply.

Seriously, the scientist in you ought to want to smell this. I'm not sure what I've got working here.

Chad looks tired, unscientific. Boy, he says, where can I get a drink in this town?

You can't.

I wonder if your secretary might have a bottle lying about.

She might, I say. She just might. You want me to call and ask?

Aw hell I don't know.

Shy?

Naw. It's not that. Naw.

I'd prefer you cleaned my bedroom first anyway.

Give me the number and get the hell out of here.

Sweet-talker?

Don't you worry about that.

I give him the number and he starts to dial, nodding me out of the den as he does.

So you're done cleaning? I say.

Cowboy cook my ass. Hello Sheila.

Chad has managed to sweet-talk Sheila into a quiet recuperative dinner at her house. He left the apartment freshly bolo-tied and with Southern gent squint, I mean to court you maam, firmly in place. My send-off was all about instilling confidence in the old lion. Recommending the wrist corsage rather than the strap version. Complimenting his makeup wizardry. Warbling an especially heartfelt version of Puppy Love complete with cracking voice and swaying head. Tossing him the crusty tube sock with suggestions on where it might most benefit his outward appearance. And so on.

With the gelding cook out of my hair and a lemon-waxed coffee table to work on, I've come up with an initial list of people I can now pay off, namely my ex-wife, my bookie, my bartender, and my madman. The four horsemen of my inertia. Incidentally, someone has spray-painted DIE MOTHERFUCKER on the side of my building. In the euphoria of coming home, I first attributed the graffiti to another neighbor across the alley who was as tired of wiener dogs as I. Pulling into the back lot, I had silently championed his cause while simultaneously calling for harsher measures. Later, while Chad was in the shower hog-tying his sagging tits to the backs of his knees, I went downstairs to the mailbox to find, among other things, an amputated mechanical rabbit, one most often seen at the nearest neighborhood dog track. Affixed to this was a dog chain, the other side bearing a message with some similarity to the one on the side of the building, albeit with a more personal touch. It read, DIE YOU MOTHER-FUCKER.

It was then that I decided my madman, he of the wrongfully chomped backside, would be paid first.

Accounting settled, the only thing left to do is to choose between playing the messages on my answering machine or opening the other interesting piece of mail I found in the box. Sender of interesting parcel? My good old fake mom, Odelle Bailey. After much debate I decide to save the mail bomb for later and head to the bedroom to see if any of those blinking lights could be from a certain Queen Bee, who's had an interesting Sunday of her own.

The first message is from Saturday night, a certain sweaty-sounding dog lawyer named Nelson Foxx wanting to discuss, surprise surprise, a settlement. Specifically sixty-eight dollars for an unnecessary visit to the vet, which, I assume, did not result in a lifetime prescription for doggie Prozac.

The second message is from Polly, reminding me in a rather authoritarian tone that I'm to pick Katie up from school on Wednesday and attend the parent-teacher conference. And again, I must reiterate, I don't just like, but appreciate, an authoritarian tone.

The third message starts in with an ear-piercing Rebel yell. Subsequent noises include several inebriated college boys chanting Sherriff Tucker, Sherriff Tucker, a guzzle, a glass of some sort thrown or stomped in revelry, a girl saying hello, hello, sir who am

I supposed to be talking to, a muffled voice of authority inquiring about shattered glassware, a tussle of minor magnitude, a cover version every bit as bad as the Aerosmith original, and, not a moment too soon, a definitive click.

Thus ends the Saturday evening calls.

Sunday, 8:15 A.M., the Queen. In a voice best described as a restrained tremble, she says, Dev, I can't prove anything, but I've got a feeling you've been having a little fun at my expense. I don't know where you were last night. I looked for you everywhere at the party. And then that crazy late-night call. And now this.

Then you hear her call-waiting buzzing in. I've got to go, she says suddenly, perhaps a little abashedly, as if perhaps she's acted without thinking, as if, almost, she fears falsely accusing an innocent man.

Call two, 10:07, from the mobile hive. In a tone Latin scholars would call Regina iratus. Younger listeners at home best turn their dials at this juncture, for the Queen is working a blue to make old Redd Foxx blush. After the string of defamations runs its course, she says, with not the slightest bit of honey in her voice, you are so unbelievably immature. I have to go to that stupid reunion because I told your father I would, but after that I never want to see you again. Ever.

Theatrical to be sure. And so final. None of the ambivalence and ambiguity we've come to expect, none of the intrigue. But how do Dee-Dee and Hooper feel? Am I still in good Higginbothan stead?

Before I can begin basking in my freedom from the hive, from all things buzzing and buzzkilling, the phone rings and I answer with a definitive bounce in the step.

Hello, says the unmistakable voice of Gay Henry, this is Rob Montegue.

Speak up sonny, I say. Who?

Rob Montegue, fashion editor of the *Birmingham News*.

Fashion-slash-style editor? I say.

What?

Fashion-slash-style or just fashion?

Fashion and style, he says.

That's what I thought. Plenty of both in Birmingham. Plenty of style and not a little fashion.

That's neither here nor there at this point.

Here nor there, nor at the fair. Shaking your big white, big white, derriere.

Listen, he says, I don't know what in the hell you're talking about, but if you don't stop impersonating me, stop ruining my good name, I can assure you, you will live to regret it.

I'd like a large deep dish pizza extra sausage.

I don't know whatever in the world you're . . .

Extra onions too.

I seem to have no choice but to call your father. That or the police.

Hang em high hang em low, I say. Hang em on a picture show. And the same goes for Preacher too.

You'll read about this in the paper.

You'll have a pizza here in thirty minutes or no tip for you.

Gay Henry dismissed, I head back to the den to see what Billy Tucker's mom has sent him. And what does Billy find? A care package it seems. Something to make the last week of summer camp go a little quicker. The contents? A photograph, a letter, and a mangled fruitcake. Let us begin a tour of the mind of *Bayou Dog*'s only fan with the photograph, a daguerreotype which contains a list of items to be arranged however a curious mind might. This list includes a sunny day, the shadow of a tripod, an elderly woman nude save some thigh-high waders, a puffy cloud with the misfortune of having passed by at this most inopportune moment, a hiked leg, a ramshackle fence, a dog in full flight across an early cornfield, and an old-fashioned water pump with a rusty red handle. Those so inclined may do with these images what they will. Now the letter.

My dearest dearest Billy,

It seems ages since last I saw your smiling face. Have you grown? Soon now you'll be out of short pants for good. How proud I'll be to see you in a pair of fine trousers. I was going to sew you a pair this week but things got hectic when Thor ran off so suddenly. I guess you'll have to settle for fruitcake! Ha! Ha! Oh Billy, I want you to stay young forever! I fear your father will never leave that tanny young slut of a wife and come make our family whole again. I know he's been saying that I'm dead. But nothing could be further from the truth. Please inform your father, the high-and-mighty sherriff himself, that I plan on having a word with his fat ass come the reunion. I won't stand it for a minute longer. I did love the hairy son of a bitch once, but that was when you were still just a twinkle in his eyes. Oh Billy Billy Billy. I love you so much. But please don't spy on that young tart when she's in the shower. And never call her Mommy. I've enclosed a picture. Wear the red shirt when you were stuck in the well.

Until I see you again, hugs and kisses.

Mom

p.s. I caught sixteen crappie day before last.

So all and all it's been a fruitful and thought-provoking twenty-four hours, one that has unfathomably left me too tired to go out. That's right. Embarrassing to say the least. I won't go into the battle royal raging at the moment between those serotonin crackheads and the fat boys from the lactic acid factory, but I've downed the last bit of rye in the house, popped my ration of aspirin plus two, and have initiated sober, though somewhat headachy, plans to make myself semipresentable in time for the parent-teacher conference on Wednesday. Step one of rounding into semipresentable form? Face deflation. That is debloatification. The unpuff. As such, I've put out an all-points bulletin for what's left of my cheekbones and have given three day's notice to chins three and four. Second step of rounding into shape? No more than two drinks per day. For the uninitiated, please be advised that day one of becoming semi-presentable is painful viewing for all. The first-day look? Puffed red goo. Fully inflated middle school kickball.

Eightball

Wednesday has arrived not a day too soon and I'm at Katie's school for the much-anticipated parent-teacher conference. I'll not relate the totality of the horror of the last two days. But my earlier allusion to the middle school kickball stands, if you can imagine a kickball that's both fully inflated and beat all to hell down in some sewer creek wedged between a dying tree and a discarded washing machine and a couple of pimply teens smoking dope from a beer can, listening to heavy metal, and urinating on the ball as they decide which house next to burgle.

But this sleep thing is the right stuff. The old-fashioned visit from the sober sandman. And dreams, such dreams when your subconscious is hydrated and nourished. Id, Ego, and Superego are getting along like happy children. Also, I've settled up with my bookie Egg and my barkeep Ewan but have not yet mustered the energy for an all-out ghetto search, looking like a cop or a Mormon or a probation officer, to try and track down my graffiti-loving friend Eightball, whose address I can't find at the office. And since my secretary has been missing since Sunday when the old ranch hand went to work his courting magic, I'm not sure exactly when he'll get paid. But he will, he will.

I'm currently dodging the hell out of principals and hall monitors and attempting to find the teacher's room without first checking in at the office. I've managed to arrive just as classes are changing, and though the kindergartners have been out of school for an hour, the halls teem with rugrats of all shapes and sizes. Most of the girls stand in line like an elite squadron, chatting quietly and casting condescending glances at the jostling, spastic, grab-assing boys who have emptied their pockets to showcase every imaginable toy and gadget and things that go beep in the night.

I walk down hall after hall dripping with positive reinforcement, walls covered with posters and bulletin boards emphasizing self-love, self-actualization, try and you can, trying is all that matters, it's all good, feeling good and happy, happy and good. Very nice indeed. Though it might not hurt to add a little on reading and math, a TV Sucks collage, a mural on NASCAR parents raising NASCAR kids.

Hey dude, a little first-grade chap says as I walk past his line.

Dude, I say, with the proper dude half nod of head.

Which seems to work him up a bit. Dude dude dude dude dude dude, he says in hyped-up staccato auctioneer fashion, dancing the hot foot, forsaking all semblance of staying in line.

I look about for the Ritalin dispenser. The dude is now in full ant-stomping clog, the flying brogans of Jed Clampett on his first amphetamine and moonshine speedball, continuing down the hall after me, the pied piper of young dudes, repeating the cherished word again and again. Hypoglycemic? Stuff candy bar in mouth, point him back toward the line, and be on my merry way? Procure rope, video game, full box of Sugar Pops and fasten junior spaz to leg of nearest behaving child?

Tyler, a teacher shouts, and with lightning speed the future meth freak is lassoed and corralled even as he continues dude dude dude *duding* all the while.

First note to self. Never give the dude half nod to preteen Lilliputians. Short-circuits the still-developing dude machinery.

I round a corner and there's Katie at the water fountain. Behind her, a tyke dressed like a young executive out for a neighborhood barbecue poking her in the back as she tries to drink. First instinct? A sharp rebuff to the whippersnapper and a twenty-year ban of further contact with my daughter. Second instinct? Monitor aggression gene in first female Degraw in four generations.

Stop it, she says, not turning around.

The well-dressed barbarian continues to poke, in the ribs, where it tickles and it's hard to drink. I said to cut it out, Katie says, flinging back an elbow that catches the young bully in his own ribs. He doubles over, looks to me, an adult, for help, sees my smile, begins to cry, and runs down the hall looking for a teacher to tell.

Hey Katie, I say.

Daddy, she yells, running over for a hug.

You could have hurt that boy, I say.

He started it.

Well violence is never the answer, I say, looking at a poster above the water fountain that says, essentially, the same thing. Something about a friendly smile all the while.

Even when they start it?

I pause, mulling over the right thing to say, because, truly, violence is never the answer, and children need to learn the art of talking things out, settling disputes in a mature fashion. But we all know that's a load of shit when they start it. No, I say, if they start it and won't stop even when you ask them to, you're allowed to pop em one. Unless they're a lot smaller than you, then you just walk away.

Okay, she says. I will. Isn't this a great school?

It sure is, I say. I feel very positive just being here. Very positive indeed. Everyone is a winner and there are no losers if you truly think so.

She squirrels her face up a bit, instinctual defender of all things scholastic. Come on, she says, I'll show you Miss Marcum. Can we get ice cream after?

We'll see how the disciplinary review goes with Miss Marcum

first, I say. She may want you to write some sentences on the board.

No she won't. Miss Marcum's fun.

I'm glad to hear it.

She's divorced.

That happens sometimes.

Then we're in the classroom and Miss Marcum is rising to shake my hand. We exchange greetings and Katie kind of flits around for a while, showing me her drawings that are scattered about the room. The first is of a man sitting on a couch with a large can in one hand and a stove-sized remote control in the other. He looks serious and not a little fatigued. The next shows a similar-looking man with two small dogs climbing up his legs, his arms scarecrow stiff as if pinioned in eternal exasperation at the sadistic whim of the gods. The small girl beside him seems to find his plight humorous. The last portrays a happy woman in a wedding dress, a lopsided flower girl, and a smiling groom who, were it not for the confines of his tuxedo, would break into a hellacious double-herky without a second thought. From his satisfied grin, there seems little doubt that he's just let rip with a you go girlfriend and is counting the moments until he can mount the bride for all he's worth.

They're all very good, I say.

After the art showing, I'm instructed to pull up a desk next to her own as Miss Marcum walks Katie down to the always myste-rious resource room and I'm wincing manfully, painfully, when she returns. Sorry, she says, that's the biggest desk I've got. It's usually large enough for the moms. Would you prefer to stand?

I agree that I would, but it takes five or so sweaty minutes be-fore I've fully extricated myself from the menacing apparatus. During this unseemly exercise, Miss Marcum has been thumbing through a large folder of some sort, having just made a cursory referral to the old grade book. During the lion's share of my extrication attempts and the whole of her perusal, I've been sneaking glances at the young spinstress schoolmarm, sound track of Van Halen's Hot for Teacher pegged at nine on the volume dial. Oh the glasses, the pulled-back hair, the ears of corn, the quarts of milk.

Well Katie's progress is fine, she says, closing the folder and looking up at me. Better than fine. She's a sharp, fun little girl. Only here toward the end of the year has her schoolwork dropped off a bit. And she's had several minor run-ins with classmates just this month.

Is that right? I say.

Yes, she says. And I'm in a bit of a delicate position here. I have some concerns, not big ones, but concerns nonetheless, but I don't want it to seem as if I'm playing amateur shrink with you or your daughter.

Feel free, I say. I'd like to hear your opinion.

Well, you've seen her artwork. Do you make anything of it?

Well, I say, I've had no formal psychological training, but it seems obvious she's distraught about the prospect of sharing a house with a boy cheerleader for the next thirteen years. That just seems perfectly clear from where I'm sitting.

I think she misses her father.

Well, yes, maybe.

I think she's worried about her father.

There could be something to that.

She's excited about the *Bayou Dog* thing this weekend.

Oh good gosh, I say.

I told her I'd give her a ride if that's okay.

Oh that's unnecessary. It's a complete joke. It'll be you, Katie, and our one crazy fan. I mean it's fine with me if you want to take

Katie, but surely there's something better to do on a Saturday morning.

Actually, she says, there's not. And believe it or not, I watched that show when I was a kid.

Tell me you didn't.

I liked the dog.

Thor was top-notch, I say. His great-great-grandson or something like that will be there. They say he's a chip off the old stunt dog.

You remember the episode when Billy fell down the well?

An acting tour de force, I say.

You were quite bad. I remember my older brother imitating your instructions to the dog. Thor, run fetch Pa. We said it around the house for years afterward. Anytime one of the kids was looking for our dad, it was always, Thor, run fetch Pa. Somebody said it last Christmas as a matter of fact.

That's good, I say, that's funny.

Thought maybe I laid it on a little thick a minute ago. I meant what I said about Katie. I hope I didn't overstep my bounds.

No, it's okay. I'm on the case.

She stands up and walks me toward the door, a copy of the *Birmingham News* in her hand. By the way, she says, have you read Rob Montegue's column today?

I'm parked in front of my former home with an ever-quickening heart rate, the driveway filled to the brim as it is with the luxury liner my ex-mother-in-law drives, a matron known to live and die with the fashion-slash-style section, which is today, depending on how you look at it, either a clear-cut case of libel or a fairly accurate article on the Governor's son duping a female member of the Governor's staff with a series of infantile prank phone calls. The article goes on to say that during these juvenile exercises in perversity, Devaney Degraw has posed as none other than R. Montegue himself. The wounded journalist concludes by wondering aloud, or at least in writing, how the Governor feels about such shenanigans involving important members of his staff during the most hotly contested gubernatorial campaign of his career.

Rob Montegue's blatant character assassination was not the entirety of his column but merely the parting salvo, the earlier portion dealing with such weighty matters as the cheeky faux tiaras that many of the Birmingham smart set have been donning for casual nights out and a heartfelt exhortation for all show dog owners to remember to shear their pets for the upcoming summer heat. Yes, he did use both smart set and faux tiaras in the same sentence. Yes, I am owed reparations for that irresponsible and unpardonable phrasing.

As I'm helping Katie get her things together, we're toodle-ooed from the front porch by the one-woman wiggery. Without looking I know she's got the newspaper in her hands. Granddaughter and crone exchange their pleasantries as I bring up the rear. One casual stiff arm keeps Katie from ruffling the dress, the other holds up a haughty section of newsprint.

Hello Mrs. Dunlap, I say. What a pleasant surprise.

Oh I'm sure it is Devaney. So nice of you to say so. Have you seen today's paper?

I have, I say. I have seen today's paper. Have you seen the back of my hand you well-traveled prune?

Actually I didn't say that last part. Children present and back alimony and all. Rest assured, however, that voice intonation intimated as much.

The fashion column, asks the liquidless one.

Fashion-slash-style, I say, as Katie runs in the house to greet her mother.

And?

The smart set's wearing faux tiaras. Poodles should be carefully sheared.

Oh Devaney, says the mummified monkey's toe, tilting back her head in an attempted titter, you always were one for evasion.

Certain people do arouse my furtive side.

Well I've never seen Polly so happy, she says.

Nor so full of pep, says I.

Yes, she is full of pep. Oh she's peppy and zippy like she was before.

Peppy and zippy and happy?

That's right Devaney.

She seemed a little down last time I saw her. A touch morose. I've been worried about her.

Oh you're pulling my leg Devaney.

I am, I say, I am pulling your leg. Polly and Chip seem very happy together. I know Chip will welcome your daily visit with open arms.

Polly's fiancé's name is Clark. And I don't visit every day.

Of course you do, I say, as Polly makes her way down to the sidewalk. Of course you visit every day like a good mother should.

Don't prank phone call my house, she says, leatherstocking her way to the car with an abbreviated wave over the shoulder to her daughter and granddaughter.

Just be sure and visit every day, I say to her back. And don't cheat em on the daily calls either.

As always, an afternoon with her mom has Polly looking like she's just been run through the eighty-cylinder Frump Machine at

high velocity. Before she can say anything, I peel off three thousand dollars and hand it to her.

We're even, I say, heading toward the car. Be sure and tell
Matlock. And by the way, congratulations on getting engaged.
Clark seems like a nice fellow, and I know Katie really likes him.
I guess if she's going to have a stepfather, I couldn't ask for much
better. Tell her I'll see her at the reunion Saturday morning.

When I get home, I pace around the apartment for an hour or
so trying to get up the nerve to give the spinster schoolmarm old
Miss Marcum a call, the town barn dance coming up and all. As
it's been over a decade since I've made a call to a grown woman to
ask her for a date, I'm in a bit of a quandary as to what to say. For
those in charge of bookkeeping, I'm disqualifying the Queen Bee
from the category of grown woman for the penalty of imitating a
heroine from a Civil War novel and movie beyond the call of duty.
That plus, obviously, excessive higginbothanism.

After a shower or two and a healthy dose of one-on-one time
in the mirror getting to know the wan but debloated Dev, I begin
the initial round of throat clearing. Unfortunately, this takes a
while, for I seem to have a small French village stuck in my throat.
After things are cleared up as best as can be expected, I go ahead
and dial the numbers, thinking what an amateur mistake it is to
not have an unlisted number with people like me roaming free on
the planet Earth.

Hello, she says.

Hehyrkah Mishiwuye, I say. This is Doo Dadah.

What?

Hey Michelle, this is Dev Degraw.

Oh, she says laughing. I thought you were a foreigner with the wrong number there for a second.

To this, I laugh uneasily and begin a casual coughing attack.

Are you okay, she asks after several minutes of my trying to work up the last of the French villagers.

Yes, I say, I'm fine.

You sure? You're sounding a bit tubercular.

Hay fever, I say.

Ah, says she.

Well this is probably inappropriate, I say, rushing right in hurriedly and sweatily and a bit squeakily. Seeing as you're my daughter's teacher and I don't know you that well and my behavior is about to send my daughter to the best local child psychologist you can recommend, but I was wondering if you'd like to do something sometime. Something casual. You know, just lunch or something. I'm completely harmless.

She puts a merciful halt to a stream of banter that could have gone on like this forever. Harmless? she says.

An excellent fill-in until a real man comes along.

No hard feelings either way?

Only if you get upset when I won't return your desperate calls.

She laughs. Seems to consider the prospect on the line. You reckon you're ever going to amount to anything?

Oh yeah, I say. I've got a bright future.

Really?

I've got all kinds of plans.

Well, she says, this will probably sound more serious than I mean it to, but I'm pretty picky about who I go out with now. I guess Katie told you that I'm divorced.

I think she mentioned it, I say.

And it's still pretty recent.

I understand, I say. That's cool. I know how you feel. I'll try you again here in a few months.

She pauses for moment. Harmless, you say?

Like going out for ice cream with your grandfather.

How about ice cream then? Saturday night sometime after your big *Bayou Dog* reunion.

You know, I say, that I've made a living making fun of the ice-cream date. Next thing you know I'm in a sweater vest for a tennis date.

Dinner then, she says. You'd be horrible on an ice-cream date.

I was in a full cardigan sweat just thinking about it, I say. Dinner then?

An early dinner though.

Early it is, I say.

We'll firm up at the *Bayou Dog* reunion.

Sounds good, I say.

And you've got to autograph a picture for my brother.

Hurry Thor, I say, run fetch Pa.

It's Friday, the day before my reunion with public torment, and Candy Lake and I are on our way back from the Birmingham airport. Whatever amphetamine tablets Candy has taken post-flight to counteract the preflight jar of Valium have set off a particularly virulent strain of logorrhea. Attempts to replicate this speech pattern would be fruitless and irritating. Much has been made in high-speed gibberish of the all-grown-up status of Billy Tucker, the cool mountain air emitting from the Birmingham smokestacks, and the overall feeling of wellness that naturally attends the Los Angelo's respite from that vast city. I've maneuvered dangerously close a few times to working in a word edgewise only to be denied at the gate with a fresh speed-freak observation, fueled as it invariably is by whatever momentary stimulus has just come into her sensory range. To wit, fresh Southern mountain air, though nonexistent with the windows up and the amphibian-killing smog outside, leads to catalogue of childhood visits to the Smoky Mountains leads to her attempts to stop smoking leads to psychobabble description of current oral fixation leads to request for the driver to insert his fingers into her mouth to satisfy said oral cravings.

As it stands now, I've had the fingers of my right hand, excluding pinkie and thumb, well into her mouth for about ten minutes now. Despite this minor obstacle, Candy has not tottered a whit in her attempt to speak for sixty continuous minutes or sixty consecutive miles, whichever shall come first as I race, one-handed, titillated, grossed-out, and overwhelmed, back to Tuscaloosa.

Her outfit? Black sundress, black heels, lots of movie starlet tan. And the face, the face has held up despite the years of sun-blasting and other dehydrating activities. Only the hollow spaces beneath the eyes, seen from the side, around the oversized sunglasses, and the recent tighten and pull of the ears, show Candy as any worse for wear. And as Candy continues to talk, elocution unhindered by inserted and pruned digits, about spring foliage spring fashions spring chickens Kentucky fried chicken my old Kentucky home, let's survey the facts. Granted I'm no psychiatrist, but fading beauty comes back to home state, state of her first flowering, knows on subconscious level that for all the giddy references to homecoming and seeing the home folks and fresh mountain air that this excursion back is one pitiful attempt at a career resuscitator, inevitably doomed to fail. Her escort for the evening, the former wide-eyed innocent who sat on her silken lap in halcyon days of yore, now an only semirepugnant full-grown hominid somewhat versed in the ways of the rut. A crappy dinner. A crappy bottle of champagne. Some horrific dancing in the hotel lounge. An empty hotel room. Well now, it all seems perfectly clear. Perfectly right and clear.

The argument against is obviously moral and boring in nature. Taking advantage of a person at her lowest point blah blah blah. And of course karma. Such an act would unquestionably jinx the hell out of any chance with Miss Marcum, the schoolteacher. In fact, one of the only truisms as pertains to the squiring of members of the opposite sex with whom one has only a passing and somewhat limited interest is that it will cost one big-time when it comes to landing the real McCoy. That and unwanted children and syphilitic blindness. But mostly that.

To sum up, the battle comes down to not jinxing any chance I have with the kindergarten teacher plus a little moral whatever versus the fact that I have seen Candy Lake naked in that dusty movie room in my mind for the better part of twenty-five years now.

And from the passenger side, unless my ears are playing tricks on me, Candy has stated, while moving without pause from pine trees to tree frogs to Kermit the frog to the British who refer to Frenchmen as frogs, that she is a bit tired and would I mind if she placed her head in my lap and stretched out.

I gently remove my fingers from her mouth. No, I say, that's okay.

She takes off her shoes, smoothes her dress, and reclines. For a second, she doesn't speak. The view? I shan't lie. The view from here is good.

I'm so tired Dev.

I nod in response.

You've grown up Dev, she says, moving her head about, trying to get comfortable.

I guess, I say, reverting back to some long-forgotten Billy Tucker script. Were stones handy, I'd have said shucks and chucked one out the window.

Does Billy still play gin rummy, asks Candy Lake, lolling her head, running her pretty tan feet up the passenger window.

Billy answers in the affirmative, with only a slight pubescent squeaking of voice.

Candy and I have just completed dinner with Chad Kingston and Sheila in the hotel restaurant and now it's nightcaps for the gang, water for me. I figured I might as well keep the whole semi-respectability thing going while I was on a roll, my cheekbones having put in a rare appearance and the sleeping Dobermans under my eyes off chasing some cop on a motorcycle. I won't go into the gory details of the Chad Kingston courting frenzy, the trip to Mobile, the sweet movie-scripted nothings at dinner, the constant referrals to Miss Sheila. Now Miss Sheila, you order whatever you like. Now Miss Sheila, how does my toupee look in the disco light?

As tale after tale of sixties-era Hollywood has brought down the house, my attempts to savage the cagey veteran have fallen on deaf ears. And believe me he hasn't been skimping on the name-dropping. Compounding the torture, in a veritable yin and yang of monologue, each behind-the-scenes look at a swinging night at the Duke's pad has been followed by a down-home stretcher that never fails to show the old railsplitter at his sly, Southern, and oh-so-self-deprecating best. Chased up a tree by the amorous hog. Momma tanning his hide after quaffing two whole gooseberry pies cooling on the windowsill. Sheila, for her part, has taken it all with been-around-the-block style. Candy, moist eyes atwitter with seven Kirs, has said the word charming seventeen times.

Surprisingly, my stories of skateboarding in the suburbs have drawn less of a response.

I had forgotten just how charming you are Chad, says Candy. Don't you think he's charming Dev?

I was just thinking of a synonym, I say.

What?

Beguiling is the word I would use. I find both the man and his tales beguiling.

Thus far the music in the lounge has consisted of a steady diet of New Country indistinguishable ballads and every Eric Clapton song ever recorded. When I mention that a few dollars might open up the DJ's Hag vault, Chad says he likes what's playing, a squeaked-out dirge by a twelve-year-old singer named Hope or Chastity or Virginity about high school love being just like Grandma's homemade marmalade. Of course the gals agree that the song is sweet and that Chad's sweet for noticing and without missing a beat Chad has launched into a charming slice of down-home life regarding his own granny's homemade marmalade. Again, my attempts to steer the conversation around to the pros and cons of male menopause fail miserably.

As round eight makes its way to our wobbly table, Sheila and Candy excuse themselves to head to the powder room, and I'm left for a moment with the old bard. Chad, I say, tell me a story.

He smiles.

Seriously, I feel like I've been talking all night. Spin me a yarn for old times' sake.

He sips at his drink, nearly knocks down the waitress with a power wink. A new song comes on by an earnest young cowpoke fed up with the city life. He has, it seems, them Dairy Queen Blues.

Great song, I say. Do you have this album? I know they're

both great, but if you had to choose, would you pick Dairy Queen Blues or Love like Granny's Marmalade?

He laughs. Hell son, he says, you ought to be having a good time. Looks like you and Candy are getting along pretty well. She's just making you work for it. Gal turns forty she's not going to roll over for some young fart like you just because you got most of your hair. No, you got to tell a few stories, dance a little, get em to laughing. Just because you hadn't learned shit ain't no need to take it out on your old partner.

It's not going to happen, I say.

It's not?

No.

Are you crazy son? Have you lost your mind?

It's a long story, I say.

You got another gal on the line I don't know about?

Not really. A potential gal maybe. It's a long shot.

Candy does look good though, doesn't she?

Don't remind me.

Guess I shouldn't mention gin rummy either.

That's kind of you, I say.

Well at least I know why you're so ornery. But my daddy always said the good ones were worth waiting for.

I nod halfheartedly at the notion and wonder, not for the first time today, about this annoying little conscience thing that just popped up out of nowhere. Embarrassing to say the least. So you like Sheila, I say.

I do, says Chad Kingston. I do like her.

And yall had fun down in Mobile?

We did, he says. We had a great time. Best honeymoon I ever had.

No shit.

I shit you not.

That's good, I say. I'm glad to hear it. Hell it almost makes sense.

It does almost make sense, agrees the smiling Chad Kingston. After I make this *Bayou Dog* movie, I'm going to buy us a little place down in Beech Grove, near the old farm. Sheila said she'd like that. Said she was just old country girl at heart. And I always liked country girls.

Yes, there's something to a good ole country gal, I say. Especially when they look like Sheila.

The old dog smiles with his eyes for a moment, then breaks into the real thing. She's a good gal, he says.

No question about it.

You going to be in my movie?

No. Hell no. Of course not.

You don't think it's going to happen.

No. Hell no. Of course not.

I got a producer flying in from Hollywood tomorrow to talk to Candy and get a feel for how we're received by the public.

And if there is no public?

There will be, he says. You underestimate nostalgia and the American people. The script I wrote is G-rated. Folks in Sioux City, Iowa, can take their kids to it and have some good clean entertainment. And all the smart-asses your age will go just to laugh at it, just to crack jokes in the theatre about the bad dialogue.

You're keeping the bad dialogue on purpose?

Of course, he says. I think kitsch is the word they use now.

I've asked friends not to use that word in my presence.

Well whatever it is, is pure gold. Give em something sincere and kind of sappy and those young folks just love feeling smart. They have fun making fun of what is not funny on purpose.

Profiteering on the ironic finding the intentionally unironic ironic? That's ironic in itself.

It's something, he says.

You're a bit of genius.

Chad leans over to whisper as the ladies reenter the room. You and me's the only ones who ever knew that. Well hello beautiful ladies.

I'm slow dancing with Candy Lake. Chad and Sheila have already weaved their way to the honeymoon suite, and the bar is empty save for a few forlorn salesmen who hold out hope that I'll get a drink flung in my face yet and the best-looking woman ever to set foot in this dungeon will be open game for an expense-account cocktail and a lifetime of bragging back home in Hickwood. Alas, Chad's words and strong example seem to have hit a receptive chord, for I've been impersonating a gentleman for the better part of an hour now, if being a gentleman includes carrying on nonsensical conversations and dancing to what may be the worst song I've ever heard. If I could name a Bon Jovi song, I would say that this is a Bon Jovi song.

Dev, says Candy, do you think Chad's right about this crazy reunion getting us a movie deal?

I don't see why not, I say, twirling her slowly about.

Will you be in it kiddo?

No.

Too busy with your law practice?

No, I say, I've washed out of the law business.

Oh Dev, she says, we've all washed out a bit it seems since good old *Bayou Dog*.

I glance about for a street tough to plug, a kindly orphan to toss a dime. About this scriptwriter in Candy's head? He's not good. Not good at all. Then she begins to cry quietly on my shoulder. I lightly stroke her back, flip her hair around. Now she really starts in. A true blubber. Beached whale on my shoulder, fresh blubber on the house.

Now, now, I say, stroking her back, flipping her hair, trying to get her face off my shoulder before the real nose running and snorfling goes into full effect.

I never had children Dev, I never had a child.

There, there, I say, stroking her hair, flipping her back.

But what does there, there mean? How did there, there come to be a thing said that was meant to comfort? Obviously, now, now means I've heard enough, I'm being polite, but feel free to shut up anytime now, the second now simply emphasizing the urgency of the request. Shut up now. Now. Shut up now, now. But there, there? Go there? Go over there and cry. I've heard enough of your drunken bawling, go over there. Over there. There, there. Again, the repetition for emphasis.

Oh Dev, where did it all go wrong?

There, there.

We were all so young then.

Now, now.

Oh I love acting so much.

There, there now, now.

Would you like to go up to my room?

And though there, there now, now would seem a phrase that any sane and heterosexual man would want to say at this juncture, I simply nod in the affirmative manner and almost immediately I'm sailing behind the dry-eyed Candy Lake, who's smiling at the bartender as we leave.

. . .

Okay, so it's bad enough luck sleeping with a gal down on her luck when you may have found the real McCoy. When that same down-at-mouther is sloshed to the gills, pushing the emergency alarm on the elevator, proclaiming her cross-eyed devotion to dirty talk in a baby-talk voice, well you might as well start tripping nuns and tossing kittens against trees as far as luck is concerned. And while on the subject of dirty talk, I must say I'm not a big devotee. It's not so much the dirtiness as it is all that yakkety-yak. Like trying to pat your head and rub your belly at the same time. No, other than the occasional bark, the spontaneous yip, and the culminating drunken coyote meets full moon, silence is golden in Dev's book.

All of which brings me to the case at hand, namely Candy Lake and me sprawled on a bed in a pitiful attempt at a make-out. Though this technically could be construed as a jinxworthy move, the gods in charge of such matters know deep in their hearts that this is only a placebo intimacy, one which will be short-lived and unintimate and will, hopefully, prevent any late-night, drunken, I'm-no-longer-attractive, guzzling of pills and booze that could heap another well-tanned corpse on the Hollywood pile. During this bad make-out, with a really bright lamp glaring in my eyes, Candy has begun some kind of move involving the underside of my arm. Don't you find the underarm a fantastic erogenous zone? she says.

Yes, I say, trying to free my arm from her grasp.

Of all the erogenous zones, I think the armpit is my favorite. Don't you agree?

Absolutely, I say. So much better than that numb hunk of leather I sometimes call my cock.

Actually I didn't say that, but boy was I thinking it.

Oh Dev, says Candy, writhing about, sandpapering my neck with her lips, you know I've never really had one.

With this salvo, I begin a tearful reminiscence for the good old days of baby-voice elevator dirty talk. Now I'm not sure how many men have been the beneficiary of this little bit of personal news while supposedly in medias res, but this isn't a first for me. On hearing such news as a fresh-faced collegian, I was prone to attack Mt. Olympus like, well, a fresh-faced collegian. Diligent would be the word that comes to mind. Alas, yes, alas. Yes, alas, alas. When I was a boy, I thought like a boy and so on.

Really, I say.

Never once.

Until this admission we were well on our way to calling it quits and the comforts of our respective beds, our own respective numb hunks of leather. But now, well this has all the makings of a rhetorical dialogue. Interesting, I say.

My analyst says it's because I've always been stared at by men. Even as a little girl grown men would stare at me. It was like they couldn't help it. It's odd to be looked at all the time.

I guess it is, I say.

We could still try.

I think we're both pretty tired.

Do you find me attractive?

Yes. Very. Always. All my life.

Oh Dev, she says, putting her head against my chest. Then I reach to turn out the light. And before too long, she's snoozing away.

I've parked behind my building after the deflated debauch and am counting the moments until I am home again in my own sweet bed. Before I hit the sack, however, I decide to take care of a quick piece of wiener dog business. Finding a melted nub of brown crayon that Katie has left sunning itself in the back window and a fast-food sack, I whip out a quick note. The message as written is less stylistically interesting than one would hope but considering the scalded dog concert I received from Sunny and Nickel during composition, it stands up well as art under duress. To wit.

> WILL PAY VET BILL IN FULL
> PLEASE TELL JACKLEG LAWYER
> GLAD TO HEAR DOGS SEEM BARKING WELL
>   AS EVER
> SINCERELY DEV DEGRAW

As I'm sliding the note under the door, Sunny and Nickel really notch it up an octave and seem to be attempting to tap out a message to me via head-against-door Morse code. Only the rigors of my new self-discipline prevent a swift bop on the window for old times' sake. In fact, I am about to bop, the irresistible call of the sirens, and have my fist clenched in anticipation when I see in the reflection of the window a young black face just behind mine. Not very long later, simultaneously I suppose, the cool smooth barrel of a gun, also in reflection. Then gun pressing against back of head, a voice sleepy and nonplussed. I got you now mother-fucker.

Riding in the trunk of a car is not all it's cracked up to be. Especially if a person had the misfortune to end up in the trunk of my car, aromatic as it is with dirty socks, fast-food sacks, and whatever other trash I've conveniently moved from rotting in backseat to smoldering in my trunk on that rare occasion when I've had backseat passengers. Alas, irony is not what the trunk dweller longs to savor.

I'm trunk-bound for approximately thirty minutes or seven screeching corners, whichever comes first, before the car comes to a slow and moody stop somewhere, one would assume, where a cadaver broiling to a patient green might least likely be found. From the inside of the car, a gentle rap anthem, the pungent smell of below average weed. And it may be my imagination, but this trunk dweller finds it hotter and stuffier with the vehicle stopped. Really quite stuffy. By the way, I've crowbar at the ready. Equals trunk popped, homey bopped. Of course there is the leverage problem, hand, crowbar, and elbow not fully assembled at this point.

As I'm working on a solution to this, the trunk is ripped open, and caught unawares in the middle depths of deep thinking, I'm not as prepared to crush his cranium as I ought to have been and instead find myself face to gun, mouth to gun to be technical, and lambasted in a melodic stream of speculation about what I and my mother may or may not have done in the privacy of our own home.

Then, as I'm lying in the trunk, brow furrowed like a possum in the middle of the road, I'm cracked quite hard on the head with the butt of the gun. I wipe away the blood that's leaking into my eyes. I try to get out of the trunk but am pushed back. I'm a little light-headed. I try to think up something soothing to say, but come up empty.

I'll kill your fucking white ass.

No fucking shit.

I see the barrel heading my way, then nothing.

The
Reunion

I wake up in the lower rung of government housing with a woman daubing my head and the voices of little kids in mid-debate about the dying man on the couch. Even with eyes closed, you can tell this is a dwelling of the poor. It smells poor. A smell attendant with the fact of no air-conditioning. Stale and dusty. And a funky mix of warm humans on old furniture and something very close to fried bologna. Old sweat is the dominant odor, tired and unfussy. Eau de Fecund Poor. It wouldn't know this sissy thing I've got going from Adam at the Human Smells family reunion, my bouquet including as it does a dry-cleaned shirt soaked through with fearful sweat, residual and antiorgasmic perfume from Candy Lake, and a last dying hint of my own deodorant, manly and oh-so-minty. Yes, I stink, but it's a fresh stink, well-heeled and likely to attract mosquitoes at a neighborhood croquet match.

No, he is not going to die, says the voice behind the daubing to a pipsqueak who keeps reaching for the wrong side of my wrist to check for a pulse.

Is Louis gonna kill him when he wakes up?

No Louis is not.

Louis's going to jail.

To this there is no answer.

Ain't he?

You kids get on back to bed. Ain't nothing here for you to worry about. This here's Louis's lawyer. He's been in an accident.

And then the sounds of kids scuttling off to bed, arguing among themselves about how many years Louis will get for killing a white man lawyer and a running dialogue along the lines of, ain't going to kill him. Will to. Said he'd slice his meat off when he

woke up. Why don't he shoot it off? He said slice. I thought he
was gonna sic a dog on him. He said that too. Wonder if he'll get
a rockweiller. Yeah I bet it's a rockweiller. Wouldn't want to be that
lawyerman. No way.

Boys, I said get to bed now!

And then silence save for the whir of an electric fan and the
soft humming of the woman beside me. Quite nice actually, discounting the concussed throbbing of my bean. After a good deal of
coaxing, the left eye manages a tentative go at unnatural light,
blanches at the arrows fired into the optic nerve, then by god toughs
it out for the team, prodded on as usual by the incessant brain who
must know, absolutely must know, what visual accoutrements complete the experience now being experienced. Namely being in an ad-
vanced state of kidnapping. The right eye, throbbing like a grooving
bass line, waits back at camp for reconnaissance results.

Which include, first of all, a woman, large and of similar skin
tone to the napping future murderer, who watches with a worried
expression a television that isn't on. The house or duplex or whatever this is is done up in late-seventies avant garde minimalism. No
piece of furniture seems to go with any other. Assorted lamps sport
missing or busted shades. In lieu of a coffee table, an old trunk. On
the other side of the couch an empty beer bottle box serves as end
table. The walls are bare except for a poster of a shirtless rap star recently gunned down and a brown water spot that looks to be attempting to branch out from the ceiling. Only the mute television
belies the conceptual consistency of the room, new and gleaming as
a recalcitrant god in the corner. A month's paycheck that. And the
best three networks have to offer free o charge. Yes, no question
about it, a lottery is just what this state needs. Poor folks in Alabama
have way too much pocket change floating around.

As I'm about to move on to the secondary observations having to do with my escape plan, namely ascertaining whether my assailant is or is not between me and the door, I hear the sound of muffled sobs beside me. Then lamentations. Followed not too long after by beseechments to the sovereign power. Culminating in a character analysis of the madman's long-departed father as good as any roasting these well-boxed ears have ever heard. You're the Governor's son ain't you?

I nod painfully

Lord awmighty, he picked a good one for his first abduction. He'll get the chair sure enough.

Not unless he kills me, I say.

He aims to. Can you walk?

I think so.

Is that your car out there?

Yes.

Keys are right there, she says.

I sit up on the couch and it's a quick bout of double vision, double poverty fun for your money. I lie back down. I can't drive, I say. Not right now. Can you take me?

I don't know how to drive.

Okay, that's fine, I say. We'll figure something out. How long's he likely to be asleep?

Could be an hour, could wake up anytime. He hadn't been right since that dog bit him. Hurt his pride or something. Made him crazy, crazier than usual. Said it was bad enough standing there day after day while they do their business and all the folks inside yukking it up, but getting chomped on the behind on top of that was just too much. Of course, Louis ain't been all the way right since he lost his eye.

He got bit in front of the grandstand? I thought it was just at practice.

Didn't you read what we sent you? Some man came by here and took a what's it called?

A deposition. Yes, I hired a man to do that. I had some legal matters of my own at the time.

You never even read it?

No, I say.

Right sorry of you. Louis missed a month of work. And a little cash settlement might have kept those other boys from riding him like they have been. Keep calling him two-holer and mess like that.

I'm sorry about that, I say. I am. I did him wrong, and I feel bad about it.

Well, I'm glad to hear you say it.

I got what I owe him in my wallet.

You got nineteen hundred dollars in your wallet, and Louis ain't got it yet?

He seemed a bit preoccupied with popping me in the head with his gun. It must have slipped his mind. Where is that gun by the way?

Next to your keys on top of the television.

Could you bring it to me please?

What you going to do with it?

I'm not going to hurt your son, I say. I thought I'd just offer him the money I owe him and see if he'll call us square. I'll just have the gun so that he doesn't. And if he doesn't have the gun, he can't kill me. And if he doesn't kill me, this whole night will be our little secret.

You're really going to pay him?

Yes, I say. You have my word.

And not tell the cops?

Nope. Not if he calls us square.

She looks at me a while, then at the blank screen, and finally back toward the TV. Outside the sun has started to come up and the first chained dog to howl. A rockweiller no doubt. She walks back to the couch and hands me the gun.

If you could help me up, I say, I'd appreciate it.

She does so, helping me first to a sitting position. Immediately I'm confronted with two large black women in the one eye I can open without pain. Then I nod, and she yanks me to my feet easy as you please, letting me lean against her as I attempt to get my legs. And standing up it seems to me that she carries her weight better than I thought. In her day, probably quite the eye-catcher.

You all right? You look funny.

I'm okay. Which room, I ask, for there are two or four to choose from, and kiddies don't need to see a white man risen from the dead and holding a gun first thing in the morning before they've had their jelly and toast. She walks me about halfway there and then I ask to have a go at it on my own. I take a step and a half and start teetering side to side. Just before I'm about to start my leisurely descent to the floor, she's beside me quick as a cat with a broad shoulder to lean on. Through the closed door, the sound of logs being split, sawed, and chipped.

I guess I'll go on in then, I say, for she's blocking the door as if having second doubts about my good intentions.

I'll go with you, she says.

It might make him mad if he thinks you helped me. You best wait out here.

You're not going to take him to jail?

No.

You're going to pay him his money?

Yes.

And you promise you're not going to hurt him?

I promise I'm not going to hurt him.

With this, she moves to let me pass and once through the door I close it behind. The room is pitch-black except for an electric alarm clock and a fist-sized hole in the shade where the faint morning light dances above the head of our sleeping kidnapper. My head has cleared some. Enough to know that I have a gun in my hand and before me the sleeping body of the man who cracked me in the head at least one more time than he had to. And those taunts, so much more painful than the actual whack to the head. Then again, I did owe him money, did botch his case, did cause him undue humiliation at his workplace. Add in the series of promises I made to his saintly mother, and you see the dilemma I'm facing. With such a crosscurrent of thoughts to deal with, I make my way gingerly toward the snoozing figure, his eye patch firmly in place, a rivulet of saliva running down his smiling face. And he looks so peaceful sleeping in the soft red glow of the alarm clock, the pink morning light skittering above his head, that I sit down on the bed as gently as I can. I lean down close to the ear that shares a side of the face with the dead eye and whisper as quietly, as gently, as I can. Wake up my sleepy little motherfucker.

My old friend Eightball makes a few mumbling sounds, grunts a bit, seems to want to get back to whatever sweet dream he's currently participating in. I repeat my earlier admonishment, but this time I couple it with a firm tap upon the forehead with the barrel of the gun. Quite firm because immediately he is one, awake, and two, bleeding like a stuck pig.

Good morning motherfucker, I say, introducing the gun barrel to the point between his good and his bad eye. And then, though eye for an eye is never the way, I bop him again in the head with the tip of the gun. Not as hard. Just for luck really. Then I stand up, nearly faint, sit back down again, try to think of something tough and gangsterish to say, can't, stand up again, and go to the door to turn on the light.

Let's go my thuggy friend, I say, leaning against the doorframe, waving him up and onward with the gun.

What you gonna do if I don't get up?

I thought I'd shoot you in the head.

I don't think you'll do it.

You're probably right, I say. But I might do it. My head hurts, I haven't slept, and you really hurt my feelings with some of your comments last night. If I were ever going to shoot someone, today would be the day.

Shit man, you owe me money.

Shit man, I got your money.

Let's see it.

After you drive me home, I say, tossing a pair of pants rather crisply into his sleepy face.

Man, he says.

Man, says I.

After he's dressed, we make our quick good-byes to Mumsy, and stroll discreetly, gun to rib cage, into a dawning ghetto day. The early sun glimmering off acres of red concrete block, metal clotheslines, broken-down bikes, dented trash cans, and all kinds of tipped-over toys, strangely pretty. A door with a fresh coat of blue paint. Leftover Christmas lights. More than a few defiant house plants in windowsills. An old lady chopping the ground with a hoe doesn't look up with the thin slam of the screen door. And behind us, Eightball's mother saying in a hoarse whisper, Louis, I'll see you when you get back. Come right back home Louis.

In the car, unbelievably, he pulls a rap tape from his pocket and pops it in the tape player before he's even put the car in gear. And, if I'm not mistaken, it's the same sound track by which I was beaten only hours before. I rap him, pun intended, smartly across the head with the gun, then let fly with a wheeling free verse poem of curses covering, but not limited to, the modern world, gangsta culture, my vitriol about the word gangsta when gangster, a fine word, a sensible word, an actual word, seems perfectly capable of describing the job title, his gumption, his missing eye, and finally his proclivity to ride his mother's big ass till the cows come home. Then, in an act of impulsive spite, I eject the tape, throw it out the window against the side of a car up on blocks, and turn the radio to the New Country station out of Birmingham. Drive, I say, as the warbling commences, a painful ditty about lessons learned when Daddy caught the singer as a tight-jeaned tyke stealing candy from the local five-and-dime.

Shit man, says Eightball, backing the car out, rubbing his head, looking red-eyed and forlorn, you don't really like that shit, do you?

Of course not, I say, turning up the volume as loud as it will go, waving the gun barrel in front of my mouth like a microphone, swaying my throbbing head to and fro, urging on verse after verse of third-grade-reading-level platitudes extolling the simple virtues of, among other things, corporal punishment in this crazy mixed-up world of ours.

Seriously man, turn it. That's the worst shit I've ever heard.

Yes it is, I say, swaying, humming, extolling virtue on all fronts. Yes, it's the worst fucking shit there is.

Back at my apartment, I make the young rapper wait in the car, ears bleeding from a bevy of odes to earnest rurality, while I wobble in for a quick queasy shower, some modest bandaging, and a change of clothes. Afterward, I grab the money, untuck my shirt, and stick the gun in the waist of my pants like the redneck bad boy that I am and hit the door at a well-clipped limp. Downstairs in the parking lot, Eightball leans against the car, smoking a long menthol cigarette and peppering Mrs. Catching's door with pebbles. Inside her apartment, mad yipdom, insane dash.

How you like the dogs, I ask.

They poodles? he says, exhaling leisurely and flinging a handful all at once that sets them chawing upon one another's tail and chomping whichever ear is handiest.

Wiener dogs, I say.

Wiener dogs, shit. Yapping and biting, biting and yapping.

You like dogs by the way?

You being funny motherfucker?

I'm armed you know.

Yeah, I like dogs. I always liked dogs. I liked that dog that bit me. He wouldn't have done it if they hadn't starved his ass for a week, then stuck a mothball up his nose so he couldn't breathe so some fat fuck could hit his quinella. Shit, I couldn't blame him. Motherfuckers.

I nod, motion for a smoke. He hands one over without a thought. Not wiener dogs though, I say.

Nah, hell no. Not no wiener dogs. Short-legged nervous wienery motherfuckers. Now where's my jack?

I got it. But you got to drive me first.

Shit bitch driving Miss Daisy give me my fucking money and let me go back to bed.

I don't want you to take this the wrong way, I say, but if I shot your black ass right now, I could be lining up a putt by noon.

He tosses his cigarette at my feet, turns on his heel, and gets

in the driver's seat, muttering in a stage whisper a lively and unambiguous riff on white men and golf and their fevered predilec-
tions with their clubs after plaid pants have been shed.

I gimp the ten feet to the car and into the passenger seat in a
little over an hour. I roll down the window and begin puffing in
earnest on the best cigarette I've had in years.

The young man in the driver's seat, the young dog lover, turns
to me and says, you can shoot my ass right now, but I ain't listening to another fucking second of country music.

Where's your patriotism? I say. New Country is America,
America is New Country. But all right, fair enough, no more New
Country music.

He looks at me, I at him. You're going to put on some of that
old shitty rock, aren't you? Some of that classic shitty rock.

I am, I say. I surely am.

I'm smoking menthol cigarettes and listening to classic rock.
It's brutal. I've nearly dive-rolled out of the car three times, the
closest call coming during an extended Aerosmith something or
another all caught up in an attempt to blur machismo and feyness
and something strikingly similar to an arrhythmic heartbeat.
Eightball has his head completely out the window, tears of shame
and remorse welling in his eyes. His own breaking point came
during an especially, a provokingly, white attempt at a blues guitar
manifesto by the god of splotchy Englishmen everywhere. Oh the
bearded slow hand, the bearded, bearded slow hand.

We pull in the mall parking lot and I instruct Eightball to
stop short of the tent and stage and inexplicable crowd milling
about. What's all this shit, says Eightball, pulling in a space at the
farthest end of the parking lot.

Bayou Dog reunion, I say.

Bayou what?

It's a TV show.

Never heard of it.

Be glad, I say pulling out my wallet, be very glad. Now what do you say I owe you?

Nineteen hundred. Plus interest.

Here's twenty-one hundred, I say, counting the money on my leg so he can see and then handing it over.

He re-counts the money. Re-counts it again. How bout my gun? he says.

Are you kidding me? What do you need a gun for? You're just going to get your ass shot off. No, you're not getting the gun.

Man.

Listen, I just gave you two hundred more than you said I owed. You want a gun that bad, go buy you one down at the pawnshop. You could get one, kill somebody, and be in jail before dinner if you really apply yourself.

He laughs, starts to get out of the car. Just so you know, he says, I never was going to kill you.

Draw the line at kidnapping and battery?

What'd you just do to me?

Coerced chauffeuring, I say, nothing more.

He starts to walk away, back toward Tuscaloosa's rough streets. So we're even, I say. Right?

He turns and smiles.

Seriously, I say. We're even. I don't owe you a damn thing now. No money. No gun. No money for a gun. We see each other walking down the street, we're just two guys, right? No guilt. Right? No animosity. No nothing. Just two guys trying to get along.

He continues to smile. Lights a cigarette. The sun on his good eye shines like it's hitting fresh snow. We're even motherfucker.

I sit in the passenger side of my own car feeling about as tired as I ever have. Watching my former kidnapper dodge traffic on McFarland Boulevard seems to have taken the wind out of the sail. A kidnapper I might even talk to Shade about getting a job if he can go a few months without abducting or killing me first. The blessed mother and the rockweiller tykes and all. At any rate, I'm tired, quite tired, and have decided to take a quick catter before entering the strip mall bayou, have indeed tucked absconded gun under the seat, locked the doors, and closed my eyes for the sweetest of brief respites, when a peppy and persistent tapping commences at the passenger window.

Apparently fatigue-induced hallucinations have started in full. How else to explain Bunny Akins in full cowgirl regalia peering in my window? Seriously, I want to know. How else to explain? I close eyelids a second time, shooing the apparition away with my hand in the process. Apparently some hallucinations are more stubborn than others. Others still come with sound effects. A sound tinny and jangly and drummy all at once. I open an eye. I close it immediately. Entering and quickly exiting a little-known innermost circle of Hell, well before whole integers are used to designate the widening and ever-less-sinful rings of pain, around 0.3 I'd say, a small and little-traveled eternal resting spot reserved exclusively for those sinners named Devaney Degraw, I thought I saw a spliff of straw between cowgirl phantom of Bunny Akins's teeth and something looking suspiciously like a tambourine. Concocting a nifty approximation of a Protestant Hail Mary, I launch headlong back to the land of Nod.

I'm one of C.A.'s backup singers, says the hallucinatory voice in my head. I'm one of the Lightbulbs. Carter Allbright and the Lightbulbs. Ain't that cute? Dev, wake up honey. Come on little governor, the show's fixing to start. Honey, it's showtime. Got the little Bunny on tambourine. Big Daddy's looking for you. And look at this crowd. Governor might make a speech. We gonna show em how it's done. Course the Governor doesn't want to interfere with your big day. Big Daddy says this is your day and C.A.'s day and he's just going to sit back and enjoy himself. And I said, ain't it Bunny's day too and he says, every day's Bunny's day and he's right you know. Well I got to go. Come on little governor, you're going to miss the show.

And somewhere in my Kubla Khan, a thin scratch of straw against the window, the diminishing, diminishing, but never diminished, rattle and bell of a tambourine.

I'm enjoying a vigorous stretch of slumber, navigating in my narcoleptic dreamscape a particularly well trimmed craft, when I'm made aware of more window pounding, more exhortations. Get your ass up boy, says Sam Shade. Do you hear that shit? More desperate pounding. Do you? I'm blaming you boy. You and you alone.

Now that he mentions it, I do hear what I suppose is meant to be music. In my dreams, there were planes taking off, and banjos plucked with dying cats in heat, and once, for a moment, as I roughhoused with a friendly dog on the beach, a pair of gag store false teeth chattering away in a rusted wheelbarrow and behind the wheelbarrow a herd of marauding rabbits laying waste to what had once been a lovely and bounteous field.

No comprende senor, I say, tossing and turning as if in the midst of gently turbulent sleep. Try next cabana senor.

This, pounding and shouting on one side of the door, pidgin English and feigned sleep-induced fitful tossing and turning on the other, goes on for a time, approximately ten minutes, until the boy Rasputin is sufficiently roused once again from the dead.

I open the door with unstifled yawn, much long winter's nap rubbing of eyes. Accompanying my every movement, my every masterstroke of choreography is a one-word litany. Jackass you say?

Jackass, affirms the man named Shade.

Is this barnyard refrain of yours in any way connected with the hoedown I hear in the distance? Are you part of the show? Charley Pride tribute or something? Going on right after the angry mob jerks Carter bodily from the stage.

Mob's eating it up.

I plan to incite them, I say. But seriously, what song are you doing to honor the lonesome ebony cowboy?

Don't be talking out your ass about Charley Pride, says Shade. Charley Pride can go now.

My attempt at a smile sets bruises colliding with scrapes and both bouncing off various puffed and tenderized portions of the beachball sitting atop my shoulders, and soon I'm in full sour-pickle grimace.

Skip Terry's gang do that to your face?

No, I say. Car wreck's the official story for the face. Hit-and-run in a crosswalk. Tossed me like a rag doll.

I got you, says Shade. Old Skip called up with some story about you and some of his young friends being drunk and getting in a boys will be boys out in the yard. Governor wasn't around, so I took the call. Didn't apologize or nothing. Just covering his ass that he wasn't involved.

You know who he was with?

I got a good guess, Shade says. I told you he'd done switched up.

You think we botched that one? The lottery and all. Skip Terry's got a lot of swing.

What do you mean we? You was in charge of Skip Terry.

That's right I was, I say, glancing across the parking lot where a sizable and unfathomable crowd shuffles around in front of the stage and around the tent beside it. A *Bayou Dog* Reunion banner stretches across the tent and American flags, plastic ones, shiny and starched by the wind, for as far as the eye can see. On stage, C.A. wears fringy cutoff jeans, a midriff-baring T-shirt under a denim jacket, a cowboy hat that seems also to be emblazoned with the American flag, and, if I'm not mistaken, tan-tinted panty hose in the tradition of those most patriotic of tarts, professional football cheerleaders. Bunny, meanwhile, careens about with her tambourine, a threat at any moment to join C.A. at the microphone for a combination group prayer and rally-round-the-governor medley.

You could beat ole Josh Wade, says Shade.

What? Are you drinking already? How many fingers am I holding up?

You're going to have to beat him sooner or later, he says. He ain't going away, and there ain't nothing else you can do to make a living. People are used to saying Governor Degraw. They been saying it a long time. Might as well milk while the cow's dry.

What?

Weather's dry or wet, cow's got to be milked.

I don't know what you're talking about literally, metaphorically, or any other which way. Speak English man.

I don't want Josh Wade to be governor for four years, he says. Him nor that bunch he'll bring in. I don't like it, but I can stand it. But not eight years. I worked too hard too long to see it all pissed away just like that.

My father's running for governor. Not me.

Governor's tired, says Shade. He'll claim fatigue, wanting to spend time with the young wife. Give the press something to talk about. Father-son angle. Swing some momentum our way.

But he still wants to be governor.

No he doesn't. He wants to read the newspaper. Garden. Hop on the young thing two or three times a week, see if his heart's still pumping.

Garden? Seriously, have you been drinking? Give me a little snort.

Before he can respond, C.A. is exhorting someone to join her onstage. And before you can say hot fudge sundae, it's the sullen little cowpoke Dallas trudging up the stairs in a mini-Stetson to join his mother at the microphone. Posttraumatic syndrome begins its tardy assault on the senses. How else to explain the melted-record-in-the-sun effect I seem to be experiencing as mother and roly-poly son launch into the Donny and Marie classic, A Little Bit Country, A Little Bit Rock n Roll?

Aye, he's a good one, the wee lad, I say.

Shade looks at me without expression.

Plump apple of his mum's wandering eye.

What's it going to take to get you to talk seriously for five minutes?

I'm waiting for a serious topic, I say.

This is serious, he says. Governor's out. He's announcing it today.

You've got to be kidding.

No, damnit, I'm not kidding, he says. If you'd been paying attention the last three months, you wouldn't be surprised either.

Who's running in the primary?

You.

Listen, I say, I was jacking around earlier and thought you were too. There's no way in hell I'm running. I'm absolutely unelectable.

We'll get you elected, he says. Get you the nomination for damn sure. Shit, I could paint Degraw on big rock and get it the Democratic nomination.

I'm divorced.

Makes no difference this day and age.

Gossip columnists across the state have libeled my good name.

I'm sure they did, he says smiling. So it's either libel, or they got their facts wrong. We got friends at the paper give the correct version. Or worst-case scenario, we got a young fellow sowing oats. Southerners don't want no choirboy nohow.

It'll look ridiculous. The Governor's tired and doesn't want the job anymore, so let's stick his son in there? They may not want a choirboy, but they don't want desperate either. It's too out of left field.

We'd have to sell it some, he says. I'm not saying we wouldn't. If we had an angle, just any kind of angle to add on to the father-son thing, we could sell it.

Look at me, I say. I'm a wreck. I've quit my job. I'm living in a dumpy apartment. I don't have a hundred bucks to my name. And I'm getting ready to go play Billy Tucker for an hour and a half.

You ain't going to act or nothing are you? Cause that would cost us an election sure.

That's good, that's funny. Listen, I'm just playing devil's advocate here. I'm not running for governor, dog catcher, cheese cutter, or anything else.

Just think about it.

I've thought. The answer is hell no.

Well, he says, I know when I'm licked.

Good. I'm serious. No way. I'm not cut out for that. Never have been. Not now, not in four years. Smacking that flesh, kissing them redneck babies, hearing those corny old dirty jokes and trying to muster up a laugh. Not me. No sir. Not by a long shot.

It was worth a try. Guess it's Governor Wade then.

Guess so, I say. Could care less.

Governor Wade and his first lady, the Queen Bee.

Is that the best you got?

He smiles in response.

How'd you hear about that anyway?

Ain't much I don't know son. I thought you knew that by now. Well, let's get on over there Billy Tucker. All kinds of folks waiting to see the bayou boy.

Roused prematurely from my nap, I'm sitting irritably at a long table and awaiting the next autograph hound who stops by to inquire just who the hell I am again before asking, somewhat resentfully, for my signature alongside that of B-movie stars Chad Kingston and Candy Lake. Apparently, my looks don't agree with them. Not just the small bruises, which have been touched up a bit by Candy's makeup artistry, the same artistry that has Candy looking fifteen years younger than she did approximately ten hours before, but the totality of my face. It seems as if I no longer look like an eight-year-old boy. Compounding fan disappointment, Thor's progeny has yet to show, though when he does he'll doubtlessly be a Gen X version, flabby and ill-tempered and looking for the nearest cool spot to lie down.

Scene setting goes as follows. Milling about in front of me, approximately two thousand people with lives obviously not worth living. It's been unreal. People who remember specific episodes, people nearly losing their composure when shaking Chad's hand or posing for a picture with Candy. Yes, incredibly, shutterbugs do abound. Though it's worth mentioning that the human grotesquerie, Adultboy, has yet to be asked to pose for his first shot.

To my left, on the stage, a gaggle of prepubescent county swains called Little Four-Wheeler pipping about in matching urban cowpoke duds, line dancing their simplistic best, the something-for-the-kids act during C.A.'s intermission and eerie acknowledgment of my status as undisputed king of the Southern bourgeois zeitgeist. In front of the stage, my daughter and Dallas singing along to a song that will be hypnotized by professionals out of Katie's consciousness by nightfall, this singing in concert a brief interlude before Dallas, flush from his successful duet with his mother, tells Katie that not only is there no Santa Claus but no God as well.

Just behind Katie is the Governor himself, looking cheery and semifamous and about as relaxed as a man can look and talking, sly dog, to the kindergarten teacher, Miss Marcum, who is laughing, sly dog sly dog, at something he's just said. Buzzing about behind them, the Queen Bee herself, attended by a full quotient of Higginbothan. From this quarter I'm receiving hard-to-determine looks. Either the Queen Bee is worried that I'll tell the Governor about her interlude with the cherubic Josh Wade, or men in slightly battered faces hold an irresistible appeal. To my immediate left, one table over, Candy Lake holding court in front of a thirty-person autograph line, which includes Jim, the butter-eating poet, and Gay Henry, all of whom are chomping free hot dogs like they're going out of style. Past Candy Lake is Chad Kingston in a similarly stacked line, at the front of which is a sixty-year-old woman in cutoff overalls and no top underneath. This woman holds a sign with a childhood picture of me, or Billy Tucker if you will, underneath which is the one-line interrogative, HAVE YOU SEEN MY SON? In the other hand, a zucchini.

I stand and motion for Chad. He sees me out of the corner of his eye, then seems to notice, as if for the first time, Odelle Bailey in all her understated finery. This prompts a look both goggle-eyed and pleased. He promises the line of patient fans to make amends with a genial smile, then quick-steps it over my way with a peck on Candy's cheek en route, the sly dog, the master show-man. A few fans applaud on cue, TV husband and wife keeping the home fires burning. He's still got it folks, Candy says to the crowd. In response to this, my pale friends from McCrae's, expe-riencing their first dosages of ultraviolet in years and blinking like albino cave bats, begin the Sheriff Tucker chant in earnest.

You are the master showman, I say on his approach.

I thank ye. Candy thanks ye. Your old floppy-titted momma over yonder thanks ye too.

Yes, I say, about good old Mom over there. What do you make of it?

Run-of-the-mill nutjob, he says with a professional nod. Get em all the time in this business. She'll come over and look at you funny here in a bit and ask if you've seen her boy.

I am her boy.

That kid on the sign is her boy, he says. Billy Tucker. You're just some beat-up-looking old fart. Candy do that to you?

No.

Whatever she did last night seems to have done the trick, he says, nodding toward Candy who's parked on yet another old-timer's lap as his rustic and good-natured wife makes ready with the Polaroid.

Invigorated by the crowd would be my guess, I say. Puts a

bounce in the step to folks like you and Candy and the good Governor over there.

It is a fair crowd if I say so myself.

You were right all along old partner, I say.

He shakes his head modestly. You seen that producer yet?

Come again.

Him, says Chad Kingston, pointing at a youngish-looking yup job who's taking notes on a yellow pad. Not exactly the made-for-TV greasebucket I'd been expecting with cell phones in every orifice and a coterie of cocaine toadies. Actually, the producer I had in mind was either invisible to the naked eye or just striding into an office in L.A. and announcing to his secretary, no calls, repeat no calls, from anyone named Chad or Kingston or any amalgamation of the letters that make up the name Chad and or Kingston. Now oil down the casting couch and make it snappy.

And why is he here? I ask.

He just wanted to meet Candy and see the turnout and talk to some of the fans about what they'd want to see in a *Bayou Dog* movie.

He's not going to ask me to be in it, is he?

No, Chad says, I don't think so. Maybe a bit part or something. Some young tough I got to pop a couple of times before kicking his green ass out of town. Or a shy down-and-outer needing a little friendly advice on the finer points of seduction and lovemaking. Maybe something like that.

That's the B-12 talking, I say. But looky here. Your wonderdog just pulled in.

Chad turns to see a trailer pull up, a spiffy one with murals of an agile quadriped depicted in an assortment of supercanine feats painted on the side.

By god they made it after all, he says. Chip'll be glad he's here for this.

Your producer's name is Chip?

Now don't be getting cynical on me after we've just settled on the fact that you're the down-and-outer needing a little manly advice. I'd hate to cast you in that other role. Young wiseacre getting cuffed about pretty handy.

Ain't no way that dog's as good as the original.

He's supposed to be, Chad says, hurrying toward the trailer, a subdued cowboy gleam in his eye, an extra, but casual, hitch in the giddyup, reluctant hero entering the saloon, as he makes his way through the crowd.

As I'm watching him pound the flesh, my erstwhile mother Odelle Bailey pinions herself between me and my kindly thoughts for mankind. An unfortunate occurrence because I was working myself into a frenzy of optimism about dreams coming true and the indomitability of the human spirit, while simultaneously composing an insta-treatise on the whole metafictional aspect of the Chad as cowboy as cowboy actor as Chad, ergo Chad equals Chad, a thought that was in the process of spawning another round, ever-widening circles of a pebble in a pond, of joy for the human interconnectiveness and unsurpassedness spurred by a long-ago wonderdog named Thor. All for nought. Fragments in the wasteland of a low–blood sugar reverie.

You seen my boy? asks Odelle Bailey, pointing with her gourd at the promo shot of my young self fake smiling to beat the band.

No I haven't, I say.

Who are you?

I'm Dev Degraw.

A glimmer of recognition flickers through her eyes, then gone as quickly as it appeared. Why are you here?

I was an actor on the show.

You know that sheriff over there?

I do.

He knows where my baby's at, she says, leaning close to my face in a conspiratorial pose. He's the daddy of my poor bastard Billy.

I never liked him myself, I say.

She leans closer still until our unshaven cheeks are nearly touching, puts a firm hand on my shoulder to prevent any chance of a sprintaway. Bops my head smartly with the placard in the process. About her is the faint smell of old manure and mayonnaise sandwiches. A hint of musty cedar shavings. And her, she says, little miss fancy pants. Stealing my Billy's daddy away with her big-city ways and flouncing hair.

Not the least attractive, I offer, subtly, earnestly, trying to unhinge my shoulder from the gourd lady's grip of death. Behind her somewhere a dog barks three snappy times. Yes, good boy, Billy's in trouble. Fetch the nose clip quick.

Oh he's a hellcat that one, says Odelle Bailey. But I was young and naive and didn't know no better.

Have you considered confronting the sheriff? I say. If I were you, I'd go talk to him. Right now, right away, not a moment too soon.

Oh I've got plans for that one, she says. Don't worry your pretty little head over that.

She says this and lets go of my shoulder, the classic, textbook even, madwoman's smile playing on her lips. Really, as far as maniacal looks go, you couldn't draw it up any better on the board.

I got some pictures if you'd like to see em, she says, fishing around in her not-quite-coveralls, and, unfortunately, in all this fishing, modesty, discretion, and decorum take a definitive backseat to pale and sagging exposure. And why do I look? Seriously, why do I?

Really must be, love to, maybe later, there's the sheriff now, good luck with your boy, good luck and yeah, there he is, Chad, this lady's looking for you.

I'm at the snack bar woofing down hot dogs and Cokes, and the only word that comes to mind is delicious. Well that and delectable. I'm real hungry. As I begin hot dog three, Coke four, in earnest, a concurrence of events unfolds. One, Carter Allbright, C.A. yall, and the Lightbulbs take the stage for another heaping helping of peppy country girl self-realization and who-needs-that-cowboy-anyway. Two, the kindergarten teacher spots me and gives a rueful smile just as I'm about to stuff the better part of an entire hot dog in my mouth. And three, the Queen Bee symbolically conks the heads of the two Higginbothans together, leaving them disconsolate and discombobulated, and marches my way at a nimble pace.

I want to know what you said to Gibson the other night, says the Queen.

Not a thing, I say.

You didn't say a thing?

He seemed to deduce the whole of the Josh Wade affair with very little assistance from me.

Were you spying on me or something?

Actually I was hiding from Bunny Akins.

Oh I was so drunk that night, I didn't know what I was doing. I suppose you told your father as well.

No, I say, I didn't do that. Never crossed my mind.

You're a jealous mean man Dev.

You really think so? I say, demurely nibbling on the last nub of bun, tonguing delicately the tiniest bit of wiener navel.

The Governor's going to lose anyway Dev, she says. I hate to say it, you know how I feel about your father, but he's going to get beat. That lottery thing just killed him. Josh's got it all but locked up.

That a fact, I say, crunching ice in my powerful mandible, managing a wave to the kindergarten teacher, who has joined Katie up near the stage. The Queen turns, sees Miss Marcum. Turns back quickly with neck-popping speed.

Who's that girl?

Who?

Very funny. That girl you just waved to.

That's Jenny Lou Phillpott, I say. She just asked me to the Sadie Hawkins dance. I met her down at the soda shop. She's swell. I'm going to let her wear my letter jacket.

The Queen glares in a none-too-regal way, glances over her shoulder for someone to make out with, realizes she hasn't played, tossed, or reconfigured her hair in a minute and a half, and turns on her heel without another word, fingers busily pulling and ply-ing at her locks as she heads for the comfort of the small hive of Higginbothans.

Sated and quenched, I head in the direction of Katie and Miss Marcum, neither of whom has joined, thank god, in the crowd's un-rhythmic clapping of hands. I keep waiting to catch the song's rhythm, but it seems less an actual melody than a swiftly paced herky-jerkydom of guitar solos by a beefy tattooed former sailor, a good deal of spoken verse boasting punctuated by fist-flying squeals on C.A.'s part, and some sort of jumping jack regimen meant, I take it, to be a distant cousin of dancing. In other words, hard rocking pop country. In other other words, not good. Very very not good.

I'm nearly to the oasis of sanity and good taste, nodding politely as I make my way through the crowd of gawking, pink-faced white people who seem to recognize me as one of their own despite my assortment of well-heeled abrasions, seem also to recognize the innate Billy Tuckerdom within, such is the kindness in their free-concert-glazed eyes, kindness to the point where I am almost one with the reunion, one with the bayou and the dog. Alas, no. These, my people, constituency of my blood, salt of earth, supporters of all things untaxing to the bean, not a word can we share, not a NASCAR high five, nary a chain restaurant steak. But what then? What alternatives? Higginbothans and yet more Higginbothans? Weekend lacrosse and keggers with the gang? Good guys, solid guys, as far as the eye can see?

I've begun to lament oh this mark of Cain, to wander the desert alone and so on, when suddenly the great-grandson of Thor, that offspring of the greatest wonderdog of all, kicker up and down of lame Lassie's ass, begins to work his way through the crowd at a quick trot. He maneuvers here and there without breaking stride before coming to a stop directly in front of my path. What follows is a formal lifting of paw, an understated and kingly panting of tongue, and one short ruff of recognition.

Don't leave Comet hanging, says the handler at the other end of the leash.

So I take the paw of the great-grandson and begin a frank appraisal of his merits as canine and progeny. First off, and I'm somewhat loath to admit it, the resemblance is startling. The same uncanny bearing, the old and whimsical eyes. He barks once with a friendly damn glad to see you, then starts moving his paw up and down to initiate the shake proper. By now Katie and Miss

Marcum have come up beside me and the crowd has rounded out a bit to give dog and boy room.

It's like he knows you, says the handler, as Katie begins petting and rubbing his neck.

I knew his great-grandfather, I say, moistness in my eyes.

The great Thor, says the handler.

Then someone behind me, a loud man with a zesty voice, cries out, are you Billy Tucker?

I look at Katie, at the lovely kindergarten teacher now petting the dog, at the Queen and her retinue glaring from the concession area, C.A. in midkickbox onstage, the blue sky above the stage, the minimall, this wonderdog.

I am, I say. I am Billy Tucker.

And a few of the gathered crowd applaud politely.

Another voice, this one feminine and curt. Ain't you the Governor's son?

I am, I say. I am the Governor's son.

More polite applause.

And then Comet is led away, looking back once over his shoulder at Katie, the teacher, and me, his handler shouting out, he'll be back for the show in a few minutes folks.

And then I am walking away, in the opposite direction, needing, inconceivably, a moist moment alone.

Restored if shameful after my sensitivity interlude and well cursing the Oprahfied brainwashing of my hairy-assed soul, I make my way back to Katie and Miss Marcum.

Daddy, what happened to your face? says Katie.

As I gaze down with parental tenderness, Miss Marcum looks

on with bemused interest. Well, I say, I don't want you to be worried honey, but Daddy was hit by a car this morning.

Dallas said you were in a fight, that somebody beat you up.

All those Twinkies Dallas eats can give him an overactive imagination, I say. Sugar and blubber can calcify in the brain and prevent enough blood from getting through. Dallas probably needs to go lie down somewhere out of the sun.

I hope you're all right, says the kindergarten teacher, an insincere twinkle in her eye.

Oh, I'm fine, I say. Rolled right over the hood, bopped my head on the pavement a bit and popped right up. Not even a headache.

Did you get his license plate number, asks the future hall monitor, the little goody two-shoes.

No, I say. It was just some crazy college kid. Probably late for intramurals or something. He stopped for a second to see if I was all right, then just took off.

Miss Marcum gives me a look of much dubiousness, accompanied by a series of fake sympathy agreement nods.

Katie, I say, why don't you run over and suggest to Granddaddy that Dallas get out of the hot sun? Mention what I said about sugar and blubber.

Calcifying?

Yes calcifying. Tell Granddaddy I suggest a sugar-free diet from now on and twenty immediate jumping jacks.

Katie looks at me like I might be joking. Her face though remains serious and scrunched a bit as she tries to remember the exact wording of the message. Oh, the poor little perfectionist, hard for a proud daddy to watch. Not a bit of Degraw in her double helix. Not the slimmest of chromosomes.

Just go up to Granddaddy and say blubber, Dallas, immediate jumping jacks.

What about calcifying?

Blubber, calcifying, Dallas, jumping jacks. Granddaddy will know what you're talking about.

Then she's off, pushing past Dallas and pulling on the Governor's shirt.

Who's Dallas, asks the kindergarten teacher.

C.A.'s son, I say. Great kid. Super kid. His mother is a fan of the Lone Star State you know.

She looks at me. It's one thing to be weird. It's one thing to be battered. But battered and weird? I vow to tone it down a bit, though I'm flush with wieners and caffeine and goodwill for the canine world and could really get a good case of free-form logorrhea going, and have concluded, incidentally, that if she takes off running, a shoestring tackle should do the trick nicely. I'm just the slightest touch jacked up.

I guess you're looking forward to C.A.'s new album, I say.

Do you remember the one with her in that Confederate flag bikini on the cover? My brother kept the album on his wall. Never played it once. Just liked that picture.

My father married her for her voice and gentle spirit, I say, and out of the corner of my eye, the Queen and Hooper Higginbothan giving yours truly a double set of fish eyes.

Had nothing to do with those legs?

He was so overcome by her simple, heartfelt lyrics I don't think he even noticed.

I see, she says. And who's the little chickie who's been staring over here and just now started making out with the guy in the glasses?

I turn to face them and, sure enough, Hooper's diligence has paid off. Apparently *Bayou Dog* reunions and a couple of C.A.'s finest have brought out the best in the old lacrosse player. However,

it looks as if he wasn't prepared for this turn of events and can't quite seem to find a place for his hands.

That's my father's press secretary, I say, just as the Queen stops chomping lip and glances again in our direction.

I thought it might be one of your girlfriends.

No. Not at all. A minor player during a minor portion of my life.

Just for curiosity's sake, she says, when did this minor portion of your life come to an end?

You mean the girl?

No.

This other stuff? Late nights and such? Getting hit by cars and sending glasses of water to strange women and all that?

That's the one.

I've about got that wrapped up. That one seems to have about run its course.

Another dubious nod is the best the kindergarten teacher can work up for this comment.

I'll miss the Barkley Brothers though, I say.

Was that you screaming Free Bird or not?

No, I say. Absolutely not.

I think it was.

To this I don't reply.

Then she is smiling ambiguously at the Queen and Hooper, who are hard if awkwardly at it beside the concession stand. Well, she says, I guess I better get Katie back home. I've still got to get ready for my ice-cream date with Sweatervest.

After she's gone, I stand in the same spot and try to soak in the moment of my pending date with a grown woman. A grown woman with a sense of humor. Interrupting my soaking-in-moment

moment, however, is the fact that C.A. has called Dallas to the stage for what I fear, if fear is a strong enough word, will be another mother and son duet. A shrewder man than I would set his hair ablaze and take off running for the hills.

The Queen continues to make out with Hooper Higginbothan, pauses again to see how torn up I am about it, then back at it again with gusto. Dee-Dee Higginbothan, meanwhile, is crying behind the concession stand.

The Governor has moved to the edge of the stage, near the steps, and looks, call security, as if he's about to join C.A. and Dallas onstage. But surely not. Surely not the whole Osmond clan.

Miss Marcum has left to take Katie home and more than likely begin plans for the severe migraine or surprise shark attack that will force her to cancel our date at the last moment.

Chad Kingston guffaws, motions for his new bride Sheila, who is just arriving, to come over and hear what pleasant comment the producer has to offer regarding Chad's shining moment in the public eye.

Candy has remembered she's gorgeous and seems to be enjoying the recollection, such is the shoulder rubbing, the tittering, the earnest down-home shake of the head with each new wave of codger, each shuffling, wood-catching teen.

Bunny has remembered her hobby, forgotten her tambourine, walks in front of the auditory effrontery, and pauses, Leaning Tower of Pisa in front of the stage, calling for the Governor as a coterie of Lightbulbs tries to garner her in without resorting to Apache leg sweeps.

Comet has begun warm-up maneuvers in front of the Bayou Dog tent, speedily fetching Frisbees with nonchalant ease.

The aberrants from McCrae's have begun the first chants for Billy Tucker.

Shade comes out of the portable toilet, sees crying rich girl, making-out rich girl, a vaguely familiar fellow with higginbothanish spectacles, textbook Oedipal psychodrama being played out under the guise of art onstage, a frighteningly happy-looking Governor, a frighteningly happy-looking Bunny scarcely restrained from stage-diving her sixty years and forty pounds into the unsuspecting arms of the Governor, a red-faced band of alcoholic vampires chanting at manic speed, and makes his way toward me, the lonely Charley Pride, wondering, understandably, about the strange ways of whitey.

They're fixing to bring the Governor onstage and make the announcement, says Shade.

Stylish, I say. Announcing the culmination of twenty-five years of public service in the parking lot of a minimall? Seriously, his dotage is a wonder to behold.

Figures it might help C.A. out, Shade says. Get her a little attention. Help out your buddy Kingston too. Governor knows a little about publicity now. And says there's no reason to wait.

Now Shade points to the stage, where Bunny is rousing the confused crowd as the Governor takes his place next to Carter and Dallas. One of the Lightbulbs leaves quickly and gathers up everyone still in the *Bayou Dog* tent. Comet's trainer holds a burning hoop to his side, Comet beside him looking ambassadorial and ready to take his place onstage as the next, logical, and eminently most electable choice for the Democratic nomination.

Thank you, says the Governor, smiling, waving, shrugging off Bunny in a friendly way that nearly sends her to the ground as she tries to kiss him from behind. The crowd applauds politely, perfunctorily, likely a few Republicans in the mix, *Bayou Dog* and family values and all that.

Thank you, says the Governor again. He looks over the crowd, hand shielding eyes in the standard I'm-looking-for-someone pose. My son out there? he says. Anybody seen my son in the last few minutes?

Instantly I assume the dazed facade of a statue of an amnesiac hidden quietly away in a never-visited park behind a lush grove of elms. Shade meanwhile pokes said statue in the ribs, prompting yelp. Get up there boy, he says. You ain't got any choice.

So I walk, stiffly, cursing the choicelessness of my life, the predetermined and predestined life of Bunnys and stepmothers and gawking friendly crowds of amber-necked rubes, until I am upon the stage with the present version of stepkin and the Governor smiling as if a mighty band of trombones is welcoming his sour fruit of the loin. And now I'm beside my father, as tall as he, nearly as broad, his arm around my shoulder as he begins to address the people, his people, Alabamians all, in a jovial tone, cherishing the final unpredictability of his public career, namely announcing his retirement without a newsman present, without a single camera rolling, he who never met a lens he didn't like. Dear friends, he says, dear friends and Republicans, then laughter and they're his, even the ones who think they aren't.

Out in the crowd, the Queen has Dee-Dee's head in her hands by the concession stand. Pre-make-out? No. Serious talk, a serious bucking up, you're still the higgiest Higginbothan in my book, and Hooper, standing a few yards back, dazed and uncertain, a fierce stick to the head to be sure.

First I'd like to reintroduce the backup band, says the Governor, especially my very good friend, Bunny Akins.

Modest applause as the two non-Bunny Lightbulbs make their modest waves at the crowd. Then laughter as Bunny nearly knocks me down weaving her way toward the Governor. She plants a slobbery one on his cheek and makes a lunge for the microphone. Seeing this, my consciousness, which I'd just programmed for ten minutes at heavy catatonia, leaps off the stage and takes off across the highway at a fugitive's clip before the drunken prayer meeting can commence. Luckily, the Governor still has something of the old reflexes left for he makes a nimble riposte and manages to spin her back toward the onrushing Lightbulbs, all the while keeping the ever-valuable microphone out of enemy hands. Afterward, sheepishly, like an old dog trotting out from the barn after being spooked by a child's popgun, my consciousness climbs out of the ditch across the highway, looks both ways before crossing the road, then jogs on back to my cranium. On cue, the first chanting yogis begin, a bubbling brook, then slowly, sweetly, the approaching ice-cream truck of catatonia.

I'd like to introduce my wife, says the Governor, and when the crowd begins to whoop, he corrects himself, or better yet, let her introduce me. Carter Allbright folks.

Applause. Oh sincerest of yogi-slaying applause. And Shade shooting me the old shiteater from where he's standing, a sweet spot, where he's standing, yes sir.

And my two sons, says the Governor, as Dallas doffs his mini-Stetson, the minicowpoke riding the Barcalounger range, lassoing Twinkies and not a joystick in three counties he can't break. Apparently I'm standing where I am, obsessing about the small rotunderie, the conspicuous gubernatorial plural, and anything else I can get my mind around instead of acknowledging the crowd, who could give a rat's ass to begin with when Gay Henry hollers out, well do something Dev.

Which seems to shake me out of my reverie because I suddenly walk up to my father, hug him, then grab the microphone and begin shouting, Four More Years, Four More Years, Four More Years.

Which does the trick all right because the little brainwashed

Pavlovians can't resist a chant of any sort, especially not when juiced to the gills on free hot dogs and free bad music and free pictures of Candy Lake in all her candied fun-ness. Throw in the comforting familiarity, the mother's teat if you will, of the local minimall in the background and about ten miles of asphalt and what you've got I dare say is a veritable pep rally. Seriously, they're mad with chanting, even the Republicans, even the Republicans without baseball caps. And Shade in the back, shiteating. And me on stage shiteating back. And now Bunny joins me at the mike, shouting, vodka over frankfurters, Goh Mah Gooh, Goh Mah Gooh, Goh Mah Gooh.

The Governor gives me a look, 90 percent certain I've been informed that this is to be his moment of departure and am just being perverse for the hell of it. The other 10 percent he gauges, correctly it turns out, that I've just struck a blow of retribution, unpremeditated or otherwise, for twenty years of being dragged onstage for no other purpose but to prove his family-manness. He mouths something in my direction regarding an ass that needs to be kicked, but with the chanting and all, it's impossible to determine who he's referring to. Then he holds up a hand to silence the crowd, smiling professionally, then warmly, won over after all by the response, the nostalgic surge of adrenaline, the siren call of demagoguery.

Thank you, says the Governor. Thank each and every one of you. But in the interest of full disclosure, I must admit I'm not the one responsible for this fine day. That is why yall were cheering, isn't it? In fact, before my son so kindly decided to boost the old man's ego, before you kind folks decided to honor me with your cheer, or pity as the case may be, I was just about to introduce a native son of Alabama, hero of stage and screen, better known to each of you as Sheriff Tucker of *Bayou Dog*. Ladies and gentlemen, Chad Kingston.

The Governor steps back from the microphone to lead the Chad Kingston cheers, then walks toward the stairs, brushing past me in the process. Cute one, he says.

I answer with a smile of earnest devotion.

Then he and Chad are shaking hands at the edge of the stage, hearty big man to hearty big man, and Chad is waving up Candy Lake, waving up Sheila, who is, attagirl, shaking her head hell no. And the Carter Allbright, C.A. yall, contingency is making way for the Bayou Doggers, all except Bunny who, seeing an open mike, has started up the Goo Mah Gooh chant once again before being briskly pulled away by C.A. herself.

It's a fairly chaotic scene, half-ass band meeting half-ass actors with half-ass gubernatorial family as mismanaging intermediary. Basically I've backed away from the confusion and am looking for a low place to leap off the stage when Chad grabs me by one arm and Candy by the other and we march, in kind of a skipping fashion, Scarecrow, Tin Man, and Dorothy up to the front of the stage, where I am once again confronted by a microphone and a small sea of sunburned mouth breathers who couldn't be less interested in my presence.

Chad takes the lead, leaning into the mike, smiling and stepping back a moment as if there's no way he can be heard over the tumult. During this smiling at fake tumult, I subtly maneuver a combination jerk and lurch out of his grasp, so that I'm no longer in the middle, where an unsuspecting eye might accidentally fall upon my battered and unfamous noggin, an aspect certainly most foul to the star-crazed masses.

Thank you *Bayou Dog* fans, says Chad Kingston with a rally-round-the-flag arm motion and whoop. Then placing hand above eyes, again in classic searching-for-missing-someone pose, he says, and speaking of bayou dogs, where is that canine wonder Comet?

From the middle of the crowd, the trainer's hand goes up. Be there in two shakes, he shouts.

Comet himself can't be seen for all the yeomen and wives of yeomen in front of him, but it's fair to surmise he's expressing some reluctance at joining us up on the stage.

And as I'm looking for Comet, silently praising his good taste and decorous manner, I come across my erstwhile mother, Odelle Bailey. Who, now that I notice her, is impossible not to notice, standing as she is with one mottled and forlorn jug completely unencumbered, nay untethered, by any kind of restraining device as she feverishly shakes the sign inquiring of my whereabouts. Three steps to either side of her, the crowd has cleared, and Comet, eschewing all prior good sense, stands patiently behind her as if protecting her right to most indecent exposure. In the anti-matter world, or more specifically antimatter plus old-fashioned schizophrenia, said teat of said hag first suckled yours truly. Contemplating such, ill-advised as it may be, my life, here on the stage with two fathers, bearish and insatiable, and two stepmothers, kittenish and posing as insatiable, seems about what you'd expect, seems little different than that of any of my pink-necked brethren out in the crowd. For aren't we all products of strange stories, improbable couplings, negotiating as best we can the great maze of predestination and chance encounter that makes up that which we call human life? And isn't it that commonality of weirdness, for lack of a better word, shaded by degree, darker here, lighter there, that perhaps we share more than any other human trait? That I am, in fact, completely normal, the product of a completely normal upbringing in a completely normal society, going, as we must, by the historical precedent set by centuries of sacrificed virgins and orgiastic Rome and Indian lacrosse games played with a human skull?

Food for thought, I say, food for thought. And Chad has finished with his lengthy introduction of Candy Lake and her assets as a human on this planet and has called me, once again, up to the microphone, where I stand between my TV father and my biological one, who has come up to give a friendly and encouraging and yes fatherly pat on the shoulder. And everything seems normal now, normal and right, Dallas muttering asshole every time Chad says my name and Bunny snoring where she stands held upright by the other Lightbulbs and my two beautiful stepmoms on the farther edges of the crowd, and Chad describing to the crowd the many homegrown, homegrown in Alabama, talents I brought to the role of Billy Tucker. And I've begun to feel just a bit woozy, just slightly warbled, when I see Odelle Bailey pulling the pistol from the inside of her overalls where once only gourds would dwell.

A shot is fired and Chad goes down at the microphone and without thinking I lunge in front of the Governor as two more echo across the stage and in the corner of my eye, a leaping dog frozen in midair.

When I come to, I'm beside an ambulance with an oxygen mask over my face and several menacing tubes attached here and there to my body. I am, to be sure, surprisingly undead. No emergency workers are around me. Shade, however, is. I pull the mask from my face and lose a couple of important-looking tubes in the process. Quite likely, I've just cut off the flow of hemoglobin and written my death sentence in the bargain. Where's the Governor, I ask.

In the ambulance, says Shade. He's all right. Precautionary tests. Wasn't hit at all.

And Chad?

He's fine. Twisted his ankle jumping out of the way. Trying to get them medics to take him to the hospital for the publicity.

I try to nod but can't quite muster the energy. Is Bunny dead?

Shade smiles. Slept right through it, he says. Never came to. She's sleeping over yonder under the concession stand.

I shake my forlorn head.

You're the only one hurt, he says, you and that crazy woman shot you. She lost about half her ass in that dog's mouth. He'd still be holding on if the cops hadn't made the trainer pry him off.

Just how paralyzed am I by the way? I can't feel much of anything in my legs.

They got you strapped to the stretcher and loaded up on painkiller. You ain't paralyzed. Took one in the thigh, and another glanced your hip.

I smile a thankful smile. And actually I'm not feeling that bad, just a little unreal, this day, my life, a minor fiction over which I haven't and never will have anything resembling control. While I'm working this theory, Comet and his trainer come by. There's the hero, I say.

Comet wags a modest tail, looks as if he wants to lick my hand, then, concerned about hygiene and the excitability of the patient, thinks better of it and settles for a friendly and earnest bark.

He'd been watching that old bird for half an hour, says the trainer. That's why I couldn't get him on the stage.

He's a chip off the old block, I say. Old Thor'd be proud to claim this one.

Ruff, says Comet. Ruff ruff.

And then Comet is gone, off into the fading sun, tail wagging, one last yip of farewell, just like, exactly like, a wonderdog from a TV show of a bygone era.

I'm about to get a little emotional about the whole dog saves boy aspect of the thing, the weird wonder of it all, when I notice a television truck pulling into the parking lot.

TV folks is here, says Shade.

From Birmingham? How long ago did this happen?

Bout an hour, he says. Once I saw you all was all right I called em.

Photo-opping the Governor after this? You have no shame.

Ain't photo-opping the Governor, says Shade. Photo-opping you.

Man, you've trotted me out for the Governor for twenty years now. I can't get some peace after getting my ass shot?

Governor never did get to announce he was pulling out of the race you know.

Good, I say, now that he's got his adrenaline kick-started he'll be ready to go.

Governor's out, you're in.

No I'm not.

We got our story line, he says. Assassination attempt on Governor. Son jumps in front to save Governor, takes bullet in the process. Episode shakes up Governor, makes him consider whether he wants to spend his twilight years working or picnicking with his lovely young wife. Son declares for race to show you can't keep the Degraw family down even with a bullet. Not to mention that he's firmly against the state lottery. Heroic son of Governor against the lottery? The only thing Josh Wade had going for him in the first place? It's a landslide.

You're a piece of work.

Listen, he says, when that television lady starts talking to you, just say you're glad no children were hurt. Keep it short and simple.

I'm going to say that my only regret is that I wasn't carrying a firearm so I could engage the madwoman in open fire. And God bless the NRA.

You want to win this election don't you?

To this, I don't reply.

That teacher's done gone to tell Katie you're okay before she hears it on the news. Said she'd be down to the hospital later on to check on you.

No shit, I say.

No shit, says Shade. Should have got your ass shot years ago. By the way, you reckon she's more interested in an unemployed lawyer or a gubernatorial candidate running on a proeducation platform?

So we're proeducation now.

We're a bunch of things.

I would smile, but my cheeks have gone numb and begun to burn slightly. From across the parking lot, the reporter and her cameraman have started with some earnestness in my direction, spurred on it seems by the medics, who are reattaching me to the proper tubes. So the kindergarten teacher's going to meet me at the hospital?

She is, says Shade.

That's good, I say, as the reporter shoves her way through the crowd.

You had to know this day was coming, says Shade, making way for the reporter and shouting, here's the hero, saved the Governor's life.

Then there's a microphone in my numb face, and I find my self speaking with what sounds like unpracticed modesty. The dog's the real hero, I say. I'm just glad no children were hurt.

And saying this, two images begin a battle royal for dominance in my tired, tired brain. The first involves Bunny Akins rousing from her slumber with a hot dog wrapper stuck to her back and lumbering toward me with a drunken prayer for the next four to eight years. The other, much nicer admittedly, the one I'm pretty sure I'm going to go with, is of a kindergarten teacher waiting at the hospital, who will never once have need to ask if I am happy.